Praise for J. C. Wilder's *Winter's Daughter*

"The depths of J.C. Wilder's story drew me in immediately. Her characters walked right off the page and engaged me, as real as any person I know. Intrigue, magic, romance--Winter's Daughter captivated me and left me wanting more."

~ *Cheyenne McCray, USA Today Bestselling Author*

"I can not wait for the rest of the Coven series. It is an absolute keeper!"

~ *Enchanting Reviews*

"I read Winter's Daughter one Saturday, totally ignoring everything around me. Engaging, gripping, and page-turning are a few terms I would use to describe Matt and Syn and their path to the truth and lasting love. I will be keeping a close eye on Ms. Wilder's site to see when the next sister's book is going to come out. For all of these reasons and some I can't seem to put words to, I Joyfully Recommend Winter's Daughter."

~ *Joyfully Reviewed*

"Winter's Daughter is an excellent tale that is well balanced and one of those rare finds that you will want to revisit again."

~ *eMuse Mag*

Rating: Recommended Read "If you buy no other book this month you have to get this one"

~ *Fallen Angel Reviews*

Look for these titles by
J. C. Wilder

Now Available:

Thief of Hearts
(Thief of Hearts in digital, In the Gloaming print anthology.)

Stone Hearts, Paradox I
(Titled Paradox I in digital, titled Sacrifice in print.)
Deep Waters, Paradox II
(Titled Paradox II in digital, titled Deep Waters in print.)
Sacrifice, Paradox III
(Titled Paradox III in digital, titled Stone Hearts in print.)

Winter's Daughter

J. C. Wilder

A SAṁHAIN PUBLISHING, LTD. publication.

Samhain Publishing, Ltd.
577 Mulberry Street, Suite 1520
Macon, GA 31201
www.samhainpublishing.com

Editing by Eve Joyce
Cover by Anne Cain

First Samhain Publishing, Ltd. electronic publication: December 2007
First Samhain Publishing, Ltd. print publication: October 2008

Dedication

For Lucas

Sometimes lies are easier to believe, though seeking the truth is well worth the adventure.

Acknowledgments

I also want to give a shout out to the ladies who keep me sane and cheer me on...

Carolan, Isabo, Cheyenne, Tina, Susan and ALL of The Ladies of the Club.

"Courage is doing what you're afraid to do."
~ *Edward Vernon Rickenbacker*

Prologue

Caramel cake. How could Mama be dead when a freshly baked caramel cake waited in the kitchen?

Synnamon Angelov could no longer feel her body. It was as though she stood outside of herself, watching the events unfold around her.

Her three younger sisters sat on the couch next to her, their eyes as big as saucers while their safe, familiar world crumbled around their feet.

It was late, near midnight, and way past their bedtime. Judging from the number of people in their house, it didn't look like they'd go to bed anytime soon.

Their once-quiet yard was filled with police cars, their red and blue strobe lights casting eerie shadows on the living room walls. Officers crawled over the house like crows pecking at fresh road kill. It made her sick.

One of the twins whimpered, and Syn couldn't make herself move to comfort the girl. Her mind and body had disconnected from each other.

Police Chief McNutt had been the one to tell Syn the terrible news in a brisk, unemotional manner. Not a hint of sympathy evident on his hard face. He'd left her to tell the younger girls their mother wouldn't be coming home. For a fourteen-going-on-fifteen year old, it was by far the worst moment of her young life.

Her sisters received the news with tears and disbelief. All Syn could do was hold them as they cried. But how could she hope to ease their pain when she too was bleeding on the inside?

Chief McNutt said Mama had been hit by a car on Winding Oak Road, less than a quarter-mile from their driveway. If that was where she'd been found, why were the police taking items from the house?

Uniformed officers walked to and fro, carrying Mama's belongings in bags marked with bright red labels that read, "Evidence."

Tears stung Syn's eyes and she blinked them away. There was no time to give into her pain; she had to be strong for her sisters. It was up to her to make sure they came through this together. Later, when she was safe in her bed, she'd allow herself to cry like a baby.

Chief McNutt stood in the dining room smoking a fat cigar. Noxious smoke hung in a cloud around his head as if he were the devil himself, straight from hell. He was a large man with pale hair and big, heavy shoes. A long stick hung from one hip and a mammoth black gun from the other.

Syn wasn't sure if the weapons of his trade or the man himself scared her more.

An officer hurried past the chief, bringing with him a whiff of cigar fumes. The scent made her want to gag. Mama had always taught her girls to pay close attention to their instincts. If a situation or person felt bad, they probably were. Syn's gaze landed on the chief. It wasn't anything she could put her finger on, but her senses were screaming that this was a bad, bad man.

More than anything else, she wanted her sisters out of here. But where could they go? Their immediate family was in Boston, more than sixteen hours away by car, and Syn wasn't old enough to drive. Not that it was really an option, as they didn't own a car to begin with.

As if he felt her looking at him, Chief McNutt turned, and his sharp gaze pierced hers. Her throat tightened and pain hit her between the eyes, forcing her to look away.

He was dark, unholy.

Shocked, Syn wasn't sure where the thought had come from. Mama had taught her how to recognize dark magic, but that was about it. She'd always said there was time for learning how to counteract the dark side when Syn was older, but that time had just run out. Mama had taken great pains to shield her daughters from the darker side of witchcraft, and in that moment Syn regretted Mama's decision.

How could she hope to protect her sisters if she didn't know what they were up against?

Looking up, she caught the chief's gaze fixed on the twins. Reaching over, she tucked the blanket securely around her youngest sisters. Several times since they'd been commanded to sit here she'd thought his attention had lingered on the twins longer than necessary. Fear nipped at her toes. Was he one of those men who liked children?

A uniformed officer came down the steps and made a beeline for the chief.

"We have a problem, sir."

Taking a long drag on his filthy cigar, Chief McNutt exhaled a thick column of smoke before he spoke. "And what would that be, Johnson?"

"There's a room in the attic we can't access. We've tried picking the lock, ramming it and dismantling the doorframe. It won't budge."

"That's because Itsy is in there, biding her time."

Clear as anything Syn heard Chloe's words in her mind, though her sister hadn't spoken out loud. She caught the faintest smirk on her sister's thin face. Reaching over, she pinched Chloe and the smirk vanished.

"You went through all the keys I gave you?" the Chief asked.

"Yes, sir, several times." Johnson said. "It's almost as if the door doesn't want to be opened."

"Horseshit, Johnson. Don't tell me you're going to turn into a pussy like the townspeople." McNutt snarled. "A door can't want anything, it simply is."

"Yes, sir," Johnson said.

"That's what you think, commoner."

Chloe's voice sounded in Syn's head again, and the smirk was back in place. Syn had only an inkling of what lived in the room, as that was Chloe's domain and Syn was happy to keep it that way. The only thing she knew was, whatever was in there

13

was not of this world. Mama had declared the room off-limits to everyone except her and her second daughter. She'd also forbidden all of them to speak of the secret room to anyone outside the family.

Chief McNutt looked at them again and this time his dark gaze landed on Syn. A jolt of distaste shot through her gut. Her nails dug into her palms. She was unwilling to show fear, so she forced her gaze to meet his.

A bolt of unnatural energy stabbed her square between the eyes, then slowly spread across her forehead. She caught Chloe's hand and without a second thought, cast a protection spell around herself and her sisters.

"White light, healing light, protect us from the darkness tonight."

Chloe's voice echoed in Syn's head, and the cooling magic of the light surrounded them. When they finished the spell, Syn felt calm and centered. As long as they remained together, the light would protect them.

"Johnson, I want you to do whatever it takes to get that door open. If you need dynamite, call the Defense Supply Company and see if they can spare someone to come up here and blow that damned door."

"But sir—"

"You heard me." Chief McNutt took his nasty cigar and stubbed it out in a pot of pansies Mama had been coddling for weeks. "Get moving, boy. We have a lot to do before the sun rises."

Syn's gaze remained fixed on the smoldering cigar in the midst of the flowers. Mama loved flowers, and if the temperature threatened to hit freezing, she'd haul those pots into the house and arrange them on the dining room table to keep them safe.

Angry words perched on the end of her tongue, and it was only by biting the inside of her cheek she managed to prevent them from spilling out.

"Girls." Chief McNutt walked toward them sporting a smile, as if trying to convince them he was harmless. "What do you

14

know about the room in the attic?"

"It's a room. It has a door with a handle and it opens from time to time," Chloe's words dripped with angry sarcasm. "What else is there to know?"

His smile vanished. "Mind your manners, child. Shoot your mouth off one more time and there will be consequences."

Syn squeezed her sister's hand.

"There is no darkness without light, Chloe."

"Mama had the only key to the room, Chief. We were forbidden to go in there," Syn said.

"And what did your mother keep in there?" The smile was back, though now it was sharper, as if he smelled fresh blood.

"I don't know," Chloe said. "As my sister said, Mama forbade us from entering the room."

His smile vanished and his cold gaze moved from one sister to another until finally coming to rest on the youngest, Autumn.

"And what about you, little one? Did your Mama ever take you into that room?"

"Syn?"

Autumn's voice sounded in Syn's mind, and Syn responded.

"Autumn, be silent, be still, be silent, be still."

The twins took up the chant and Autumn shook her head before burying her face in Syn's side.

"So none of you have any knowledge of what is behind the door?" His gaze met Syn's. "You're lying."

"No, sir." Her head came up and her chin shot out. "Mama taught us to respect our elders, and we do not lie."

"Like hell—"

"Hey Chief," another officer called from the front door. "They're here to pick up the kids."

Syn looked out the window to see a white-paneled van headed toward the house. Behind the van were two sedans. They parked on the far side of the turn-around with their engines idling.

"Right on time." The Chief waved at his man, then turned his attention to the girls. "Your rides are here."

"Where do you think you're taking us?" Chloe spoke up.

"We've arranged for you to stay elsewhere for the night."

"And in the morning our Aunt Bethany will be here to get us?" Summer spoke, fear thick in her voice.

Syn patted her sister's shoulder, trying to comfort her, but it was hard when she was just as terrified.

"Of course. We've already contacted your aunt, and she's taking an early flight out tomorrow. By lunchtime you'll be reunited."

In that moment, Syn knew he wasn't telling the truth. Aunt Bethany wouldn't be here in the morning. She doubted Beth even knew what was going on. Why was he lying? What was he up to?

"Syn, I don't want to leave," Autumn wailed. "Why do we have to go? Aunt Bethany knows where the house is, can't she pick us up here?"

Syn's grip tightened on Chloe's hand, and she threw an arm around her youngest sisters. Her gaze met the chief's and she spoke in an even tone. "And we'll be kept together until then?"

"Of course. The Baptist Church of Salem will be taking all of you in for the night. Your aunt is well aware of the arrangements, and she told me to tell you she'd be here as soon as she could." He smiled, and once again it didn't reach his hard eyes. "Now come along, girls. You don't want to keep everyone waiting, do you?"

Syn was in a silent panic as she ushered her sisters to their feet. What did they do now? Try to run away? The woods were thick and it would be simple to conceal themselves, but Autumn still wasn't well. Who knew what a night in the woods would do to her cold?

There was no one in town Syn could think to contact. The residents of Salem had shunned them years ago, and none would welcome their call for aid. Bethany was many miles away, and Syn had her phone number in the book by the phone. Would they let her get it?

"Chief, I need to grab—" she began.

"No time for that now. You can pick up your stuff in the morning." He moved between Syn and the living room door.

"Now you need to get in the cars so your sisters can be put to bed soon. The littlest one isn't looking very good."

Syn bit her tongue and did as she was told. Wrapping the blanket tightly around the twins, she and Chloe herded them outside.

The door of one of the sedans opened and a woman stepped out. Syn stared hard at the woman, stunned to realize it was Ms. Belcher, her second grade teacher. What was she doing here?

"Autumn, Summer. Over here, girls," the woman called to the twins.

The girls stumbled over the long blanket, but they walked toward her without hesitation. The twins had never attended public school, but they'd seen Ms. Belcher at the library where Mama had taken them every week.

Ms. Belcher opened the back door and helped the girls inside. An alarm bell went off in Syn's head when the door slammed shut. What should she do?

The driver's door to the second sedan opened, and out stepped another woman. It was Ms. Stubbs, the wife of the owner of the grocery store in Salem. Dressed in a heavy wool coat, she waved to them.

"Chloe, you're to ride with me, dear," she called. "Hurry now before you catch your death!"

"What's going on, Syn? I don't want to go with her."

"I don't know, Chloe. I don't know what to do!"

Syn gave Chloe's hand a squeeze, then released her. Dragging her slippered feet through the grass, her sister walked toward the car. Her back was arrow-straight and her bright red hair was caught in a tangled braid. She'd been waiting for Mama to return and help her braid it properly.

Syn's heart gave a jerk when she saw her blue butterfly ponytail holder in her sister's hair. When Chloe climbed into the car and Ms. Stubbs slammed the door, terror took hold of Syn.

"Why do we have to ride in separate cars?" She faced Chief McNutt with all the bravado a fourteen-going-on-fifteen year old could muster. "We can fit in one."

His steely gaze moved over her face, and for a few moments

she didn't think he'd answer. "Little Synnamon, of all your sisters, you look the most like your mama." He gave her an odd smile. "You're almost a carbon copy, aren't you? She was a very beautiful woman, you know."

Revulsion made her skin crawl. There was something wrong with this man.

"Why do we need separate cars, Chief?" This time she spoke a little louder.

"Your mother was the kind of woman men desired and other women hated. You'll learn about this when you get a little older." His voice grew soft and his gaze distant. "She was also a very smart woman, far more so than we'd ever dreamed." He reached for Syn's arm.

She jerked away and her head came into contact with the lamppost, hard. Stunned, she was unable to move when his big hand captured her chin and forced her gaze to meet his.

"You look just like her. Skin softer than silk, eyes the color of violets and hair like coal dust."

"What do you want from me, Chief?"

His voice dropped. "You know what's in that room, don't you, Syn?"

"I already told you I didn't."

"You and your sisters lied to me, didn't you?" His grip tightened. "I think we both know what lurks in the attic."

The thought that this man knew about the attic sent dread shooting through her. No one outside of the family could know what was in that room. It was too dangerous. Only Mama or Chloe could control Itsy—

"I see from the look in your eyes you know more than you let on." His eyes gleamed. "How do I access the room? How do I control it?"

"No."

His grip tightened until she feared he'd break her jaw with one hand. She clawed at his fingers, her short nails did little to soften his iron grip.

"Don't deny me girl. I will have my way."

"I can't answer you. I don't know!"

His gaze narrowed. "We'll just see about that."

18

Keeping a punishing hold on her jaw, Chief McNutt dragged her across the drive toward the white-paneled van. The driver's door opened and a blond man Syn didn't recognize stepped out.

Stumbling behind the chief, Syn's eyes welled with tears as her sisters began to scream her name. Their voices were muffled by the closed car doors, but she heard them all the same.

The blond opened the double doors of the van and by the time Syn reached it, tears ran down her face. The pain in her jaw was unbearable, and the world around her had disintegrated into a watery wasteland of distorted images.

The chief's face came into focus, just inches from hers. "Sooner or later you will tell me everything you know, or your sisters will pay the price for your stubbornness."

Syn's feet left the ground and she hit the cold steel floor of the van with a jarring thud. She scrambled to her knees and the doors slammed shut before she could reach them. With a cry, she threw herself against the door then pressed her nose against the window.

The chief and the stranger were talking just a few feet away, but she couldn't hear what they were saying. The blond seemed to be agitated when he gestured toward the house. The chief grabbed his shoulder and gave him a gentle shake, then the blond nodded.

"Chloe!"

"Are you okay, Syn? Where are they taking us?"

"I have no idea."

"Syn, Syn, Syn, Syn."

The twins' frightened voices sounded in her head.

"Hush, girls. Calm down, and we'll get through this together."

Tears continued to stream down Syn's face, and even though every fiber in her body objected, she knew what she had to say to her beloved sisters. Pressing her palm against the window, she strained to see them in either of the cars.

"Listen to me, girls. It's possible these people will separate us. Do you remember what Mama told us to do if something bad happened?"

19

Silence.

"*Sisters!*"

The twins began to whimper and Chloe's voice sounded.

"*Yes, Syn. If we're separated, and Aunt Bethany can't find us, one day we will be called to return to Angelov House.*"

"*Perfect, Chloe. Mama would be proud.*"

The blond stranger opened the driver's side door and climbed behind the wheel of the van without a word. Starting up the engine, he put it in gear and Syn had to brace herself from sliding across the cold, metal floor as they headed down the drive.

Syn's fingers curled against the glass, then straightened when the two sedans followed the van.

"*How will we know, Syn? What do we do then?*" Summer's voice was high, strained.

"*Trust in the universe, Summer. We are Daughters of the Light, and when the time is right, the Goddess will tell us when it's safe to return. We will be reunited, girls. It is our destiny.*"

The van pulled out of the long drive and made the left turn to head west into Salem. Syn's eyes widened when the second car turned right and drove east.

"*No!*"

The final car carrying Chloe went straight out of the drive and headed toward Columbus.

Goddess, do not let this happen!

Her sisters' screams threatened to tear her head apart. Grabbing her ears, Syn began to sob. Within moments, the voices faded altogether and for the first time in her life, she was truly alone.

Chapter One

Fifteen years later

Turning his police-issued SUV into the overgrown drive, Salem Police Chief Matthew Whitefeather couldn't explain what it was about Angelov house that fascinated him. There were many beautiful homes in and around Salem, but there was something about this one that pulled at his soul.

The house sat on a large hill overlooking the town of Salem, Ohio. Only a few acres nearest the house had been cleared, and the rest of the property remained wooded and unimproved. It was an amazing piece of property, the kind of place he could easily envision living out his golden years on the wide porch with a beer in one hand, a wife in the other, and a dozen grandkids romping through the yard.

The house was an elegant piece of architecture, with turrets and balconies along with a wide front porch. It sported at least twenty rooms, and at the very top a widow's walk between the two main turrets.

Legend was, the wives of fishermen would await their husband's return from the sea up on a walk such as this. The property sported unfettered access to Lake Erie, where many made their living from the waters, as the Angelovs probably had in the past.

The place had been empty for many years and the locals believed it was haunted. The Angelovs, the family who'd built the place centuries before, were just a few of the ghosts said to be wandering about terrorizing people. Some even believed just coming onto the property was bad luck.

After pulling in behind the crime scene van, Matt threw the

SUV into park. Pausing only long enough to grab his flashlight and secure it on his belt, he slammed the door and headed for the van.

If the house wasn't already haunted, it might well be now. He'd been stuck in a meeting with the City Council when the ten-twenty call, unknown emergency, had been received by Dispatch. It was only when the first officer arrived on the scene that the call was re-dispatched as a ten-eighteen, a dead body found.

"Chief." Officer Bryan Haines stood by the van with a clipboard in one hand. "We searched the house and came up empty."

"Not surprising."

Several feet from the porch steps was a small body covered by a white sheet. He'd been notified the deceased was a child, and the body barely registered under the cotton drape. Matt walked toward the scene and Haines fell in step beside him.

"The other kids were taken to the station and their parents are there now," Hayes said.

"And the psychologist?"

"On his way in. The Chaplain Corps was notified and Father Fred just happened to be at the station. He's sitting with the kids, too."

Matt dropped into a crouch beside the body, steeling himself for what was to come. Dealing with death was never an easy task, but the demise of a child was heart-wrenching, no matter how hardened the cop.

When Matt pulled away the sheet, the pale face of Robert Young, Jr. was revealed. Already his skin was the mottled bluish color of the dead. His hazel eyes were open, and the child stared sightlessly at the blue sky. Matt had seen him playing with his friends on the square only last week. His jaw clenched. Only eleven years old, and already his life was over.

Christ.

"Medical examiner should be here any minute. Upon visual inspection of the body I could find no obvious source of trauma." Haines began flipping through the pages on his clipboard. "According to his friends, he's been dead approximately forty-five minutes."

"Who was with him?"

"Billy Steele, Seth Greene and Thomas McNutt."

"Chief McNutt's grandson?"

"That's him."

"Did they give any indication as to what happened?" Matt dropped the sheet over the child's face, knowing he'd see it again in his sleep.

"According to Billy, the boys dared Bobby and Tommy to knock on the front door. When Bobby touched the door, it flew open and Bobby began to scream. Tommy fell down and Bobby flew backwards through the air as if he'd been shot out of a cannon."

"Interesting."

"Chief." Haines sounded distinctly uncomfortable. "Everyone in town knows this house just ain't right."

"Give me a break, Haines. All I want is the facts, not some paranormal mumbo-jumbo. There is no such thing as ghosts, and this house is just that, an old house. Chances are we're going to find evidence that a homeless person had shacked up in there. The kids startled whoever was in there and he panicked."

"Yes, sir." The officer's lips tightened.

"Did the kids say anything else?"

"Seth said when Bobby came flying off the porch, he saw black smoke in the doorway."

"Smoke?"

"Yes, sir."

"Did anyone get a statement from Tommy?"

"Not yet, sir. The paramedics took him to the hospital. He's in shock."

Hell, if his best friend had been killed in front of him when he was eleven, Matt was sure he'd have been in shock too.

"Get on the phone to the M.E. and ask him what the hell the hold up is. I don't want this child lying out here another minute if we can help it."

"Yes, sir."

"I'm going to take a look inside," Matt said.

"Yes, sir."

Crime scene officers stood on the porch while a K-9 officer swept the area of yard closest to the house. Several other officers watched the dog at work, waiting for any sign the canine had located more evidence.

Matt headed up the walk, taking care to steer clear of the area the K-9 team worked. Angelov house was isolated, and even for a fleet-footed eleven-year-old boy it would take close to ten minutes to run through the surrounding woods to reach the nearest phone. If someone had been staying here, he'd be long gone by now.

The moment Matt stepped over the threshold, instinctively he knew the house was empty. Of humans, at least. Long years of police work and his acutely developed senses were enough to tell him this. Both he and his twin, Micah, had what their father called "preternatural senses," which gave them an unusual edge over many cops.

The house was dim, thanks to the shutters over every window. Pulling out his flashlight, Matt entered the living room. The white-sheet-covered furniture was arranged on the right, and the rest of the room was bare. Dozens of footprints marred the dirty floor, and he'd bet they were all from his officers.

The dining room was next, and like the living room, everything was covered in sheets, even the chandelier. Thin ribbons of light penetrated the gloom, and dust floated lazily through the air.

Embossed wallpaper hung in dirty, tattered strips and he couldn't help but admire the hand-carved crown molding and recessed ceiling. Someone had put a great deal of care into the building of this house. This place had to be worth a fortune. In today's economy, buying the woodwork alone would cost Matt at least a year's pay.

A swinging door led the way into the kitchen and it was much brighter in here. A shutter had fallen away from one window, and golden sunlight streamed in through the dirty glass. At first glance, he thought the room was empty, then he saw a filmy gray smoke near the opposite door. He blinked, not quite sure if his eyes had betrayed him.

The smoke swirled into a column and the air turned cold. Every hair on his body leapt to attention and he reached for his gun. Before his eyes, the smoke vanished through a crack in the floorboards.

Matt stood there shocked, his mind unable to absorb what he'd seen. For a moment it felt as if he'd been struck in the head.

"What the fuck was that?"

With his hand on his gun, he moved toward the other door, taking care to test the floor as he walked. Was there some kind of trap door? Maybe it had been coal dust swept up from the basement? Slowly he moved into the next room, and when he did, the tension left his body.

Damn, that was...spooky.

Shaking off his unease, he realized this had been a family room. More sheet-shrouded furniture was grouped in the center of the room. Dozens of boxes were stacked along the outside wall, and one stack had fallen over. Paint was chipping off the walls and had curled on the ceiling like hundreds of commas. Moving his flashlight over the damage, Matt realized it would take a crew of painters weeks to repair what years of neglect had wrought upon this room alone.

It was depressing.

His light swept over the wall when something caught his attention. Moving forward, his light caught on words that had been carved in the plaster. The scrawl was childlike, stiff.

Now they come,
Now they die

Matt reached for his radio to raise Haines. "Four-ten to three ninety-seven."

"Three ninety-seven."

"Send in the photographer. I'm in family room on the east side of the house."

"Copy that."

Matt pulled a latex glove from a small, billfold-like pack on his utility belt. Crouching, he poked at the plaster powder with one finger. It was perfectly white and free of dust, indicating it had landed here recently.

25

Rising, he moved toward the kitchen and began checking the windows. All of them were secure, and the locks were covered in a thick layer of dust. The massive wood-burning stove was also gray with dirt, as was the kitchen table. Nothing appeared to be disturbed.

"Sir?" The photographer appeared in the doorway with a digital camera in hand.

"Hawkins, there's a carving in the wall just through this doorway. Please document it, along with the plaster dust on the floor."

"Yes, sir."

The kitchen cabinets were the glass-fronted kind, and to Matt's surprise there were dishes still inside. He opened one of the doors. Everything had been neatly put away, the glasses lined up and the coffee mugs stacked in twos waiting for their owner to use them. He closed the door.

Where was the Angelov family now?

The hair on the back of his neck prickled, and he had the distinct feeling someone was watching him. He turned but the kitchen was empty. There was something about this house—

"Sir?" Officer Hawkins called from the other room.

"Yes?"

"Where is the carving you wanted me to photograph?"

"I'll show you." Matt walked into the room and swept the beam from his flashlight over the walls. "It was right here—"

The carving was gone and the expanse of peeling paint undisturbed.

"Wait a minute."

Starting from the kitchen doorway, he re-traced his steps and swept every inch of the wall, only to find it intact. Now he was starting to feel more than a little squirrelly. Surely he wasn't starting to see things?

"Three ninety-seven to four-ten," his radio squawked.

Matt keyed his mike. "Go ahead."

"We found footprints out here near the barn. When you're done with three-ninety can you send him out?"

"Copy that."

Ignoring the gaze of his perplexed photographer, Matt told him to head outside to the barn. After the other man left, Matt searched the wall again and came up empty-handed.

"It was here," he muttered. "It was. Why else would I have put on a glove?"

Irritated beyond words, Matt headed for the kitchen and his heart leapt into his throat. On the floor where he'd seen the smoke was a photograph that hadn't been there moments before. A single beam of sunlight illuminated the glossy photo. It was the only thing in the room—besides himself—that wasn't gray with dirt and age.

Crouching, Matt examined the photo. It was a candid shot of a dark-haired woman and four children. Was this the Angelov family? From what little he'd heard, the mother had been killed in an accident and the children had been shipped off to live with relatives somewhere in the east.

"Three ninety-seven to four-ten."

"Four-ten."

"M.E. is on the scene."

"Copy that."

With his gloved hand, he picked up the photo. The woman was exquisite, with pale skin and hair as dark as night. Her arms were around the two older girls, one of whom was the spitting image of her mother and the other, a redhead. In front of them a set of twins sat cross-legged, each with pale blonde hair and wide blue eyes.

A beautiful family.

Photo in hand, he rose. With the M.E. on scene he needed to get outside and start the paperwork. Then he'd head to the hospital and check up on Tommy McNutt. Sooner or later someone would have to take the boy's statement, and it might as well be Matt.

A hollow thumping noise from the dining room had him reaching for his gun again. Senses on high alert, he moved through the kitchen then opened the swinging door. A small rubber ball was rolling across the floor toward him.

After tucking the photo into his shirt pocket, Matt retrieved the ball and rubbed off a layer of dirt with his gloved thumb. The ball was clear rubber with a pink-tutu-clad ballerina in the

27

center, forever suspended in a pirouette.

One of his men must've knocked it loose—

Something or someone in this house is playing with you.

"Like hell they are."

He headed for the front door. He didn't believe in ghosts, witches or any of that nonsense. In his line of work, he'd learned long ago the dead were the last thing he'd have to worry about. It was the living that would stick a knife in a man's back.

ʚ

Matt was sitting by Tommy's bed when the boy's eyes finally opened. It was near midnight, and it had been an incredibly long and exhausting day. If Matt hadn't been focused on the boy's face, he never would've seen the slight movement.

Laying his hand on the boy's arm, Matt leaned forward. Tommy's mother was sound asleep on the bench seat under the window, worry evident on her tired face. His father had been here earlier, and he'd left with the promise to return at first light.

Tommy's gaze was empty, and after blinking several times, he slowly focused on Matt. The child said nothing, his blank gaze was enough to give Matt a chill.

"Tommy, it's Chief Whitefeather," he whispered.

The silence was thick and the boy continued to stare at him.

"Do you remember me?"

Tommy gave a faint nod.

"Good job, son. I know this afternoon was very frightening for you. Can you tell me what happened?"

The boy looked away. His gaze traveled to his sleeping mother, then returned to meet Matt's. He gave another tiny nod.

"Tommy, can you tell me what happened to your friend?"

Tears began to fill the boy's clear green eyes. His lips moved but no sound came out.

"Wait, let me get you a drink." Matt poured a glass of water from the plastic pitcher, then helped the boy sit up to drink it. "Better now?"

Tommy nodded.

"You know you're safe here, Tommy. I won't let anything hurt you again."

The boy nodded and continued to stare at him for a few more moments. When he spoke, his words were whisper-soft, forcing Matt to lean in.

"It was the Devil. He came after us."

Chapter Two

Five years later

The small metal sign marked the city limits of Salem and had Syn biting her lower lip. Cresting the rise, she steered her Jeep to the shoulder of the road and took her first look at her hometown in twenty years.

Nestled in a slight valley, Salem was a picture postcard with its gleaming church spires and large, well-kept homes. On the outskirts of town, the properties were much larger and the number of horses and cows increased dramatically.

In the center was the square with its covered bandstand and towering Christmas tree decked out in red bows and gold bulbs. Stores lined the square, and people walked to and fro picking up last minute items before heading home for dinner. Even the municipal buildings were decorated for Christmas with evergreen boughs and enough red ribbon to overload a landfill.

The hypocrisy of the scene made her sick.

From a distance, Salem didn't look as if it had changed at all. To some it was a paradise in the scenic rolling hills of Ohio, and even Syn had to admit it was lovely. To others, those who knew the truth, it was a beautiful façade hiding a black heart. To a casual observer, it was here the pillars of the community raised their offspring to be upstanding citizens and live the American Dream. Only its residents knew Salem was not as wholesome as it seemed.

This town hid its secrets well.

Her gaze scanned the hill on the other side of town, searching for any sign of her childhood home. The trees had grown a great deal, and at this distance she couldn't pick it out.

Releasing the brake, Syn pulled onto the road and headed for town. According to Aunt Beth, the house was in decent shape, though it was beginning to show its age. Beth was fond of saying houses were like people, they didn't do well if left on their own for too long.

Her aunt had been pushing Syn to return to Salem for the past five years but Syn had resisted. She'd known her instincts would tell her when the time was right, and hurrying the process would be a mistake.

Turning onto a dirt road, Syn hoped to avoid going into town today. She was exhausted and didn't want anyone to spot her before she was ready to deal with them.

Had any of her sisters returned? What if they'd come and gone, thinking she was dead? Maybe she'd be alone with Itsy...

"Stop that."

Her words were loud in the relative quiet of the car. With a scowl she pushed a CD into the player. The screeching heavy metal music did nothing to calm her nerves.

Syn's instincts were telling her she'd be the first to return. She'd had a dream about the long, rocky path ahead of her, and the first steps needed to be completed without her sisters. This would be a journey of courage for her. Mama had believed the universe took care of its own and Syn could only pray this belief held true in the coming weeks.

Feeling moderately calmer, Syn took a deep, cleansing breath, her gaze focused on the road. What would the house look like now? Would it be as she remembered?

Upon Victoria's death, Beth had hired a Trust company to hold the deed for the house. Beth told her that Angelovs had come out of the woodwork and tried to lay claim to the property when the girls vanished. Most had tried to convince Beth the girls were dead and it was nonsense for her to maintain the property for them.

For centuries the house had passed to the first-born daughter in each generation, and Beth had been determined to uphold the tradition. The trust successfully held off the family claims and oversaw the maintenance of the house. Syn hoped they'd done a good job and wildlife hadn't taken over. She wasn't too excited to share her space with creatures of the four-legged variety.

Turning up the music, she didn't want to think about the work awaiting her. For now she'd stick to her immediate plans of making camp and getting a good night's sleep. Tomorrow she could ponder the first item on her list, making the house habitable so they'd have a roof over their heads when her sisters returned.

Her sisters.

The ever-present ache in her heart grew sharp, and her grip tightened on the steering wheel. As she turned left onto Winding Oak, her stomach tightened. When she was a child, accidents on this stretch of road had seemed like a weekly event.

Lying in her attic bedroom, she'd hear the screech of tires and the sickening crunch of a car hitting either the guardrail or one of the trees along the road. She'd send up a silent plea for the driver's health, but it was inevitable some would die. She'd just never dreamed it would be Mama.

Keeping her gaze fixed on the road, she passed the spot where she'd seen her mother's body. The curve was sharp, and it was no wonder she'd been hit. It would be hard for a driver to see someone walking on the road at night at the bend. All these years later Syn was still haunted with the niggling feeling the so-called accident wasn't all there was to the story.

She slowed the Jeep when the driveway came into view.

Here. It was right here that I saw them last.

Pulling into the foot of the drive, she scanned her surroundings. The road was recently paved and the grass and weeds were dormant with the oncoming winter. Without a house in sight, it made for bleak surroundings for some, but not for her. She'd always loved it out here, it was so wild and untouched. Her nearest neighbor was a mile up the road and Syn liked it that way. The less she had to deal with the residents of Salem, the better off she and her sisters would be.

Chloe.

Summer.

Autumn.

Silently, she repeated their names over and over, as if doing so would cause them to appear. In the years since that dreadful night, she'd performed the ritual thousands of times. Even though they'd been separated, she knew as long as she repeated their names they couldn't be forgotten. Never would they be taken from her as long as she retained that sliver of their identity, even though she barely remembered their faces without the help of a photo.

Syn wasn't sure what hurt more—losing them or being unable to remember their faces, their laughter or how they smelled after bath time. What kind of a sister was she if she couldn't recall even these tiny details?

How she longed to see the women they'd become. Did Chloe still love chocolate ice cream with marshmallow fluff? Even now, did the twins run in the rain and splash in the puddles with their bare feet?

Did they miss her as much as she missed them?

Syn released her death grip on the steering wheel. Try as she might, she'd never been able to shake the feeling she'd failed her family when they'd needed her most. It broke her heart just thinking about it.

A soft whine snapped her attention away from her thoughts. Maddie, her dog and constant companion, popped her head between the front seats and braced her front paws on the console. Automatically, Syn reached up and gave the dog a good scratch under her chin.

"Don't worry, girl. We'll be free of this tin can in mere moments, I promise."

Putting the car in gear, she pulled further into the driveway, surprised by the obvious signs of neglect. Long gone was the neat gravel lane, swallowed by a multitude of dead weeds and brush. Her nose wrinkled. Whoever the trust had hired to keep up the place wasn't doing a very good job.

Guiding her Jeep up the drive, she spied a heavy chain spanning the drive and blocking the way to the house.

"Where the hell did this come from?"

Slamming the gearshift into park, Syn exited the car to inspect the roadblock. Judging from the condition of the chain, it was safe to say it had been there quite some time. In the center hung a "No Trespassing" sign, though it was barely legible. Time and weather had taken their toll, bleaching the sign to a uniform gray.

"No trespassing," Syn muttered. "We'll just see about that."

After a quick examination of the wooden posts that secured the chain, she marched back to the car. The wood was old and it would take very little effort to remove the chain. After retrieving a hand ax from her camping gear, she returned to do battle.

Taking aim, she swung the ax, gratified when it sank into the soft wood.

"Nothing like a little destruction to burn off excess tension." She took another swing.

Now the question was; who'd ordered this chain to be placed here? The only people with the authority to do so would be the trust company, Beth or herself. Neither had mentioned blocking the drive, so that left only one other option.

The police.

Annoyance forced her to swing the ax harder than before. When it made contact, the reverberation sang up her arm, giving her a sense of satisfaction. With one final strike, the post gave way and the chain dropped with a rattle. Satisfied, Syn braced the ax against her shoulder, then spat on the sign.

"No trespassing, my ass."

Turning on her heel, she headed for the car. The Salem police had betrayed her family in the worst way and she wasn't about to forgive them. Even though she had no hard evidence, she knew it was McNutt who'd orchestrated the separation of her and her sisters.

Getting into the car, Syn tossed the ax onto the floor of the passenger seat.

The only information she'd been able to uncover was that McNutt ordered the sisters to be put into the foster care systems in California, Wyoming and New York. As far as she knew, the girls had been put on planes within hours of their separation.

As for Syn, she hadn't been quite so lucky.

Putting the car in drive, she shrugged off the disturbing memories of the weeks after her mother's death. Tonight, she didn't want to think about anything to do with the dark times.

Tomorrow would come soon enough, and that's when the real work would begin. For now, her only responsibility was to breathe and wrap her mind around the fact she was finally home.

The gravel was long gone, though the lane was in surprisingly good repair. The trees lining the drive seemed to close in around her car. Even bare of leaves, they struggled to shut out what little light was left. She'd tried to time her arrival so she wouldn't arrive in the dark, but an accident on highway three had delayed her homecoming.

"It doesn't matter if it's dark, it's only a house," she muttered.

Famous last words...

Maddie whined and nudged Syn's shoulder.

"I hear you, girl."

She didn't know what she'd do without her dog. She'd found the mutt hunting for scraps behind the diner where Syn worked several years ago. When Maddie crossed her path, Syn hadn't been in the market for a dog. At that time, she'd had enough problems keeping herself fed, let alone keeping a second belly full.

As it turned out, Maddie was anything but a burden.

The beagle-boxer mix shadowed Syn better than a stalker, rarely letting her mistress out of her sight. The dog was a steadfast companion and warm to sleep with. That was a bonus, as they'd slept in tents more often than not over the last few months.

The driveway curved to the left and when Syn made the turn, the trees and weeds gave way to a neatly trimmed lawn, though the grass was brown. Here the driveway had been well-maintained, complete with fresh gravel.

"Ah, so the maintenance money didn't go up in smoke after all."

The fading sunlight illuminated Angelov House with golden-pink rays. Tears stung her eyes and something inside her chest loosened. The sense of homecoming was so strong it threatened to steal her breath. After being away for so many years, she'd forgotten just how attached she was to this place.

From its turrets to the wrap-around porch, Syn loved every

board and creaky joint of her home. Pulling up just to the right of the porch steps, she put the Jeep in park and shut off the engine.

"I'm home."

The only response was the tick-tick of the cooling engine.

Opening the door, she took a deep breath of icy air then shivered. It tasted like snow. How in the world had she managed to live more than half of her life in the South when winter was her favorite season?

Maddie made a dash for freedom the moment Syn got out of the car. With her nose to the ground and her floppy ears dancing, she began scouting her new territory.

Staring up at the house, Syn marveled at its sheer size. It was so much bigger than she'd remembered it, but then as a child she'd never thought of the size. It was simply home. Built in the late 1700's by the first Angelov to set foot in America, it was truly a marvel to behold. Pieter Angelov had built this house for his lovely and very rich young bride.

In the early years, the Angelovs had earned their living by working the land and fishing the Great Lakes. It was by chance Pieter had married into the powerful Westin family from New York City. Their multi-millions combined with his business acumen had secured the financial future of his descendents. The Angelov Fishing Fleet had been born, and even though the business had diversified many times over, the fleet still pulled in a tidy profit on its own.

Syn didn't care about the money. All she'd ever wanted was to live in this house.

It was a beautiful old place perched on a hill overlooking both Salem and the shores of Lake Erie. Her childhood in this home, on this land, had been idyllic. As children they'd been forbidden nothing, given free run of the house and the surrounding acreage.

Then it was all gone in the blink of an eye.

Shaking off her dark thoughts, she bounded up the steps. Not now, not yet. In the light of day she could excavate those wounds, but not here in the darkness.

Up close she could detect evidence of neglect. The paint was peeling, and one of the front shutters was askew. The porch swing where she and her sisters had spent many happy hours had broken, one half still hanging from its chain.

So much had changed and yet, it was still the same.

Angelov house possessed an air of loneliness she hadn't anticipated. Standing on the porch, it hurt to think of the house empty for so long. This was a special place and it never should've been abandoned. Her jaw tightened. It never would've happened if it weren't for the corrupt Salem Police.

Hardening her heart for what was to come, she withdrew the house keys Beth had sent to her in Arizona. Her hand shook when she turned the key and stiff tumblers ground together. Behind her, Maddie raced up the steps in a scurry of toenails and fur.

When Syn opened the door a rush of stale air assailed her. Withdrawing a flashlight from a jacket pocket, she flinched when the beam illuminated a line of bright red on the dusty wooden floor.

Brick dust.

To those who practiced voodoo, brick dust was used to protect the inhabitants from anyone who wished to do them ill. Literally, those with a black heart would not be able to cross the threshold and do harm to those inside. It wasn't something Mama believed in and they'd never used it around the house. Just who had left it here?

Or what?

Careful to not disturb the line, she followed Maddie into the house. The entry hall was filthy; inches of dust and dirt coated everything in sight. To the left was the hall tree that used to hold their coats, though now it was bare.

Beyond that was the family room, and when she entered, Syn's heart gave a queer little jerk. It, like the hall, was covered in dust and dirt. They'd painted the walls an appalling pink shade only months before her mother's death. She smiled at the memory.

The furniture with sheets as shrouds lined one wall, and the closed shutters blocked what little light was left outside. Stacks of boxes were arranged against the far wall. One stack had fallen over, and what looked like clothing lay on the floor.

The mantel over the fireplace was covered with

candleholders. Wax had overflowed and secured the holders to the carved marble. She ran her finger over the cold, dusty wax. Mama would cry if she could see this destruction. While she might not have been a meticulous housekeeper, this never would've happened on her watch.

Syn turned away. She could take heart that it had survived and with some hard work it could be salvaged.

On wobbly legs, she headed into the kitchen. Very little light penetrated this room and she could hardly see her hand in front of her face. She made out the dim outline of the table and chairs. Her stomach tightened. She and her sisters had spent many hours around that table doing their schoolwork.

Maddie nudged her leg and whined; her tail wiggled a mile a minute.

"Hold on, baby. I know you're hungry, and so am I."

Missing her family to the point of physical pain, Syn turned and headed for the front door. Maddie had kept pace with her, pausing only to snuffle her nose through the dirt, which had her sneezing for her trouble.

The wide stairs leading to the second level loomed in front of Syn, but the darkness on the landing above made up her mind about venturing on. Walking upstairs now would not be a smart thing to do. She was exhausted, her dog was hungry, and finding a place to sleep was top on her list of immediate needs.

"Come on, girl. Let's go setup housekeeping."

Leaving the house, Syn couldn't help but feel as if a weight had been lifted off her shoulders. The house had a dark, almost oppressive feel to it. Maybe it was the brick dust causing her to think this way? One of the first things she'd do tomorrow was clean all of it up. Voodoo had no place here.

After retrieving her gear from the back of the Jeep, she picked a sheltered spot under an ancient oak tree near the house. Setting up camp was as familiar to her as eating a sandwich. Within a half-hour the tent was up, her bags were stowed and her bed was ready. Maddie dined on canned dog food while Syn munched on a cardboard-flavored protein bar.

All in all, not a very satisfying dinner after such a long day of travel.

Making a mental note to get food first thing in the morning,

Syn, followed by Maddie, climbed into the tent and Syn zipped them in. The dog took her favored spot at the foot of Syn's bed, created from a blow-up mattress and multiple sleeping bags.

From her duffle bag, she dug out her warmest pajamas and long underwear. It took only minutes to change, and by the time she was done the word "chilled" did not begin to describe how she felt. Tomorrow she'd heat up some water so she could bathe, but tonight, it wasn't going to happen. She could sleep dirty; it wasn't like she'd never done it before.

Climbing into her nest, Syn zipped shut her sleeping bag. The moment she was settled, Maddie got to her feet and stretched out by Syn's side. She pulled a sleeping bag over the mutt, and the hound fell asleep quickly and began to snore in Syn's ear.

She smiled for the first time that day. Having Maddie with her was a definite comfort, as she was never alone with the dog by her side.

An unexpected sense of homecoming settled over her.

Finally, an Angelov had returned to Salem. There was no doubt that any number of people in town would be shocked to see her, as her resemblance to Victoria was strong. Many would be dismayed, and more than a few would be downright angry.

That's what she was counting on.

Taking a deep breath, she willed her body and mind to relax. For now she was safe, anonymous. For the next few days she'd avoid going into town until she had her feet squarely beneath her. The last thing she wanted was to be caught off guard by the people who'd destroyed her family.

Mama had raised her daughters to seek the truth in all matters and avoid taking revenge upon those who'd wronged them. Over and over she'd told them no good would come of hanging onto a wound, as the other person probably wouldn't care how they felt. Hanging onto old hurts would further damage them, not the person who'd inflicted the pain.

In her heart Syn knew her mother was right, but she'd never been able to shake her anger and the need for knowledge. She needed concrete evidence to answer what happened to her mother that night. As a child her voice had been taken from her, but not this time. This time would be different.

She was a mature, intelligent woman who could stand on her own. Not only would she reclaim the child they'd damaged, she'd find her sisters and reassemble her family. At the same time, she would ferret out the answers to her mother's death. Someone in Salem knew what happened that night, and it would take time to draw them out, but time was one thing Syn had plenty of.

Her sisters would know when it was time to return, and once they were reunited, all hell would descend upon those who'd torn them apart.

ȣ

At the very top of Angelov House, tucked under the eaves, was a small, octagonal window. A soft breeze sprang up and gently tugged at the shredded lace curtain. Beyond the window in a small, sealed room, shadows shifted then coalesced into human form. Drifting toward the window, the figure peered out into the night, its gaze fixed on the tent.

With ghostly fingers, the creature reached out toward the woman now sound asleep. Pain lanced its ghostly form and for a second it lost shape, turning to a smoky gray before repairing itself.

Finally, she was home. Synnamon Angelina Victoria Angelov, Victoria's eldest daughter. Many years had passed, and it was time to set things to right. Soon the daughters would be reunited and here where they belonged.

In the sleepy town below and places closer than the girls could ever imagine, secrets would be discovered. Victoria had lost her life in the face of another's jealousy, and it was time for her daughters to reclaim the heritage that was theirs and theirs alone.

The witches would return to Salem and many humans would die for their sins.

Chapter Three

Since she'd arrived earlier than anticipated, Syn was on her own in finding a habitable space in the house. Normally she didn't mind sleeping in the tent, but it had been many years since she'd been subjected to a northern Ohio winter. Both she and Maddie would be far more comfortable with a solid roof over their heads and a fireplace to cozy up to.

Armed with a notepad and pen, Syn wasn't too surprised to find the house looked worse in the daylight. After opening the shutters and getting her first look at the mess, she'd been tempted to close them and go in search of a hotel.

The darkness had hidden the thick dirt and dust that accumulated on every available surface. The sheets covering the furniture were no longer white; they'd turned a mottled combination of yellow and gray. Cobwebs, bigger than any she'd ever seen, hung like ghostly drapes in the corners and doorways. One web large enough to catch a human hung from the living room chandelier, causing her to look around for the mythical creature who'd created it.

"Thank the Goddess I didn't run into that last night." She sidestepped the monstrosity. "I'd be back in Arizona by now if I had."

As far as she was concerned, there wasn't much worse than walking face-first into a spider web. Just the thought of those invisible strands against her skin was enough to send her scurrying from the room with Maddie at her heels.

Since entering the house, the dog had glued her amazing nose to the floor so as not to miss any scent worth wiggling her tail for. Every now and then she'd raise her head, let out a ferocious sneeze, then continue on her journey.

Jogging up the steps to the landing, Syn leaned against the rail and looked up into the attic two floors above. Her eyes widened when she spied more cobwebs, some the size of the one in the living room.

Somewhere in this house was a spider the size of a Volkswagen.

"Eww!"

Just the thought was enough to make her skin crawl. Maybe she should go back to the car and grab the ax—

Maddie yanked her back to reality by galloping up the remaining steps to the second floor. There she stood, with her head down and an expectant expression on her funny face.

"Chill, girl. It's not like the dirt is going anywhere."

Climbing the remaining steps, she wasn't surprised to see more of the same. Dust, dirt and yellowing sheets covered everything. The paintings that had once lined the walls now leaned against some boxes in a corner. Yet another sheet covered the paintings and the discolored patches on the wall, the only testament to their once having hung there.

The second floor of the house had rarely been used unless family visited. Apart from her mother's bedroom and the sunroom in the back of the house, this floor held little of interest.

But what of her secret hiding place?

The grandfather clock stood where it always had, though a sheet now covered two-thirds of it. Tucking the notepad and pen in her pocket, Syn dropped into a crouch, her nimble fingers moving along the ornate carving at the base of the clock. As if guided by some inner force, her fingers located the latch and a small door opened in the front.

She and Chloe had found this little treasure while playing marbles one rainy afternoon. Chloe had made her move and the shot went wide, hitting the clock instead of Syn's marble. After swearing each other to absolute secrecy, they'd used this drawer for notes or presents to each other.

Had anyone else found it?

Reaching inside, her fingers touched something cold and

round. Pulling it out, she smiled when she saw the amber gazing globe. About the size of a softball, it had been a gift from her maternal grandmother and Syn had always considered it one of her prized possessions. With great reverence, she cleaned the globe with the hem of her shirt.

Reaching into the drawer again, she found some colored pencils, a necklace with a ballet dancer charm and a piece of tourmaline. Staring down at her childhood treasures, Syn yearned for a time when life was simpler, though she knew it would never be again.

Reluctantly, she replaced the items and closed the door. Later, when she had a clean room, she'd retrieve her treasures and place them where the sun could cleanse away the darkness.

As she rose, sadness washed over her. Much like the globe, she'd existed in darkness for many years and it was long past time to stand in the light. The Salem police had dealt her family the first blow and she would deal the next.

Salem would never be the same.

Armed with her notepad once more, she began checking the rooms. They were empty. All of the furniture was located in the back bedroom and it was crammed full of bed frames, dressers and other odd bits of furniture.

Backing out of the room, it was then she realized Maddie wasn't with her. Pulling the door shut, she called for the dog.

"Maddie?"

A snuffling noise caught her attention and she found the dog sitting in the middle of the hall. She was looking at the door to Mama's sunroom with a curious expression on her funny face.

"Maddie, what are you—"

Her voice faded when she realized the dog didn't stir at the sound of her voice. Frowning, she walked toward her, coming to a stop when Syn saw what she guarded.

A neat line of crushed brick dust crossed the hallway from wall to wall.

She dropped into a crouch and absently rubbed Maddie's head. More brick dust. What was up with this? The dog nudged her hand.

"It's okay, baby. Mama has to check this out."

Prodding the dust with her finger, she felt nothing. It was apparent the dust had been here for some time, but why was it here in the first place?

On her notepad, she made a note to call Beth and ask her about this. Rising, Syn stepped over the dust with Maddie at her heels. Straight ahead was the sunroom where Mama had grown herbs and taught her daughters to create healing potions and salves. With the glass walls and ceiling, being in the room gave one the feeling of working outside under the trees. The leaded glass in the door caught her image and for a second Syn thought she caught a glimpse of Mama over her shoulder.

With her heart beating madly, she avoided looking at the glass and instead headed for her mother's bedroom. Taking a deep breath, she opened the door, and all of the air rushed from her lungs.

Her mother's room was intact.

If one could ignore the dust and spider webs and the fact every drawer had been opened and dumped on the floor, it looked as if Mama had just left the room. The broad mahogany bed was neatly made and her mother's favorite lotion sat on the nightstand.

On the dressing table, her makeup and perfumes were scattered across the top. The closet door was open and inside the clothing still hung on the hangers. On the fireplace mantel, candlesticks and photo frames jockeyed for space.

On leaden feet, Syn moved across the room and picked up one of the frames. Running her finger over the glass, a row of smiling faces appeared.

Her sisters.

Syn was first in line with her hair in a wild tangle around her head. Her dress was overly large but it still didn't hide her scabby knees. Standing next to her was Chloe, with a sullen look on her face and a paperback book tucked under her arm. Her yellow dress was neat though she wore a lopsided bow in her red hair.

The twins looked like angels in their matching pink-and-white dresses, though Syn knew they could be little devils when they wanted. Mama had never wanted to dress them alike, but the twins had insisted that day.

One summer they'd worn matching princess dresses complete with tiaras. The girls refused to change until one night Mama had snuck off with the garments and burned them as the twins slept. Oh, the tears and cries of utter despair would've been heartbreaking if it hadn't been so amusing.

She ran her finger over their smiling faces. Where were they?

A strange clicking noise in the hall caught her attention. Maddie's head came up and the hair rose on her back. With a low growl she darted out the door, her nails scrabbling for purchase on the wooden floor. Syn followed, coming to a fast stop behind her dog.

In the center of the hall were two miniature rocking horses, and they moved in unison.

She recognized them immediately. The toys had belonged to the twins. On their fifth birthday, Beth had given the girls the horses, thus setting off their carnival period. For months they would wear only ballet tutus and leotards. Until the night of their mother's death, the girls had kept these horses on their nightstands where they could play with them before going to bed.

The hair on the back of her neck prickled.

Reaching out with her finely tuned senses, she could detect nothing threatening, inside the house at least. Then again, there had never been a time when she'd felt unsafe here.

Mama had maintained the house would always protect her girls, as if it were a living, breathing entity. Until that moment Syn had thought it was Victoria's active imagination that had caused her to use those terms.

She picked up one of the toy horses. Now she wasn't so sure.

∞

If Matt had known how much paperwork was involved in being chief of police, he would've turned and run the moment he'd been hired.

He shoved the computer keyboard he'd been pecking at for the last two hours. Kicking back in his chair, he rubbed his tired eyes. His neck ached from remaining hunched over and his ass was sore from sitting in a hard chair for so many hours.

Paperwork was the root of all evil.

Even though he hated being tied to a computer, Matt had to admit his technical staff had done an amazing job in computerizing most of their paperwork. The reporting process was now streamlined, which helped with the year-end statistics and, in turn, made budgeting much easier.

No longer did he have to argue for hours with city council to get more money for the department. Now all he had to do was hand them a neatly printed report and it was all spelled out for them, in simple language of course. Even though automated reporting had cut his paperwork hours, it still didn't change one basic fact.

He hated computers.

Today was a good day where paperwork was concerned; he'd only had to kick back two incident reports due to missing information. Considering it was usually three or four per shift, two bungled reports for a twenty-four-hour period was excellent.

His computer dinged, and an email appeared in his once-empty Inbox. As he glanced at the sender's name, the pain in his neck increased. It was from the lieutenant mayor, who was a pompous ass in Matt's opinion, and it would seem he was requesting a meeting.

Flicking off the monitor, Matt decided he could avoid his email for the rest of the day. After spending most of his morning in paperwork hell, he could afford to ignore the lieutenant mayor and anyone else emailing him for now.

Damn, he missed being on the streets.

From the moment he could walk, law enforcement had been the only job he'd ever wanted. His father was a sheriff in southern Ohio and his mother had just retired from police dispatching. He and his siblings had chosen law enforcement as their career path, and none of them regretted the decision.

His twin brother, Micah, was a police officer and SWAT team member in Haven, Ohio, a small town about two hours south of Salem. His youngest brother, Nakoa, was a K-9 officer for a Sheriff's department in Kentucky, and his sister, Storm, was a crime prevention officer in Cincinnati.

The day he and Micah had graduated from high school, they'd both signed up for the Marines. Micah was trained as a sharpshooter before moving to the law-enforcement arm of the armed forces, while Matt had gone straight into police training. After serving for eight years, he'd left the Marines and returned home to work for his father. It was on his thirty-second birthday he'd received the job offer to come to Salem and become chief.

It had been one of the proudest days of his life.

Outside his window, the picturesque view was of the town square and the main road leading both in and out of Salem. He'd been here six years now and found he quite enjoyed small-town life. It was a nice place, with a low crime rate and friendly atmosphere not seen much anymore. Other than Robert Young, the last murder had occurred the year before he'd arrived and it was part of a domestic violence case. A woman shot her husband after he'd gotten drunk and almost beaten her to death.

The bastard had gotten off easy.

Salem had the usual problems with drugs, alcoholism and domestic cases. They dealt with the occasional runaway, petty theft from the stores and vandalism. All in all, for a cop it was the equivalent of working in Mayberry, USA.

Reaching for his coffee mug that read, "Member of the biggest gang in the world...COPS", he grimaced when he saw it was empty. Looking through the glass windows that made up two walls of his office, he saw his administrative assistant, Mary, headed for her desk with a coffee cup in one hand and a fat muffin in the other.

His stomach rumbled.

"Hey, Mary, is there any coffee left?"

She stopped in the doorway, her usually animated face deadpan. Taking a sizeable bite of the muffin, she chewed before answering. "Yes."

She walked the few feet to her desk, then sat.

"Would it be too much to ask you to get a cup for me?"

Amusement tugged at the corner of his mouth. It was a familiar game they played and he already knew the answer to his question.

"Yes."

Grabbing his cup, he rose and headed for the door, stopping by Mary's desk. Already the woman was typing madly.

"Just in case you didn't get the memo, I am the chief here and that makes me your boss," he said.

"Really? Let me alert the media. Chief Takes Charge of Office Staff." She didn't stop typing as she spoke. "That should be good for the front page, much better than the exposé on the ingredients of the high school's Mystery Meatloaf."

This time he did smile. "I could fire you, you know."

"Good luck. If you fire me, then you'll have to find your butt with both hands. At least when I'm here I do keep my eyes on your butt."

Rolling his eyes, he reached for her muffin.

"And get your dirty paws off my snack. There's more in the break room."

The woman had eyes in the back of her head. How did she do that?

Matt headed into the lunchroom. She always seemed to know what was going on around her. Maybe it was a parental thing that kicked in upon the birth of children? Whatever it was, it was too bad she wasn't a police officer. She'd make one hell of a detective.

After filling his coffee mug, he snagged a fat raspberry muffin from the box on the table. Returning to his office, he eyed the files that had magically appeared in his absence.

Damn, what he'd give to be outside in a cruiser right now. Bright afternoon sunlight poured in the window and even though the temperature hovered near forty, it was one of those days to be outside jogging and drinking in the sunlight. Winter was fast approaching, but this was the kind of day that could make one forget the coming ice and snow.

As Matt reached for his muffin, Mary called to him from her desk.

"Chief, Ms. Whitlow out on Winding Oak called in and said

that the chain was down at that old house out there."

"Who's available?" Turning on his monitor, he flipped to the CAD screen for call tracking. All of his officers were tied up on calls and two more were holding.

"You're the only one sitting on your butt twiddling your thumbs, Chief. Isn't it about time you pull your weight around here?"

Ignoring her smart mouth, he was already unlocking the cabinet to retrieve his gun belt. With Mary, you got what you paid for. If she wasn't such an excellent admin, he'd have her replaced in a second. Lucky for him he had a good sense of humor.

"I hear you."

"You'd better get out there, Chief, I'm sure some kids are in that old wreck committing lewd or depraved acts. They might even be listening to that wild rock-and-roll music and smoking mary-juan-uh."

With his muffin in one hand and gear bag in the other, he headed out the office door.

"I'll be out, Mary, and God help us but you're in charge. Please try not to piss off the public, will you?"

"Well, I'll try, but I make no promises. Sometimes the people who call in are dumber than rocks and they just have to be set straight for their own good."

With a huge grin, Matt walked out into the bright sunshine. It looked like he'd get his wish after all.

Chapter Four

Stopping his SUV in the driveway of Angelov house, Matt keyed his microphone.

"Four-ten, on scene."

"Sixteen forty-four."

Exiting the car, he walked toward the chain now lying on the ground. After the death of Bobbie Young, he'd decided the best thing to do was restrict people from coming out here. While the chain didn't stop people on foot, it did prevent the kids from coming up here by the carload.

The sign was warped, as if a car had driven over it several times. It took only a glance at the posts to see what had happened. Someone had hacked at the support until the eyebolt gave way. Chunks of freshly chopped wood littered the ground, and the bolt was still attached to the chain.

He fingered one of the marks. Someone had wanted in here pretty badly to take an ax to the post. Beyond the chain he detected several distinct sets of tire tracks in the fallen leaves.

Instinctively he knew this wasn't the work of kids looking for a quiet corner to get high. This property consisted of several hundred acres and most of it was forest, making it the perfect location for any number of crimes. With the dense underbrush and distance from town, someone could toss a body out here and it might never be found.

He keyed his microphone. "Four-ten."

"Four-ten." The dispatcher's voice was tinny.

"Do we have any officers free for a five-seven?" He headed back to the car.

"That's a negative."

"Copy that."

It looked like he was going in alone. Matt returned to the SUV and took a few seconds to remove the shotgun secured between the front seats. He'd just put the cruiser in drive when an officer marked him on one of the back channels.

"Three ninety-seven to four-ten."

"Go ahead, three ninety-seven."

"What cha got out there, Chief? Kids playing house, or did Ruprect's cow get out again?" Bryan Haines was chuckling as he spoke.

"Not quite."

"The only ones fool enough to go out there are either pill-heads or drunks. Everyone local knows that house is haunted, so you know there aren't any townies out there screwing around."

Matt rolled his eyes. "You're a pussy, Haines. How many times do I have to tell you ghosts don't exist?"

"Just a few more, sir."

"The driveway chain support was destroyed with an ax, and I have fresh tire tracks on the drive. Somehow I don't think it's a bunch of stoners coming out for a party."

"Copy that." All amusement was gone and Haines' voice had assumed its usual no nonsense tone. "I'll head your way, should be there in five, six minutes."

"Copy that."

Easing off the brake, Matt steered the SUV along the drive. Over the past few years he'd picked up bits and pieces of the outrageous lore associated with the Angelov family. The locals believed the owners were witches and now the house was haunted by long-dead family members.

A mother and her four children, witches.

Matt shook his head. Just what were people thinking? Yes, he'd had some odd experiences out here that he'd yet to explain, but that didn't mean the house was haunted or witches existed, let alone had lived in this place.

Many of the townspeople went out of their way to avoid this section of Winding Oak. Some were foolish enough to drive miles out of their way to avoid getting anywhere near the property.

On several occasions he'd witnessed some of the strange rituals people performed as they drove past the drive. Some went so far as to make the evil eye symbol, while Mrs. Cabot, the PTA president, would clutch a cross and mutter prayers of deliverance.

In all of his years of dealing with the public, he'd never seen anything quite like it.

After spending time out here investigating the boy's death, he had a much clearer understanding of how the townspeople felt, though he still firmly disagreed with them. No matter how many times he'd tried looking at the strange experiences, he always came back to the same conclusion.

There was something just not quite right with this house, but it didn't mean it was haunted.

What the hell would his twin say to that? After he was done laughing, that is.

Every instinct in his body objected to pulling up next to the house. Procedure dictated that he park out of sight, but the layout of the property prohibited that. He'd much rather take his chances in the SUV than running from the woods to the house. At least the vehicle offered some protection.

Near the porch steps was a battered brown Jeep and just feet away was an industrial-sized dumpster. All of the shutters on the first floor had been opened and there were numerous garbage bags lying in and around the dumpster.

It looked like somebody was doing some illegal housecleaning. His mouth quirked. They didn't even have a ten code for that one. Illegal use of a broom and mop had never come up before now.

About ten yards to his left was a tent and a few pieces of clothing hung on a makeshift clothesline. It looked as if whoever was here was looking to stay a while. He reached for his radio.

"Four-ten."

"Four-ten," the radio bleeped.

"I don't have a computer in my car, so I need you to run a twelve for me."

"Go ahead."

He read the license plate to the dispatcher.

"Copy that, four-ten. LEADS is down, so I'll have to call Arizona. This could take a few minutes."

"Copy that."

Shotgun in hand, he exited the SUV and headed for the Jeep. Heavy-metal music poured through one of the open windows and he winced at the sound of shrieking guitars. It was some kind of death metal with dark, morbid lyrics. He flicked off the safety on the shotgun.

The Jeep's ragtop was off, giving him easy access to look inside. The rear was empty and in the backseat there was a generous quantity of dog hair and a half-chewed fabric toy. It was on the passenger-side floor he found what he was looking for, an ax. The sharp edge glinted in the sunlight.

"Gotcha."

As he moved toward the house, a piece of broken furniture come flying out one of the windows. It landed on the porch, then rolled down the steps, missing him by inches.

"Nothing like being made to feel welcome," he muttered.

Shouldering the shotgun, he walked up the steps and in through the open door. Here the music was much louder, disorienting. With that much racket going on, a serial killer could sneak up behind him and cut off his head before Matt would even realize he wasn't alone.

Some attempt had been made to straighten the entryway, though it was still filthy. A broom and dustpan leaned against the wall and there were bristle marks in the dirt. It would take more than a broom and dustpan to clean up this disaster. Maybe a HazMat team should be called.

Taking up a position left of the doorway, Haines entered the house a few seconds later with his shotgun at the ready. Matt motioned him to remain on the other side of the doorway. When Bryan reached his position, Matt used a series of hand motions to indicate he wanted Haines to cover his back. Bryan nodded his acceptance of the plan.

Matt dropped into a half-crouch and began pie-ing the room. With slow and deliberate movements, he peered into the room then moved back to safety. After doing this several times, he had a good idea of the layout of the room and the figure near the window who was tossing things onto the porch.

Given the curves, the intruder appeared to be a woman. She sat on the floor near the open window and was sorting through a cardboard box. By her side was a plastic storage bin filled to overflowing.

Next to the bin was a medium-sized dog with its nose on its paws as it slept. Judging from the white on its muzzle, it was an older animal, but no matter how old dogs might be, they always had some bite left in them.

Haines trained his shotgun on the woman's back, then Matt stepped inside the room. When the obnoxious song ended, he called out to her.

"Police! Freeze! Put your hands where I can see them."

The woman's head came up, but to Matt's surprise, she didn't follow his order. Instead she reached toward a portable stereo and turned it off as the dog rose. A low growl sounded from the mutt, and the fur on its back stood at attention.

When the woman turned, all thought went out of Matt's head. It was her—the woman from the photograph.

Her ink-black hair was tamed into a fat braid that hung to her waist. Her skin was milk-pale, and black brows arched over the most amazing violet eyes he'd ever witnessed. Her lips were full and she had a small mole at the lower right corner. Dressed in oversized jeans, a black hooded jacket and battered boots, she looked like any of the hundreds of drifters he'd encountered in his career.

One dark brow rose. "Can I help you?"

ʚɞ

Shocked, Syn stared at the cop who held a shotgun pointed at her chest. For a moment, the past and present collided and she vividly remembered the last time an officer had pointed a gun at her.

You've done nothing wrong; you're as clean as the day you were born.

A second officer came in behind the first, also brandishing

54

a wicked-looking shotgun. Judging from his strawberry-blond hair and freckles, this man could be one of the Haines boys or a close relative. The resemblance between this man and the eldest Haines son was too strong to deny.

"Who are you, and what are you doing here?" the first cop spoke.

Her gaze shifted back to him and she couldn't help but notice that for a cop, he was really hot. She'd bet in his bare feet he was at least six-five, and his broad shoulders were the kind a woman would swoon over. His face was strong, and while he had the ever-present hard-ass look all cops carried, she could tell by the wrinkles at the corner of his eyes this man enjoyed a good laugh.

His black hair was shaped in a ruthless military-style cut that accented his high cheekbones. With his coppery skin and black eyes, she'd bet her last dollar this man was at least half Native American.

"I said, what are you doing here?" the first cop spoke again.

More than a little irritated by his tone, she held up her filthy gloved hands. "What does it look like? I'm cleaning."

"Haines, I'm going to pat her down." The first cop lowered his gun.

"You'd better ask first, or my dog will damage a kneecap." Syn nodded toward Maddie, who'd glued herself to her mistress' leg.

"Then I will take great pleasure in shooting her dead," the second officer spoke.

Syn's gazed moved from the first man to the second then back again. "I hope you're in good shape, because if he shoots my dog you'll be taking him out of here in little itty-bitty pieces."

"Threatening an officer is a felony offense in Ohio," the first man said.

"And I'm pretty sure shooting without provocation is as well." Her tone was dry.

The handsome cop slung the shotgun over one shoulder and walked toward her. Maddie's growls increased in volume. Syn dropped her hand to the dog's head and gave her a reassuring pat, letting the dog know this man was a friend.

When he was about a foot away, he stopped and held out his hand toward Maddie. The dog gave him a few suspicious sniffs then sat, still on guard but no longer in attack stance.

"Unzip your coat," he ordered.

Syn hated being crowded by men larger than she, but she refused to move away. Ever since the night she'd been taken away from here she'd learned there were some men to be feared, though she didn't get an uneasy feeling from this one.

"If you insist." First she removed the rubber gloves and tossed them into the trash pile before reaching for the zipper. "Is this how you normally pick up women, Officer?"

He ignored her jab and began to pat her down. His touch was as impersonal as a visit to the gynecologist. With his big hands he patted her torso from waist to armpits before moving to her breasts. Her gaze didn't leave his face when his hands slid along the bottom of her underwire bra, then down over her belly.

Judging from his hard, closed expression, Syn knew this man didn't understand how it felt to be treated like a piece of meat. To be stripped of everything, then treated like an animal. She'd bet her life he'd never experienced shame such as hers.

"Turn around."

Later she wouldn't be able to explain why she responded as she did, but at the time she wanted to see some kind of humanity from this man.

"So polite." Syn's gaze met his and she gave him a hard smile. "That tone makes me want to do anything for you, Officer."

When she turned, he flipped up her jacket and searched her back before moving to her belt.

"I usually know a man's name before I let him into my pants," she purred.

"Chief Whitefeather." His words were clipped, and his hands continued their search, moving over her buttocks and between her thighs.

"Chief? I thought you were an Indian. What's your first name, Big Dick?"

"Keep it up, witch—"

"Quiet, Haines."

Syn smirked. She could pick out the Haines offspring from a mile down the road. That red hair and freckled skin gave them away every time.

"You're clean."

Whitefeather spoke and his voice sounded strained. So this man was human after all.

"I'm so glad you approve." She turned toward him, noting Haines still held the gun pointed at her chest. "Can you put that away now, Junior? You might hurt someone, namely me."

The officer's green eyes narrowed and she knew he'd come to the conclusion she looked familiar. Would he be able to put a name to her face? He'd been but a child when they'd left town; it was quite possible he didn't remember her family at all. Slowly, he lowered the gun and Maddie growled again.

"Your dog had better stay put," Haines said.

"Then don't annoy her. She's cranky today." Her gaze flicked to Whitefeather's. "Is there anything else I can do for you? Maybe you'd like to perform a body cavity search for fun?"

"Just your name, ma'am."

"Synnamon Angelov."

She didn't miss the narrowing of Haines' eyes. By this evening it would be all over Salem that the witch's daughter had returned.

Her gaze met Whitefeather's. "The house is mine, and I'm cleaning it out before the renovations begin."

"I'll need some identification."

"It's in my car outside."

"After you then." He stepped back and allowed her to lead the way.

Calling for Maddie, Syn left the house and jogged down the porch steps. She caught sight of two marked vehicles beside the house and a third coming up the drive. Mentally she cursed. She should've paid closer attention to what was going on. Instead, she'd been caught in the painful memories of her childhood, so she'd turned up the music to drown out the voices in her head.

Reaching the Jeep, she opened the glove box to retrieve her

wallet. "Were you expecting a den of thieves to be out here or what? How did little ole' me rate two officers to roust me out of my own house?"

"I'm sure you can understand an abandoned property is the perfect place for kids who are up to no good." He took her license.

"The property was hardly abandoned. We have a caretaker keeping an eye on the place and—"

His radio squawked, cutting her off.

"Four-ten."

He keyed the microphone attached to his shoulder. "Four-ten, go ahead."

"Nineteen ninety-nine Jeep Wrangler, brown, registered to one Synnamon Angelov, age thirty-four, five-ten, black and blue, one-sixty, at a Sedona, Arizona address. Break."

"Go ahead."

"This Angelov has a lengthy arrest record. We're currently checking to see if she has any outstanding warrants. Break."

Syn's gaze met his, and even though she was withering on the inside, she offered him a brazen smile and a shrug. "Some of us were born to be bad, Chief."

He keyed the mike again. "Go ahead."

"She has both a juvenile and adult record. Petty theft, vagrancy, drug abuse, trespassing, and fifteen years ago she was convicted of involuntary manslaughter."

Syn's skin crawled and she wanted nothing more than to slink away, but she wouldn't give any man the satisfaction of seeing her shame. While she wasn't proud of her criminal past, she'd accepted the dark and twisty side of herself a long time ago. If she hadn't walked that road, committed those crimes and lived on the streets, she wouldn't be the woman who stood before him now.

No longer was she the lost, broken woman who'd lived the life of criminal. Her desire for death or the mindlessness of drugs was gone, banished by years of hard work and intense therapy. But no matter how many times she'd wished the past could remain just that—in the past—it never did. Always, when she least expected it, the old Syn would make her presence known.

Whitefeather's gaze never left hers as he spoke into the radio mike. "Copy that."

She'd seen the look in his eyes many times before. He'd already passed judgment and found her lacking. Most people who learned of her dark past did the exact same thing. So what did it matter if one more small-town cop thought she was some sort of drug-addicted, murdering skank?

"Is there anything you'd like to add, Ms. Angelov?" Whitefeather's tone was noncommittal.

"Hardly. I'd really hate to ruin any future surprises for you. I just love the anticipation."

"An explanation might go a long way toward my trusting you more." He handed her license back to her.

"Oh, my life is over, the chief of police doesn't trust me." She rolled her eyes. "Your dispatcher will come back and tell you I have no warrants. I've been clean for fifteen years and I'm not going to make excuses for a difficult time in my youth. I don't owe an explanation to you or anyone else." She stuffed her wallet back into the glove box and slammed it shut. "I did the crimes, I did my time and I'm a law-abiding citizen now. That's all you need to know."

"Fine." His handsome lips tightened and she would almost swear he was disappointed by her response. "In the morning I will verify the ownership of the house, and if everything checks out, you're good to go."

"You do that." Crossing her arms over her chest, she propped her hip against the Jeep. "The house will be listed as held by a trust company in Boston. If you call them, they will assure you I'm the legal owner of this place."

"We'll see about that."

"Suspicious, aren't you? Did you ever stop to think maybe a person is innocent until proven otherwise? Isn't that a tenet of our judicial system?"

His dark brow arched. "People who are innocent don't usually talk back to the law, nor do they have lengthy criminal records."

"Ah, the unforgiving type I see. I'll bet you never made any mistakes growing up, did you?" Syn's smile was icy and thin.

"Thank you so much for coming all the way out here to harass me. What's the matter, not enough crime going on in Salem to keep you busy?"

"Unfortunately, there is always something to be taken care of in Salem." He crossed his big arms over his chest. "This was considered much more important."

"That just warms my little heart, Chief."

"I'll bet."

Haines walked out of the house with a troubled look on his face. In retrospect, this one probably didn't remember anything of the dark times, as he'd been pretty young, possibly the same age as the twins. Still, she had little doubt he'd heard the rumors and speculation that must've run rampant in the town after they'd left. The destructive side of her personality would not let her leave it at that.

"Officer Haines, please make sure you give your daddy and mama my regards." She walked toward the steps.

"Do you two know each other?" Whitefeather asked.

"This one here was but a child when my sisters and I left Salem." Syn's laugh was careless. "But I surely did know his older brother, Donnie. He spent most of my fourteenth summer trying to get into my panties or shove his tongue down my throat. I think he was almost eighteen. If he'd succeeded, wouldn't that have been statutory rape?"

"No, Chief." Haines' face looked as if it were carved from stone. "My family didn't associate with common trash."

"Just the uncommon kind." Syn reached the top of the steps and she turned to face the men. "Yeah, well, if anyone in Salem knew what trash was, it was your mama, boy. Edina Mayhew Haines could spot a bad seed, couldn't she? How do you think she and your daddy got together?"

His face turned bright red, and for a moment she thought his head might explode. If looks could kill, she'd be dead where she stood.

Without another word, Haines spun on his heel and stalked to his cruiser. Slamming the door hard, he took off in a spray of gravel.

"Hmm, maybe you need to think about anger management for your officers," she said to the chief.

"I apologize for Officer Haines. He's been under a great deal of stress lately." His tone was stiff.

Syn shrugged. "I can tell he must've been the whiner of the Haines brothers. He probably had a lot to live up to, with an upstanding brother like Donnie. And how is Trent? Is he still as crazy as hell?"

"I'll check out your story, Ms. Angelov," Whitefeather continued. "Then I'll be by tomorrow around noonish, so I'd recommend you don't leave the county."

"How very Hill Street Blues of you, Chief. If you have so much spare time on your hands, why don't you look into my mother's murder instead of harassing those you're supposed to be protecting?" She struck a look of surprise and snapped her fingers. "Oh wait, now I remember. The Salem Police only look out for their own, isn't that right?"

Chapter Five

When Matt returned to the station, he couldn't shake the memory of Synnamon Angelov announcing her mother had been murdered and the police had somehow covered it up. She was obviously crazed; an entire police department would not be able to cover up a murder, not in Salem at least. The gossips usually knew a crime had occurred before the police did. But she didn't seem unstable. She had ancient eyes, eyes far too old for a woman only in her mid-thirties. Then again, if her record stood up, she'd packed a lot of living into her short life.

And what the hell happened between Haines and Ms. Angelov? Obviously she knew Bryan's family; was that why he had acted so out of character? Matt had worked with Bryan since he'd been hired as chief, and he'd never seen the other man go from zero to sixty so quickly. He was a good officer, a good man who knew when to hold his tongue and when to draw his gun.

Then again, if there was a woman skilled at getting under someone's skin, it was Synnamon Angelov.

That mouth of hers would get her into trouble. On one of Mary's good days, Synnamon would put her to shame with her sarcastic comebacks. With those mysterious purple eyes and a toned body built for a hard night's ride, she wasn't a woman men would easily forget.

Mary was still at her desk though it was well past six o'clock. Her reading glasses were perched on the end of her nose and she was working her way through a stack of reports.

"Mary, I'm glad you're still here."

"Well, I'm not." She looked at him over her glasses. "My

husband is madder than a wet chicken, but if I don't get these damned CCHs processed, the officers will make my life hell tomorrow."

Matt gave her a sympathetic smile. "Some days the paperwork never ends around here."

"I'll second that. First shift was busy today and ten detective's reports just came down. They're sitting on your desk."

"Great."

"So you've said about twenty times since you walked in the door." She wrote a badge number on the page, then placed it face down on her desk.

"I need to ask you a question, Mary." Matt dropped into a hardback chair positioned in front of her desk. "What can you tell me about the Angelov family?"

"Not much." She shrugged and continued working her way through the printouts. "I was in college when all the craziness went on."

"What happened?"

"The townspeople believed the Angelovs were witches. In my early teens there was a story going around that Ms. Angelov was cooking up spells against some of the menfolk." Mary chuckled.

"You don't say."

"Hell, some of them deserve to have spells cast on their butts. If I had my way, I'd cast a few around here too."

"The Angelovs..."

"I'm getting there. All I know about Victoria Angelov was she was always nice to me. I think the women were wagging their tongues because she was very beautiful and those old biddies were jealous.

"Daddy always said she had the kind of curves a man would have to be dead not to notice. Mom suspected Ms. Angelov was keeping company with some of the married men around town." Mary shrugged. "That rumor was enough to set the Junior League women on their collective ears."

"What about the father of her children? Where does he come in?"

"Doesn't. Nobody knows their fathers, and she never kept company with any man in public, at least. Ms. Haines told Mom she thought both Synnamon and Chloe were from the devil himself, what with their coloring and all." She snorted with laughter. "Synnamon looked just like her damned mama, even the village idiot could've seen that. Then again, Ms. Haines probably still tells everyone all four of her kids were found in the cabbage patch."

"And she's still a virgin?"

"Of course. That woman was so tight Mr. Haines got her drunk on their wedding night just so he could pry her legs apart."

Matt had to look away or start laughing. Edina Haines was a very stiff, arrogant woman who took her position in Salem seriously. Far too seriously, in his opinion.

"Anyway, to make a long story short, Victoria and the four girls lived out at that house all alone. Just before the twins started first grade she decided to pull them out of public school because the other kids were always picking on the older girls. One of them—Chloe, I think—was held down and one of the Haines boys shaved her head bald. The very next day all of his hair fell out. They say Chloe cast a spell on him and I say it serves the brat right. There's something wrong with that boy."

"I don't believe in witches," Matt said.

Mary shrugged. "It doesn't matter what you believe, Chief. You don't have to believe in something in order for it to be real."

"Don't you think this is strange, for a town to believe in witches?"

"Hell if I know, nor do I care much." She shrugged again. "All I know is Ms. Victoria and her girls had a way about them. They were always smiling and laughing when I'd see them on market days. Town folk would grab their kids and walk to the other side of the street just so the Angelovs couldn't put a hex on them. The residents are a superstitious bunch."

"So what really happened? Why did they abandon their home?"

"I was in college, and all I know is what my sister told me. Ms. Victoria was hit by a car, killed on impact, and the kids were taken in by family."

"It was an accident?"

"According to Chief McNutt it was. By the time I started working here, the case was long closed. Curiosity had me digging out the case file, and I must tell you, for an accidental death that file is pretty thin."

"In the morning, can you locate that file for me?"

Her gaze met his and she laid down her pen. "Are you sure you want to stick your nose into this? There are some in Salem who will not thank you for looking into that case. Some of Salem's most upstanding citizens will be very unhappy that an Angelov has returned to that house."

"I see you heard already."

"Just got off the phone, actually. What can I say? It's a small town. People don't have anything to do other than gossip."

"Synnamon Angelov believes her mother was murdered. Considering what you've shared with me, I have to admit I'm rather curious as well."

Mary blinked. "She thinks her mama was murdered?"

"She does."

"Well, then I guess I'll be digging that file out real soon." She removed her glasses and laid them on the desk. "I'm about to leave, and I'd recommend you do the same. You've been working some long hours the past few weeks."

Matt nodded. "I'll be going home shortly. I have a few things to finish up, then I'm out of here."

Mary picked up her bag, then gave him a stern look. "I'd better not find you here early in the morning, Matthew. You need to take more time off; you're not getting any younger, you know."

Matt grinned. Mary was one of the best assistants he'd ever had, and even though he wouldn't admit it to her, he enjoyed their little sparring matches as much as she did.

"And I'm not on death's doorstep either, but thanks for watching out for me."

He rose and went into his office. A large stack of reports were perched in his "In" box, and several forms were on the blotter awaiting his signature. Wasn't that just the way it worked? He risked his neck protecting the people, and in turn he received three more hours of paperwork.

ℬ

Just after midnight a soft rain began to fall. The patter on the nylon roof should've made it easy to fall asleep. Syn stared upward, her body exhausted while her mind continued to race.

She'd chosen the living room to clean first and she'd be able to move in tomorrow. During the process she'd found little bits and pieces of her childhood. A few tattered snapshots, some books, and her very first wand now packed into a plastic tub for safekeeping.

After cleaning the room from top to bottom, she had to admit it still needed a lot of work. It seemed the more she'd swept, the more dust and dirt she'd stirred up. Just how long would it take to get the house clean, really clean? Lucky for her Beth had arranged for a team to come out to give her a hand.

It had taken some effort but she'd managed to get a bed frame down the steps and set up near the fireplace. Now all she needed were mattresses and bed linens. She grinned and hugged her pillow tight. What a luxury it would be to sleep under a solid roof and in a proper bed again.

According to the radio, the weather was going to turn very cold in a few days. Hopefully by then she'd have a working kitchen and fireplace. That alone would make the house look like the best hotel in the world to her.

An image of Whitefeather's face floated through her mind.

"Hard-ass." She turned onto her side and jiggled Maddie hard enough to interrupt her snores.

Well, maybe that wasn't a true description of the handsome cop. She'd been quite rude to him and Haines, so if he had been a hard-ass then it was probably because she'd been behaving badly.

Haines.

Syn tucked her hands beneath her cheek. Who would've ever thought one of the Haines offspring would go into the cop business? His brother Donnie was one of the biggest jerks Salem had ever harbored, even if he was good-looking and fast with his mouth. Who knew how many unsuspecting girls he'd lured into his bed?

And where did this Whitefeather come into play? Salem was the whitest town on earth. How had they ended up hiring a Native American? She remembered when the first ethnic family had moved to town, the shockwaves it sent through the residents. She grinned. The hiring of a Native American had probably had Old Silas Ruprect ringing the church bells for an emergency town meeting a time or two.

Then again, one look at the handsome man had probably set the Junior League members' panties on fire. His uniform had obviously been tailored to fit his big body. Those black pants had a perfect break in the front and she'd bet she'd cut herself on the crease. His waist was slim, and the gun belt only served to accentuate it. His broad shoulders were made all the more spectacular by his black shirt and sweater. She'd bet her next meal his arms were ripped with muscle.

All in all, Whitefeather was one delicious man.

She wondered if he had a girlfriend. Probably. Anything that hot would be snapped up pretty quickly. It only took one look at the man to know he was good in bed. One glance into those black eyes, and she'd imagine it didn't take him much effort to get a woman to lose her panties. He'd probably defrocked half the women in Salem.

And how about you, Syn? Could the chief tempt you to give up your vow of celibacy?

"Hell, no!"

Maddie's head came up and the dog gave her a sleepy look.

First off, having sex with a cop was out of the question. She'd been arrested too many times to ever feel safe with any man who carried a gun. Most of the cops she'd dealt with had thought the badge and a weapon made them law unto themselves. There was no way in hell she'd ever get tangled up with a lawman.

Second, she was celibate and would remain that way.

The moment she'd set foot in prison, she'd made the decision to remain celibate. Her prison time had been spent getting counseling, along with a college degree in computer graphics design. After her mother's death, her childhood had been turned into such a train wreck. She had no idea how to be in a relationship with a mature, adult man.

Her counselor had spent many hours trying to convince her otherwise, but Syn refused to budge. She'd accepted long ago she'd never marry, and while it pained her, she didn't want to be responsible for destroying another life. Her self-destructive tendencies were bad enough without inflicting them on another innocent person.

Chapter Six

The next morning Matt was well into his second cup of coffee by the time Mary walked into his office. Her dark hair was askew and she had a smudge of dust on her chin.

"Damn near took me an hour to find the Angelov file, Chief. Somehow it ended up in a box of misdemeanors from the early seventies." Mary dropped an interoffice envelope on his desk. "I had to go through nineteen boxes before I found the damned thing."

"Thank you, Mary. I appreciate your hard work." He reached for the file.

"Lucky you asked for it now, or it would've been purged next month." Mary drifted out of his office. "And you will have to pay for my dry cleaning."

"Send me the bill."

"And my hairdresser—"

"Not likely."

"Cheapskate."

When Matt had taken this job, one of the first tasks for the administrative team had been to go through all the existing police files to organize and box them according to year. How would a twenty-year-old closed case file have been so badly misplaced?

Opening the envelope, he withdrew the file folder. It was well-handled, the cover smudged and the edges split in several places. In the bottom left corner was a lopsided red CONFIDENTIAL sticker. Below that was a hand-written addendum stating only McNutt and Corporal Pine were privy to the information contained within.

What nonsense was this? Closed cases were public information and anyone could request a copy. So why would McNutt or his corporal put a warning on a file? If anything, it would guarantee anyone coming across it would read it.

As he opened the cover, a woman's face stared up at him. At first he thought it was Synnamon Angelov, then he quickly realized his mistake. The writing on the bottom edge of the photo confirmed it.

Victoria Angelov.

He opened his right-hand drawer and withdrew the photograph he'd found at the house five years ago. It only took a quick glance to confirm it was the same women in both photographs.

Beautiful was too small a word to describe her. Her ink-black hair was wavy and tumbled about her shoulders in a careless cascade. Her skin was quite pale, unlike her daughter's, and Victoria's eyes were more black than purple. Her lashes were thick and her nose pert, but it was her mouth that drew his attention. With that wide smile, her lips were painted a shiny red with a tiny mole on the corner of her mouth, like her daughter's.

There were other subtle differences between the two women. This woman had a romantic look to her, which was reflected in her clothing. He squinted. Was that velvet? Her daughter struck him as more the thrift-store type who would turn up her nose at feminine bits.

Synnamon also lacked her mother's apparent softness. This woman looked as if she hadn't worked a day in her life, while her daughter had the weight of the world on her shoulders. Synnamon had the weariness he'd seen in his own eyes many times before taking the job here.

Judging from the worn edges, this photo had been passed around quite a bit. Flipping it over, he was disappointed to find the back blank.

Putting it aside, he picked up the yellowed incident report and began scanning the sloppily written information.

October 12, 21:30...emergency call received,...woman's body

*on Winding Oak...rain-slick streets...Officer Richard Travis was
first on the scene...found woman face down on the
road...seventy-two yards from the foot of her drive...ambulance
was called...declared dead at the scene.*

It seemed straightforward. It was likely Victoria had been
walking on the narrow shoulder when she was hit. There were
no sidewalks in that area and the bend was precarious, with
one side petering down into a ravine with a river at the bottom.

If it had been dark and rainy, then it would have been
nearly impossible for someone to have seen her, as that curve
was just short of a sharp right turn. Rather than stopping to
give aid, the driver had fled the scene and left a mother of four
to die in the rain.

Tragic, yes; murder, no.

The death certificate came next, and he read it over. She
was thirty-eight at the time of her death, the same age as him.
The medical examiner found the cause of death to be blunt-
force trauma to the head. She'd also sustained a broken femur,
four broken ribs and a shattered forearm.

It didn't take much force to severely damage a human with
a car, but to cause this much trauma, the car had to have been
traveling at a high rate of speed. That road was dangerous in
the light of day, but at night, speeding would be suicidal on
those curves. Winding Oak saw more deadly accidents than any
other road in the county.

Add to that the fact Victoria was no small woman.
According to the report, she was five-foot-eleven and weighed
one hundred and seventy pounds. A car hitting someone that
size at a high rate of speed would've been seriously damaged,
possibly totaled on site.

The final page in the file had been torn from a notebook.
Scanning the header, he noted these were Officer Travis' on-
scene notes and the bulk of it was a repeat of the incident
report. Matt flipped over the page, disappointed when he saw it
was also blank. Picking up the folder, he leafed through the
pages again.

Where were the detective's notes? Accident analysis report?
Sketches made on scene or photographs? Evidence list? Why

was the disposition paperwork missing? Where were the witness statements?

Just how the hell had that much paperwork been misplaced?

Picking up the envelope, he opened it wide and shook it over the desk. Several photographs fell out, the top one so gory it gave even him pause.

It only took a few seconds to realize there was no way in hell this had been an accident. Spreading the photos on his desk, he studied them to see what story they would tell.

In the first photo, Victoria lay face down in the road, her arm outstretched, as if seeking help even in death. The second photograph showed her on her back, and her body was torn to shreds. Half of her face was gone and much of the flesh on her torso had been torn away.

The third photograph was a standard autopsy photo. She'd been striped nude and the blood had been washed away. In the harsh light of the coroner's office, her mangled face and upper body resembled bad hamburger. Deep abrasions scored her torso down to her upper thighs. The left side of her face was gone and the white of bone showed through the gore where her cheek should've been.

Taken aback, Matt leaned back in his chair. Only a neon sign flashing murder could've made it more apparent. A simple hit-and-run accident wouldn't have inflicted the type of damage her body had sustained.

If he wasn't mistaken, somehow this woman had been either dragged behind a car or quite possibly tangled in the wheels of a large truck. Ten years ago, his father had looked into an accident similar to this and the marks on that victim were almost identical to Victoria's.

This case could very well be a murder, but first he needed to find the case disposition. Matt reached for his keyboard. Bringing up CAD, he entered the case number then waited for the results.

CLOSED, October 13 — NO FAULT ACCIDENT, Chief McNutt

No fault? Who was McNutt kidding? The victim died, and

that meant someone was at fault, even if it was Victoria herself. And the case had been closed the very next day? There was no way in hell a proper accident investigation had been completed less than twenty-four hours after the accident. Either McNutt had had the most efficient accident reconstruction team in law enforcement history or the most incompetent.

Was it possible her daughter could be correct?

A rookie on his first day at the academy would've been able to see there was something very wrong here. At the time of the case the chief would've been at least fifteen years into his career. How could an experienced cop make such a stupid mistake?

Maybe it wasn't a mistake.

The hair on the back of his neck prickled. Could McNutt have deliberately closed this case without a full investigation? Was he covering for someone? Or maybe he'd done the deed himself?

Matt sat back in his chair, his gaze glued to the photos. What reason would a career lawman have to risk his reputation by deliberately bungling this case if he wasn't somehow tangled up in it?

"Fuck."

Matt gathered the file contents and returned them to the envelope. Before he reopened the case he wanted someone else to go through the file and give an opinion. Seeing that this case involved a possible cover up, there was only one man he trusted enough to be thorough and keep his mouth shut.

Armed with the envelope, Matt exited the office. "Mary, do you know where Sherlock is?"

"In the lab. Earlier he was dusting for prints and I heard him laughing like a loon." Mary shook her head. "That man's crazier than a shithouse rat."

"That man has one of the most brilliant minds in law enforcement." Matt headed for the steps.

"Yeah, and to this day he can't match his socks to save his life," Mary chuckled.

Taking the steps two at a time, Matt reached the second floor in seconds. This area of the building was occupied by the police dispatchers, his lieutenants, and a small area they called

"The Lab".

To infer Sherlock's domain was a lab was an insult to any real crime lab in existence. It was basically one corner of a large room sectioned off with two-by-fours and copious amounts of chicken wire. The pen boasted a wall of shelves, a large worktable and more reference materials than any cop could ever read.

Hunched over the table and muttering under his breath was Simon "Sherlock" Locke. He wasn't a sworn officer, so he couldn't work the streets, but Matt would sell his soul to have ten more just like him. The man was a genius when it came to forensics and processing a crime scene.

"I've got you, you little bastard," the man muttered.

"Who did you catch?" Matt walked into the pen and laid the file on the table.

Sherlock's head came up, and from behind his thick glasses, he blinked several times.

"Uh... Hi, Matt." He held up a cola can covered in a thin layer of fingerprint dust. "I caught the jerk who's been stealing my soda from the refrigerator downstairs."

"I see." It was on the tip of Matt's tongue to ask who it was, but he decided it would be more expedient to ignore his curiosity.

"Simon, I need you to take a look at a case for me."

"Sure thing." He picked up a wet nap and scrubbed at his dirty fingers. "What's up?"

"This is an old case from twenty years ago. I'd like you to review the information and get back to me with your thoughts."

"Sure thing. I'll catch up with you later this afternoon."

"Great." Matt headed toward the door, then stopped. "Sherlock, don't mention this to anyone, okay?"

Sherlock looked up. His expression was curious, but he didn't question the command. "Whatever you say, boss."

"And whatever you do, don't let this file out of your sight. If you have to put it down for any reason, lock it in the gun cabinet in my office, got it?"

The other man nodded. "This case, it's important?"

"Very."

"See you shortly, then."

Matt headed back to his office. He had a lot of work to do, but right now, he wanted to speak to Synnamon and let her know her story was verified by the trust and she was free to come and go as she pleased.

Ω

Sitting on the porch steps, Syn was gnawing her way through a protein bar, trying to convince herself it didn't taste like styrofoam. Maddie was off chasing rabbits in the clearing on the other side of the drive, her happy baying echoing off the surrounding woods.

Several hundred yards from the house was the barn, and in front of that a white picket fence surrounded Victoria's pride and joy, her garden. Mama had insisted on growing as much of their food and herbs as they could, as nothing could beat fresh vegetables grown on your own land.

She'd taught her daughters to do the same, but early on Syn realized her talents did not include horticulture. Chloe used to say Syn could kill a plastic flower, and Syn was woman enough to admit her faults.

Being here was both unsettling and oddly soothing at the same time. For so many years she'd yearned to return, and now that she was back, it wasn't quite as she remembered. Without her sisters around, the place was lifeless. Sometimes she felt as if the house was holding its breath, waiting to see what was going to happen next.

It simply wasn't the same without Mama.

To a child, Victoria had been a larger-than-life personality. Generous with her hugs and kisses, she'd spent most of her time with her children, teaching them the Craft and a deep love of nature and all its bounty. Her laughter had rung from the eaves, and the scent of roses followed her wherever she went.

She'd always worn loose-fitting clothing in bright gypsy colors, and she'd encouraged her children to be proud of their Romany heritage. At a young age they'd learned the honorable art of tarot cards and fortune telling.

Behind the barn was a fire pit, and on chilly nights they'd make bonfires and dance wildly in the moonlight. Her mother sang constantly and all of them played at least one instrument. They'd been taught to respect their elders, to always be polite, use their magic only when absolutely necessary and to never, ever use it in anger. Mama had done her best in educating her daughters in the ways of the world, but she'd neglected to teach them the most important thing.

How to live without her.

Syn balled up the rest of the protein bar and threw it into the dumpster. She'd been so young and clueless about how to cope when Victoria had been killed. As the eldest daughter, she'd felt it was her duty to keep her sisters safe, but she'd been unable to help herself, let alone her siblings. Stripped of her family, her home and everything familiar, Syn did the only thing she knew how to do, survive at all costs.

With a sigh, she put the brakes on her sadness. Just what good did it do to think about her past? What was past, was just that, past. In life there were no Do Overs, no way to change what had already happened. She'd had to just suck it up and move on.

Syn rose and dusted off the seat of her pants. Pursing her lips, she was about to call for Maddie when a flash of light caught her attention. A 4x4 was coming up the drive, and she flinched when she saw the police beacons perched on the top.

Back for more, was he?

Whitefeather pulled up beside her Jeep and when he got out of the SUV, she was immediately reminded of just how big he was. Walking toward her, he moved easily, and he seemed to be a man comfortable with himself. To her surprise, he was smiling.

She gulped.

Oh boy! The addition of a smile on his rugged face was enough to tie her stomach in knots. Chief Whitefeather was the kind of man who caused women to forget chocolate ever existed.

"Looks like you've been working hard." He nodded toward the dumpster.

"The trash won't carry itself out here, so I guess I'll have to do it."

"It's a damn shame this house was empty for so many years. It's a fascinating piece of architecture."

"Thank you."

"Has it always been in your family?"

"Yes."

His brow rose. "Care to elaborate?"

"Not really, but if you insist, an ancestor built this house for his bride. The story goes that while he was building the house they lived in the barn over yonder."

"That must be true love, to live in a barn." His smile was disarming and she couldn't help but respond.

"Yeah well, some women will do anything for the men they love, even if it is stupid."

He walked up the steps toward her, and her breath caught. In passing her, his jacket sleeve brushed against hers and his clean male scent surrounded her, titillating her long-dormant senses. Goose bumps broke out all over her body, and it was in that moment Syn knew she could be in over her head with this one.

"They don't make them like this any more." He was examining the joint that attached the support to the roof. "I'll bet not a nail was used in building this house. It looks like the builder used pegs to hang it all together."

"I'd hazard a guess you're right." Feeling defenseless, she crossed her arms over her chest. "When the winter storms come in from the lake you can feel the house shift and it creaks like an old woman."

"That's probably one of the reasons the house survived when others didn't." He moved to examine the doorframe, his attention focused on the workmanship. "This house would be able to give with the wind, even if only millimeters. This would greatly increase its strength in the face of a storm."

Handsome really didn't do this man justice; gorgeous was more like it. With his direct gaze, coppery skin and big body, just being near him was making her shivery all over. When he bent over, Syn's gaze became glued to the most amazing male backside she'd ever encountered. His uniform trousers delineated a taut ass and hinted at muscular runner's thighs.

"Yummy."

Mortified that she'd spoken out loud, Syn slapped her hand over her mouth. Her cheeks flamed and she turned away.

"It is, isn't it?" He chuckled. "I'm probably boring you, sorry. It's sort of an obsession with me—restoring homes, that is..."

Speaking of obsessions, I think I've fallen in lust with your bottom.

"...really enjoy working with my hands."

Plastering a lazy smile on her face, she turned. "And I'll bet you're really good at it."

"I haven't had any complaints yet."

Their gazes clashed and Syn silently cursed her wayward mouth. Flirting with handsome men was her way of keeping them in their place. It reduced them to sexual objects, rather than humans with thoughts and feelings. According to her therapist, it was an unconscious reaction that allowed her to turn the tables and feel in control when really she was intimidated by men.

"So why are you here, Chief?" She braced her fists on her hips. "I assume you've learned I'm not some squatter who's moved in to steal the riches of the Angelov family?"

"I have. The trust assured me you wear a white hat."

"So I'm allowed to leave the county?"

His grin widened. "Yes, you may."

"Well, that's a relief." Her tone was dry. "Now I can continue my out-of-state crime spree."

He propped his hip on the porch rail. "People should have hobbies."

"Yeah, well, both you and I know my criminal record is the elephant in the room," she said. "It's just going to have to stay that way."

"I looked into your record, read it from top to bottom." His gaze met hers. "You've been clean for the past ten years, give or take a few. You served your time and the state of Arizona declared you rehabilitated. We all make mistakes, and I can only assume you've seen the error of your ways and have decided to stay on the path of a law-abiding citizen."

Syn was impressed. Usually most people tried to grill her for all the gory details. Maybe he was one of those nice guys she'd been hearing rumors about.

She tossed her braid over one shoulder. "Only until I get bored. That's when I get dangerous."

"I guess we'll have to keep you occupied, then." His smile was easy, flirtatious.

One point for the cop...

"I was thinking I might rob the Winkie Mart for kicks. I need to clear them out of chocolate and dog food."

"You'd better be careful." His eyes twinkled. "Ms. Winkie keeps a loaded gun behind the counter."

"Wow, is that legal?" She blinked. "I mean, she must be a hundred years old by now."

"Ohio does have a concealed-carry law but no, I don't want her waving a gun at the teenagers in town. I removed the bullets and replaced them with Simunition rounds. All they do is shoot wads of cotton at high speeds."

Syn laughed at the image of old Ms. Winkle firing cotton balls after a shoplifter. "Well, that's safer at least."

"Just don't tell her. It would break her heart. I think she has a secret desire to become Dirty Harry." He pushed off the rail then headed down the steps. "You know, you have a beautiful smile. You really should laugh more often."

"Ya think? Then I guess you'll have to come around from time to time and make me smile."

The moment the words were out of her mouth, she froze. It was rare that a nice man wanted anything to do with her kind, and she wasn't quite sure how to respond to him like a normal woman.

"You might be right." He opened the car door, then paused. "At some point we'll have to share war stories. You and your past, and me and mine. I don't think we're all that different, you know."

Astounded, Syn couldn't say a word when he tipped his head in her direction then got into his vehicle. Her feet felt as if they were welded to the porch. Even after he left, she still couldn't move.

Damn, he was *hot*.

A bolt of feminine excitement seized her chest, and she began to laugh. Sheer wonderment took control of her body, and she was laughing so hard she had to sit or risk falling down the steps.

Maddie, hearing her laughter, came at a run. With big, bright eyes and her stump of a tail wagging madly, she smashed her muscular body into Syn's legs.

Wrapping her arms around the dog, Syn held on until the laughter slowed, then finally ended with a hiccup. She took a long, deep breath.

"Oh, Maddie, we just might be in trouble."

Chapter Seven

"In my opinion, at the minimum there was procedural misconduct in this case. At the worst, it was a complete cover-up." Sherlock pulled the file from the envelope and tossed it on Matt's desk. "I took the liberty of enhancing the photographs, and I want you to pay particular attention to her ankles. The bruising looks like ligature marks to me."

Matt studied the blow-up of Victoria's lower legs. The discoloration had the distinctive ribbed pattern, a hallmark of a rope digging into her skin.

"Good call."

"The only parts of her body that didn't resemble chopped beef were her back, buttocks and legs from the knees down," Sherlock said. "I think she was dragged either behind or beneath a car."

"I suspect you're right." Matt flipped to the next photo, an enlargement of Victoria lying face down. "Feet first?"

"Sure looks like it. If you take a look at the shoulder of the road near the rear tire, I can't say for sure, but that looks like some kind of rope to me. I tried to enhance that particular section, but it was too grainy to tell."

"I don't know. It looks like a mop head to me," Matt said.

"Yeah, too bad there wasn't more light on that side."

"Let's go with the idea Ms. Angelov was dragged behind a car." Matt's gaze met Sherlock's. "Just by looking at these photos, I would say she was either dead or unconscious by the time they tied her up."

"How is that?"

"Her back was untouched. I would surmise a conscious person being dragged behind a car would try to do anything to get off their stomach. When threatened, our first instinct is to protect our torsos if at all possible."

"Sounds reasonable."

"Another issue is her fingernails. One photo shows them to be intact. Wouldn't you try and grab onto something, anything if you were being dragged?"

"Damn straight." Sherlock took the photo. "So she was either dead or unconscious before they tied her up."

"*If* they tied her up," Matt corrected. "We still have no real proof of that. For me the bottom line is, her fingernails indicate she didn't fight back. So if she was hit by a car, it could've been a quick death."

"You think she wasn't?"

"I have nothing to verify it was a vehicular accident. No mention of the car or driver, not even a license plate number or description in the report. If someone did hit her, there would've been some kind of skid mark, and none is mentioned."

"Man, she died a horrible, vicious death," Sherlock murmured. "Someone must've really hated this woman to do this to her body."

"Someone who was very passionate in their hatred," Matt said. "Another option is, by dragging her they could've covered up another cause of death, such as a gunshot, knife wound or bludgeoning." Matt spoke more to himself than Sherlock.

"What are you implying?"

"I'm not implying anything. It's simply an observation."

Sherlock pointed to the photograph with the mop head-looking object. "Or a cover-up."

"It's possible."

"Wow." The other man looked astonished.

"Why do you think I wanted you to take a look at the file? If this is a case of incompetence by the department or a deliberate cover-up, either way this woman was killed and her children were left without their mother. This department owes her daughters the truth."

"You know, McNutt was an asshole, but he wasn't stupid,

Chief." Sherlock began to rub his forehead. "This crime occurred in the middle of a very distinguished and unblemished career. I would be hard-pressed to think he would've done anything to jeopardize his job and standing in the community."

"And I've seen men kill for five dollars. No one can predict what someone will do in certain situations. Even your best friend can be a serial killer if the stakes are high enough."

"Nice thought."

"It's human nature." Matt nodded toward the photographs. "I have an old case on my hands and it's obvious it was mishandled. What are the odds of someone being able to orchestrate a cover-up of this magnitude?"

"Slim to none."

"This means we could be looking at a complex crime with quite a few players. In all my years of law enforcement, I've learned nothing is ever immediately apparent, X never marks the spot, and it's difficult to predict why anyone does anything."

"I still have to say, I find it hard to believe that with so many cops on the scene, someone didn't say or do something to rectify the situation. There must have been at least eight officers there, and you know how cops are. They're as gossipy as a group of old women at Ms. Rose's salon. How could someone guarantee they'd all remain silent?"

"There has to be a uniting factor, or McNutt had something pretty serious to hold over their heads."

"All of them?"

"It's slim, but still a possibility."

"Hmm, there's the situation that transpired in the New Orleans Police Department in the 1990's. A large portion of the department was on the take, and the rest looked the other way. This went on for many years before it was busted up."

"Point taken." Matt's gaze met Sherlock's. "Tell me, if you were a career cop, what would cause you to engage in a cover-up that could end your career?"

"Loyalty? The thin blue line runs tight in this department, and some of these guys would take a bullet before they'd tell stories on their brothers."

"Which could indicate the possibility one of the officers or a family member was involved in this crime."

"Blackmail material?"

"Possible, but farfetched. Blackmail would affect only one or two people, not an entire department." His gaze caught on a dime sticking out from under his blotter. "The most common cause for most crime is money. According to the trustee in charge of maintaining the property, the Angelov family is loaded."

"Really?" Sherlock's head came up. "You mean that old dump is worth something?"

"It's lakefront property, how could it not be?"

"So who was the beneficiary of the victim's will?"

"A question that begs an answer. I'll have Mary get that information." Matt made a quick note. "Victoria's eldest daughter was only fourteen when her mother was killed. Something is telling me this is a crime of utter, blind rage, and that kind of rage would indicate someone who was involved with the victim."

"Crime of passion."

"Exactly. That said, I don't think any of our possible scenarios fit, not yet anyway."

"So where do we go from here?"

"Theoretically, any and all officers who were employed here twenty years ago are potential suspects. I need a complete roster and a way to determine which officers were on duty that night."

Sherlock gave a low whistle. "That won't be easy to do, Chief. I doubt if the timecards are still around after this long and the only officer we know was on the scene and still works here is Lieutenant Pine."

"Well, we're assuming he was. If he was the on-duty corporal that evening, then yes, he would've been there.

"If this is a crime rather than shoddy police work, the only aspect I'm certain about is McNutt and Pine are involved. As the chief, McNutt was probably on-scene, and the confidential sticker points to their involvement."

"So far we have McNutt, Pine and Travis on the scene, and one of them has to know the truth about what happened out there."

"And chances are I'll have a sizable list of possible suspects on my hands."

Both men went silent. On his desk, Victoria's smiling face stared up at Matt and his gut twisted. No person should be condemned to die as she had.

"Well, if you don't need anything else, I need to check my prints." Sherlock rose. "I'm lifting them from the can using heated crazy glue."

"Isn't that overkill?" Matt chuckled.

"No." Sherlock looked offended.

"Thanks for your help."

"Anytime." The other man reached the door then stopped. "Oh, I almost forgot." He pointed to the photos. "It wasn't raining that night. I couldn't detect the sheen of rain in any of those photos. What with those floodlights out there, that pavement should have lit up like it was noon."

"I'll be damned." Matt picked up one of the photos.

"Not yet, Chief, but you might be by the time you close this case." With that, Sherlock left, closing the door behind him.

Matt turned to stare blindly out the window. The sun was beginning its descent, and the bandstand in the center of the square was filling up. This was probably one of the last good days Salem would see before winter set in. Soon the cold would take over and freeze everything within an inch of its life. His golf clubs would gather dust and his running would be confined to the gym on a treadmill.

He rubbed his eyes.

Returning the case file to the basement and walking away wasn't an option. From the time Matt could walk, his parents had preached the morals of honesty and integrity to their offspring. He had to reopen the case or risk not being able to look at himself in the mirror each morning.

Picking up the portrait, he stared into Victoria's dark eyes again. Who could've hated this woman enough to kill her, then take the extra step of mutilating her body?

Spurned lover, possibly. She was a beautiful woman, and she had at least two lovers or ex-lovers. The twins with their pale hair probably didn't have the same father as the elder two. Maybe one of the fathers sought to cover up his infidelity by killing her? Men had committed murder for much lower stakes.

Synnamon's face materialized in his mind. A fourteen-year-old girl was a curious creature. Chances were, if her mother had been having an affair, her daughter must've had some indication. Just how much did she remember? Enough to convince her it was murder, rather than an accident, that had taken her mother's life?

Another question concerned the girls directly. In Travis' on-scene notes he'd mentioned Children's Services had been called, but there was no indication of where the girls had been taken. The missing pages of the incident report required an entry for their whereabouts, or at the very least a mention of them being turned over to Protective Services.

Where were they now?

As a resident of Salem, he'd never seen or heard of anyone coming to town and claiming to be one of the Angelov sisters. Other than the caretaker, no one ever went up to the house with any regularity.

He dropped the portrait on his desk. At least a million questions buzzed around his head, and he needed to slow down, take a deep breath, or he was going to miss something vital.

First things first, he wanted to drop in at the diner and see if he could pick up any gossip concerning the Angelov family.

After gathering the file contents, he secured them in his gun cabinet before leaving his office.

"Hey, Mary, getting ready to leave for the day?"

"Yes, on time for once. My husband won't know what to do, with me making dinner for him."

"Listen, I need you to research something for me when you get in tomorrow."

Mary picked up her pad and pen, "Shoot."

"Look up some historical weather information, specifically the date October 12, 1987."

Mary's pen froze. "You're opening that case again, aren't you, Matthew?"

Ah, she's used my first name. Ms. Mary is displeased.

"There are quite a few unanswered questions about this case, Mary, and I can't let this slide."

"When Victoria Angelov died, this town was torn apart." She dropped her notepad and pen on the desk. "When I returned from college, this town was a disaster. It took years for all the bad feelings to die down, and you're about to stir it all up again."

"I'm the Chief of Police, and this investigation was badly mishandled by this department. It's past time to go back and make it right."

"By reopening old wounds," Mary snapped. "Do you even care who might get hurt in the process?"

"Are you talking about the Angelov family or the townspeople?" Matt pulled on his jacket. "From what I can tell, that family was also destroyed by this department's mistakes. Four young girls lost their mother and their home. Why aren't you defending their honor?"

Mary looked away, her shoulders stiff.

Matt stepped into her line of vision, bracing his hands on the desk. "You need to make a decision. If this case is going to be a conflict of interest or difficult for you to handle, you'd better speak now so I can replace you."

"Replace me?" She looked shocked. "As if anyone could do that—"

"Good." Matt turned and headed for the door. "I've got news for you and everyone else in Salem. No one is above the law."

∞

Syn made quick work of picking up the myriad supplies she'd bought to begin cleaning the other rooms downstairs. The trust had arranged for a cleaning team to arrive tomorrow, along with plumbers and electricians, as Syn didn't want to take a chance on turning on the water or electricity without each system being inspected first. Who knew what kind of damage time and mice had done to the place? Hopefully she'd have both working by Saturday.

Buoyed by the thought, she left the hardware store with her final bag of supplies. Her Jeep was parked several yards away, and Maddie was sitting patiently in the driver's seat, her gaze fixed on her mistress.

Syn had no sooner deposited her shopping bags in the back end when the hair on the back of her neck stood at attention.

Someone was watching her.

Her gaze scanned the surrounding area and caught on a man walking toward her with a determined expression. Distaste coated her tongue, and a feeling of unreality descended over her.

It was John Haines, the patriarch of the Haines clan. She'd recognize him anywhere, with his reddish hair and freckled skin. Anger burned in his pale eyes. He'd aged gracefully, just a little graying at the temples, and his skin was loosening on his jaw. He smiled wide, but his eyes were cold.

"Well Johnny, imagine meeting you here," she said in a jovial tone.

Maddie began to bark.

"You may call me Mr. Haines," he spat. "It's little Synnamon Angelov, all grown up." His leisurely gaze took inventory of her body, leaving her feeling exposed, dirty. "Damn, girlie, you're almost as hot as your mama."

Her smile was hard. "And look at you, only twenty years older and forty pounds heavier." She slammed the tailgate and tried not to laugh when his cheeks flushed. His smile vanished.

"What did you come back for, Synnamon?" He moved toward her. "Didn't we make it clear enough your kind isn't welcome in Salem?"

"Can't honestly say I remember that conversation." She shrugged. "Maybe I wasn't impressed with what you had to say?"

"Well," he chuckled, "I just might have to refresh your memory."

Haines was a tall, broad man, and he was trying to use his size to intimidate her. There was no way in hell she was going to budge. No man, especially this piece of dirt, was ever going to bully her again.

"Well, it's easy to act like a big man when you're dealing with a child." She tilted her chin, and her gaze met his dead on. "Now it takes quite a bit more than a little testosterone and a tiny dick to scare me."

"Your mama always acted like she wasn't afraid either, but she was a fool. Just look what happened to her." His smile was distinctly unkind. "Another dead whore on the highway."

Syn wanted to knock his legs out from under him, and it would only take a little spell. Instead, she bit her tongue until the taste of blood forced her to release it. There was no way she would show this man how much pain his careless remark had inflicted.

"You say Mama may've been a whore, but that didn't keep your kind away from her, now did it? Sneaking up the hill, trying to coax Mama out into the woods to do things your wife wouldn't." She shrugged. "You have no idea how foolish she thought ya'll were. She said the men of Salem were nothing but a bunch of posturing limp-dicks—"

The speed at which Haines moved took Syn by surprise. Grabbing her by the throat, he slammed her against the side of the Jeep. Stunned, all she could do was clutch his hands and dig her nails into his flesh.

"Your mama learned her lesson, and now that you're home, it looks like we'll have to teach you one too," he hissed.

Syn tried to swing her knee up into his groin, but he sidestepped her. The position left her unbalanced, his hands squeezing on her windpipe.

Hell, this bastard was going to kill her on the square in the middle of town. Where the fuck was everyone?

"Mr. Haines, Ms. Angelov, do we have a problem here?"

When she heard Whitefeather's voice, it was the sweetest sound she'd ever imagined. Instantly Haines released her, and she stumbled, grabbing the tailgate handle to avoid falling down.

"Why no, Chief, this young lady stumbled and I was just helping her up is all."

"By the neck?" Whitefeather's arms were propped on his gun belt in a deceptively casual stance. Syn couldn't help but notice the safety strap had been moved back from his holster for easy access. "Is that a southern thing? I've never seen that technique before."

Haines chuckled, and it was so incredibly fake Syn was struck by the urge to spit in his face.

"I was headed to the diner, Chief. Can I buy you some dinner? Ms. Mamie has her famous fried chicken on the menu."

The chief shook his head. "No thanks, John. I just came from there. You go on and enjoy your dinner."

"I'll do that. 'Night, Chief." He turned to Syn and the jovial expression vanished. "And you too, Ms. Angelov. You be careful now. Salem's beautiful façade is just that, a façade. For some people, this town can be a dangerous place."

"Thank you for the warning, Johnny. Don't you worry your little head about me, though; I can take care of whatever comes my way."

His gaze narrowed and when he faced Whitefeather, the smile was back in place. He nodded at them both, then headed across the street to the diner.

"Bastard," she muttered.

Her throat was swollen, and she had no doubt she'd be bruised come morning. Her gaze didn't leave Haines until he vanished into the diner. In the future, she'd be more vigilant and he wouldn't take her unawares again.

Next time, she'd be ready for him.

"Do I need to lock you up?" Whitefeather asked.

"Me? Some cop you are." She scowled at him. "In case it escaped your notice, Haines was choking me, not the other way around."

"I noticed. Would you care to explain what was going on here?"

"Not hardly."

"Judging from the look on your face when he left, I'm pretty sure you were wishing him dead."

She rolled her eyes. "If I'd wished him dead, you'd be calling a coroner now."

Spinning around, she stomped to the driver's-side door, where Maddie was still barking. She opened the door and the dog lunged at her, threatening to knock her off her feet. Syn pushed her back onto the driver's seat. If Maddie had gotten loose, Haines would've received a bite out of his ass.

"Are you going to cause problems for me, Syn?" The chief stood close behind her.

"That's what I'm good at, Whitefeather, and the boys like it that way." She forced a saucy tone into her voice. "You saw my record. I'm a bad girl through and through."

Waving Maddie into the backseat, she climbed in and slammed the door. When he tapped on the window, she reluctantly lowered it.

"I'll be stopping by your house tomorrow. There's something we need to discuss." The scent of his aftershave tickled her senses, and it was all she could do to not take a gargantuan breath and sigh with pure feminine pleasure.

"Another titillating conversation with the po-po. Be still my heart." She turned the ignition key and the engine leapt to life. "When I said you needed to drop by more often, I was only kidding."

"Well, I'm not. I'll be by around one in the afternoon."

"Whatever. You know where the house is." Putting the car in reverse, she backed out of the parking spot, not caring he had to move in order to avoid being hit by the mirror.

Driving down Main toward the turn-off, she felt as if every person she passed watched her. On one level, she knew she was being paranoid. Even in Salem word didn't travel that quickly. Besides, chances were most people didn't give a fig that an Angelov was in their midst.

Though there were some who would be very nervous indeed.

೮೦

"That bitch's daughter was seen in town."

Chester McNutt pointed to the phone and rolled his eyes toward his wife, then moved into his office, carefully shutting the door behind him. "I told you to never call me about this again," he snarled. "What part of 'never' don't you understand?"

"Her oldest daughter, that Synnamon, is here in Salem. She's living up at the house."

"So what? It's a free country—"

"She's going to start poking around," the voice whined in his ear.

"Jesus, you're a paranoid bastard. She was a child when her mama died and I'm sure if she remembers anything about that night, it isn't enough to come after anyone."

"We have to do something—"

"Christ almighty," Chester snapped. "I'll keep an eye on the situation, and when something needs to be done, it'll be taken care of. I'm not going to chase that girl off just because she's come home for a visit."

"There's something out there, something—"

"I'm well aware of what's out there. For Christ's sake, man, pull your shit together and try to act normal. Her return isn't going to change anything for us, do you understand that?"

"Y-yes."

"Good. Now don't call me about this again. You interrupted my dinner, and I don't need this bullshit."

Chester disconnected the call. This morning he'd heard the Angelov girl was back, and he'd gotten a call from the Rotary president, who'd suggested firing a warning shot across her bow. If Chester knew anything, he'd bet his favorite slippers that Synnamon Angelov would be gone before the new year.

Exiting his office, he paused when he reached the hall mirror. Turning to the side, he admired his solid physique. Not bad, even for a man half his age. He'd lost a little hair up top, but his body was still in good shape. Of course he didn't look as good as he had when he and Victoria—

"Chester! Your dinner is getting cold," his wife called.

"I'm coming, darling." He pasted on a smile then walked into the kitchen. "I just hate it when a pointless phone call interrupts my evening. I keep tellin' those boys to not call after seven, and what do they do?"

"Call?" She smiled.

"Of course, Jane. They might be grown-ups but sometimes I think they're teenagers again."

His wife chuckled and Chester sat down to a heaping plate of meatloaf, mashed potatoes and green beans made lovingly by his wife of forty years. Spooning up a large bite of potatoes, he stuffed them into his mouth, the flavors of real butter and cream making his taste buds dance.

Yes sir, very shortly the Angelov woman would be hightailing it back to whatever hole she'd crawled out of, or his name wasn't Chester McNutt.

Chapter Eight

Sitting cross-legged on her sleeping bag, Syn finger-combed her wet hair. It was marginally warmer in the house, but she was still chilled, thanks to having taken a lukewarm bath. With luck, this time tomorrow she'd have a working fireplace. She could hardly wait.

Earlier she'd removed as much of the furniture as she could, then scrubbed every inch of the walls, floor and even the ceiling. Rather than the scent of dirt and neglect, the room smelled of pine oil and lemon polish.

It felt strange to be getting ready for bed in her childhood home again. The night Mama died, Syn had been hustling the twins through their baths. She'd been drying their hair when the officer knocked on the door and their lives were forever changed.

Stretched across the foot of the sleeping bag, Maddie was snoring for all she was worth. She'd worn herself out chasing mice upstairs. Syn could only hope the little beasts would stay up there and leave them alone tonight.

The only light in the room was the cool blue light of the moon pouring in through the front window. Thick clouds dotted the sky, making the light spotty at best, but she didn't want to light the lantern. It was peaceful here in the darkness.

For the first time since her return, she felt comfortable.

Syn closed her eyes and continued combing her long hair. It was a pain to take care of, but some of her fondest memories of her mother had to do with her hair. She and her sisters would pile on the bed while Mama brushed their long tresses and told stories.

A smile tugged at her lips. How well she remembered those evenings, Mama in her dressing gown and them in their pajamas in a giggling pile on the bed. Her smile faded. That life was gone.

John Haines' angry face floated into her mind's eye and her eyes flew open.

Bastard.

She couldn't help but wonder what Junior knew about her family. He was a cop and the son of a snake, that made for two strikes against him. The bad blood between their families was no secret. The moment Mama filed a police complaint against the oldest son, Donnie, the mutual dislike had become fodder for public consumption.

Every Angelov child was born with a gift, and while Syn might not have been able to grow a weed, her talent was reading others. If she concentrated on a subject, she could sometimes pick up on what they were thinking, though feelings were much easier for her to detect.

Haines, for all his bluster, was afraid of her. The only question was why? Was it the police report Mama had attempted to file against his son? Surely he couldn't have been holding a grudge for that long.

John Haines had been the principal at her elementary school. Back then, Salem had only one and it covered kindergarten to eighth grade. Consequently, if the twins had started school, all four of them would've been in the same building.

She'd lost count of how many times she and Chloe had ended up in his office. Attending a public school had not been a wise choice for the Angelov girls and it was one Victoria had come to regret.

Most witches were born with certain powers, and, more importantly, the ability to learn others. Chloe was the headstrong one, and it had been difficult for her to control her temper. One day she'd turned Susan Henson's hair pea-green because she'd called Mama a witch. Chloe had paid a huge price for that mistake.

Both girls had received a good whipping, even though Syn hadn't been involved. As long as she lived, she'd never forget the feel of Haines' knee in her gut. Even now she imagined she could hear his hot, heavy breathing as his big hand struck her buttocks.

"Perverted bastard," she muttered.

Mr. Haines had made no bones about how much he disliked the Angelovs. They'd been suspended for any real or imagined infractions, and between the two of them they'd accumulated more detentions than any ten students. Syn was sure he'd hated them before they'd ever set foot in the building. What would cause a grown man to have such a powerful and irrational hatred for children he didn't even know?

Little more than an hour after the humiliating incident, Mama swept into the administrative office and set everything on its ear. With anger in her eyes, she'd charged into Mr. Haines' office and claimed her children, telling the principal in no uncertain terms that she was removing her children from his school.

From then on, she'd be teaching them herself.

Syn's eyes flew open and she groaned. There were times when she wondered if she'd go crazy from chewing on her own brain. She was tired and it was past time to go to sleep—

Outside, a shift in the shadows caught her attention. Sitting up straighter, Syn focused on the far side of the barn. Again the shadow moved, this time in the direction of the garden. Whatever it was, it was far too large to be an animal, unless Bigfoot was paying her a visit.

Was it John Haines?

As soon as she had the thought, she squashed it. This person moved with the ease of someone much younger than he. The figure jumped over the low fence. No, she was pretty sure he wasn't skulking around her yard.

In the darkened room she rose and snagged her boots, pulling them on her bare feet. Maddie's head came up and her stumpy tail began to wiggle. Syn made a hand signal to hush and the dog went on alert.

Reaching into her backpack, she grabbed the only weapon she had and tucked it into her boot. With Maddie at her heels, Syn made for the kitchen door. When they slipped out the back, she made a soft clicking noise with her tongue and the dog obediently fell into step beside her.

Walking carefully, Syn was grateful her eyes were already adjusted to the dark. If she'd had the lantern on, not only would she have missed someone running around the place, she also would've been both blind and helpless in the dark.

Together they made their way along the side of the house toward the front. From this angle, her visitor wouldn't be able to see them. Maddie's fur stood on end, and every now and then she'd emit a soft snarl, though she remained at Syn's heels.

Arriving at the corner of the porch, Syn pressed her body against the house, then winced when dry rose thorns dug into her thigh.

Off to the left was the dumpster, and in front of the porch was her car. A few yards on the other side of the house, her tent was a yellow blotch against the dark landscape. Bent at the waist, she moved forward to wedge herself between the dumpster and the porch.

Nothing moved.

Maddie squeezed her body in next to Syn's. On alert, her ears perked forward and her gaze fixed on something near the far end of the garden.

"What's out there, girl?" she whispered.

Maddie emitted a soft whine and her feet danced in anticipation. Taking the dog by her collar, Syn stared in the direction of Maddie's gaze. Several minutes passed before she caught a movement.

There, beyond the garden in the middle of the clearing, was her prey. A break in the clouds painted the yard in silvery light, and she could see the intruder clearly. Standing maybe twenty yards from the forest was a man dressed in black. His head was covered in some kind of a tight-fitting hood, and he had a strange, bug-eyed appearance thanks to some type of goggles.

The figure raised a large rifle and pointed it in the direction of the house. Before she could comprehend what was about to happen, a gunshot shattered the night.

Grabbing Maddie, she smashed both of their bodies into the dubious sanctuary afforded by the steps. Bullets buzzed overhead and struck the house, windows and the porch.

Shards of glass rained down on them both, and it took

everything she had to keep from screaming. Her grip tightened on the dog as Maddie struggled to get out of her arms. Syn lost count after fifteen rounds, and she was forced to shove her fist into her mouth when something hot grazed her cheek.

They were trapped. It was all she could do to keep her head down and cling to Maddie with all her might. Moving now would be suicidal.

After what seemed to be an interminable amount of time, the shots stopped and Syn imagined any person within five miles was calling 911. When she deemed it was safe enough to risk a look, she poked her nose out of their hiding spot.

The man was now crouched, and it appeared he was breaking down the rifle. Within seconds he'd stowed it in a bag and flung it over his shoulder to make his getaway.

"Oh, hell no."

Rising, she climbed out of the tight corner and motioned for Maddie to have at him. Silently, the dog took off like a missile, running as fast as she could, her body low and tight to the ground.

Syn snatched her weapon from her boot and pointed it at a large pine directly in front of the shooter.

"I'm sorry, Mr. Tree, but I need your help," she whispered.

Focusing all of her energy into the wand, she chanted under her breath, "On this night when evil is about, I call upon you, Goddess of Storms, to ferret him out. How dare this dark one walk on sacred ground to destroy? Use this pine as your weapon to reveal the evil lurking in the Devil's toy."

Energy flowed through her body in a wave of electricity. A blast of white light leapt from the wand, and Syn was unprepared for the kick. As if scooped up by an invisible hand, her body was thrown backward against the porch steps just as the pine exploded into flames.

Startled, she staggered to her feet and heard the man shout at her dog.

Maddie!

Wand in hand, Syn took off across the drive. In the distance Maddie and the man were tangling on the ground and judging from the sound of it, the intruder was losing. An unseen obstacle tripped Syn up, and she fell face first, skidding a few feet in the frozen grass.

Cursing and scrambling to her feet, Syn looked up just in time to see the man on the ground with Maddie on top of him. With one arm, he raised the bag to use as a weapon against her beloved companion.

Pointing her wand at the bag, she screamed at the top of her lungs, "Aloft!"

The downward movement stopped, and the bag was torn from his hands. It flew through the air to land several feet away. Even with the distance between them, Syn could feel the waves of shock radiating off the shooter. His head turned and his gaze landed on her. A wave of malevolence, as strong as any physical push, slammed into her.

"White light, white light," she whispered in a desperate attempt to protect herself. "Maddie! Come!"

The man lunged to his feet to retrieve the bag, then ran for the woods. His stride was ungainly and Syn knew her dog had landed at least one good blow to his ego or backside, whichever came first.

Maddie came running and her stubby tail wiggled furiously. Something dangled from her mouth.

"Are you okay, baby?" She dropped to her knees and ran her hands over the dog until she was sure her girl was unhurt. "You are the best dog ever."

Maddie gave a muffled whine.

"What do you have?"

The dog dropped the object in her lap, causing Syn to grimace. It was wet, and if she was not mistaken, held the scent of blood.

A tense giggle erupted from her. "Took a piece out of him did you?" She grabbed the dog and gave her a bear hug. "We can only hope you don't get rabies."

Chapter Nine

Matt cursed under his breath as he jogged around the marked cars lining Synnamon's driveway. Thirty-some rounds had been fired last night, and he'd missed the whole damn thing. He'd been roped into attending the retirement dinner for the Montrose police chief. Adding to his annoyance was the knowledge he'd managed to forget both his pager and cell, so the department hadn't been able to reach him until this morning.

"Son of a bitch!"

On the far side of the house was a line of pickup trucks, each sporting different logos on the doors. A large white van had been backed up close to the porch steps and the back doors were wide open. The abandoned air the house had carried for many years had been banished.

A small army of men dressed in everything from torn jeans to suits bustled around the trucks. Two more men were on the roof, and judging from the amount of soot on their white HazMat suits, they appeared to be cleaning out a chimney.

Didn't these damned people know this was a crime scene? Where the hell were his officers? A few members of the crime scene team were in the clearing across from the house, collecting evidence and taking photographs.

He spied Sherlock sitting on the floor of the mobile command van with dozens of little baggies surrounding him.

"Why in the hell are these people cluttering up my crime scene?" Matt snarled.

"Yours?" Sherlock glanced at his watch. "Little late, aren't you?"

"Sherlock…"

"Don't worry, we've finished processing the house and I gave them the all clear." He grinned. "Come on, Chief, do you think we're amateurs?"

"No, but I didn't expect to find a circus here this morning."

Sherlock shrugged. "Neither did I. Someone else arranged for the workers and Ms. Angelov didn't know how to call them off."

"She could've sent them away," Matt muttered.

"Why bother? By the time they arrived, we were done at the house."

Matt propped his foot on the bumper of the van. "What do we have so far?"

"Thirty-eight shell casings, and one small duffle bag containing another two hundred rounds of ammunition, a granola bar and a handful of condoms."

"Condoms?"

"Yes, condoms." Sherlock rustled through the bags. "We also have blood and a piece of his clothing. Her dog literally took a bite out of this guy's ass."

Matt took the bag to examine the bloody scrap of cloth. It appeared to be some sort of synthetic material, and the pattern was distinct with its small box-and-X design.

"That's some dog she has." Matt handed the bag back to Sherlock.

"For a dog her size, she's a tough one. My lazy mutt would've run to the perp and rolled over for a belly scratch."

"I just might have to buy that dog a bone."

"Me, too."

"The moment you finish processing the evidence, I want the material sent over to the state crime lab for DNA testing. Take it down there yourself if you have too."

Sherlock pushed his glasses higher on his nose. "Chief, I have a feeling whoever did the shooting will not come up in AFIS."

"Why is that?"

"It looks like the work of a professional. I dusted a few of the shells—they're clean. I couldn't find even an edge of a print. Everything in the bag was clean. Whoever did this knew what they were doing."

"Or watches television crime shows," Matt muttered. "Keep going, Sherlock. Find me something, anything to work with. I'm going up to the house to speak to Syn—er, the victim."

"Aye-aye, sir."

Sherlock was chuckling when Matt left. If Matt wasn't so concerned for Synnamon, he might've smiled as well. For now, he wouldn't be happy until he saw her with his own eyes.

The front door was propped open, and the object of his thoughts came through the front door lugging a bag of trash. Her braid was a mess and her clothing was covered in dust.

"Morning, Ms. Angelov," he called.

Synnamon looked at him, then smiled. At the sight of her even, white teeth, his stomach flopped as if he'd dropped ten stories in an elevator. Damn, she was one fine-looking woman, and with that smile she could fell any man with a pulse. Her long-sleeved sweatshirt and blue jeans did little to hide her generous curves.

"Morning, Chief. What brings you out here so early?"

She tossed the bag into the dumpster, then came down the steps. When she got near, he noticed a scratch on her cheek. Their gazes met and he felt as if all the air had been sucked from his lungs.

"Did you get that"—he motioned to his own cheek—"last night?"

"Can you believe it? I guess a shot must've ricocheted off the dumpster and grazed me." She rolled her eyes. "If it had been any more to the left, my nose would've been pierced."

"I'm glad you've managed to keep your sense of humor at least," he ground out.

Her smile faded, and it was then he caught a glimpse of the uncertainty her forced cheerfulness masked. Circles under her eyes stood in silent testimony to a sleepless night, and her mouth was pinched. The urge to pull her into his arms and hold her was overpowering, to the point that he forced himself to step away.

"Do you drink coffee?" he asked.

She blinked. "Well, yes I do, but as you can see"—she waved her hand toward the men working on her house—"I need to be here."

"Jorge!"

Jorge Sanchez, the owner of a Salem-based plumbing company, jumped out of his van and walked toward them.

"Buenos dias, Chief. What can I do for you?"

"I'm going to take Ms. Angelov to get some coffee. Can you keep an eye on things here while she's gone?"

"*Si,* I'll be happy to watch out for the *chica*. Her dog and I are good friends already." He gave Synnamon a big smile. "You'll be well taken care of by Chief Matt. You had a rough night, so you rest and enjoy his company, *señorita*."

"Thanks, Jorge."

Matt took her arm and escorted her to his SUV.

"Are you in a hurry?" She fell in step next to him, her long legs easily matching his stride.

"We have a few things to discuss and there's not much time." He opened the passenger door for her.

"We do?"

When she moved past him into the car, he caught a whiff of her perfume, and his gut tightened. He chose not to answer and slammed the door instead. Through the windshield he caught her annoyed expression. When he got into the cab, he struggled to ignore her enticing perfume.

"I have some questions I need to ask you." He started the engine, then made the turnaround to head for the road.

"About the shooting?"

"No, about your mother."

"Go ahead." Her tone was calm, but he detected a level of reluctance in her voice.

"What makes you think your mother was murdered, Ms. Angelov?"

"If you're going to get that personal you should probably call me Syn." Her tone was wry.

"Only if you agree to call me Matt."

"Agreed."

They reached the end of the drive and he paused to allow another car to pass before pulling out. Beside him, Syn's posture was rigid and her jaw was set. Those amazing violet eyes stared straight ahead.

"That night, I saw her lying on the road."

Shocked, he couldn't think of anything to say. He'd never guessed she'd been allowed to see her mother's body. What kind of asshole would've permitted that?

He cleared his throat, waiting until he felt calm enough to speak without flipping his lid.

"You saw your mother?"

"She was maybe ten yards from the curve." She pointed to his side of the road. "Right there. She was right there."

Matt slowed the car. His gaze moved over the asphalt as if new evidence would suddenly reveal itself.

"Why were you permitted to see her, Syn? It would've been rainy—"

"Rainy?" She gave him an odd look. "Who said it was raining?"

Bingo.

"Syn, yesterday I took a look at the report associated with your mother's death. What I found wasn't quite as I'd expected."

"And?"

"I believe your mother was murdered."

ဆာ

Even though Matt's lips were moving, all Syn could hear was the roaring in her head. Slowly, she turned away, feeling as if her soul and body were miles apart. Blindly staring out the window, she couldn't believe she'd heard him correctly.

Mama had been murdered.

Her chest went tight and it was becoming harder to breathe. How many years had she waited for this moment? For thousands of nights she'd dreamed of having the chance to bring Mama's killers to justice and now she'd completed the first step.

Finally, someone believed her.

"It was late. We usually went to bed around ten, but that night Mama said we could stay up late and finish packing for Boston." Her lips were numb, but somehow the words still tumbled off her tongue. "We were supposed to leave in the morning and I was helping the twins dry their hair when someone knocked on the door."

Silent tears ran down her face.

"I have no idea what time it was when the first officer came to the house. I answered the door, and he told me there'd been an accident and he would sit with us until the chief arrived.

"I tried asking him questions. I didn't even know if Mama was dead or alive, but he wouldn't give me a straight answer. He kept saying we'd find out the details when the chief got there. He lined us up on the couch and it felt like we waited for hours.

"Finally McNutt arrived with maybe six or seven other officers. The officers came into the house and began searching." She frowned. "But there were others. It was then I realized there were at least ten other men there, too. They didn't have uniforms and they were all over the place—in the garden, in the barn, down at the cemetery. It was utter chaos.

"I still don't understand why they'd search the house when she'd been killed on the road. Now that I think about it, that wasn't right, was it?"

Matt might've said something, but it was beyond her ability to hear anything outside of herself. Her focus was on the events of that night, and reality had ceased to exist.

"Finally McNutt told me Mama was dead, killed in an accident." She shook her head. "It was so weird. How could she be dead when there was leftover cake in the kitchen? She'd just made it the day before.

"No one looked at us and they didn't speak to us. Most of them acted as if we didn't exist. Some were even laughing and talking as if they didn't have a care in the world." Her voice broke and she struggled for control.

"Our Mama was dead, and these men acted as if nothing

unusual had happened. The moment Mama left this world, we ceased to exist as well."

Never would she forget the feeling of sitting on the couch watching their lives being torn apart by strangers. She'd been in the awkward stage in-between childhood and adulthood, powerless to do anything. No one had listened to her when she'd finally worked up the courage to object. She'd been told to be a good girl and sit with her sisters. Pain clutched at her heart. How utterly powerless she'd been that night.

"That was when the cars arrived to take us away. McNutt said that they'd called Children's Services to collect us, but that wasn't who came to the house." She swallowed hard. "They drove three separate cars, and I was more than a little confused.

"Why would they want to split us up? Our family lived in Boston, and if they'd called Aunt Bethany she would've been there in hours. Our family would've never given them permission to separate us.

"But no one ever called her." She laughed, and it was a bitter, ugly sound even to her own ears. "It took me years to get in contact with her. She told me it was three days before the family found out Mama was dead and we were missing. If they hadn't expected us the next day, it might've been weeks before they realized anything was wrong.

"The girls were screaming. I still hear them in my dreams." Her hands fisted. "McNutt had me by the back of the neck and threw me into the van. I don't know who the driver was; I'd never seen him before."

Exhausted, Syn closed her eyes. "Then we left. Chloe was taken east and the twins toward Columbus. The man took me into Salem and it was then I saw Mama. I wouldn't have recognized her if he hadn't told me." She swallowed hard, the image of her mother's body sharp in her mind. "He said, 'Say goodbye to your mother, kid.'"

Her lips firmed. "And I haven't seen my sisters since. By the time Beth arrived in Salem, Mama had been buried in an unmarked grave and the house had been thoroughly searched." Her jaw clenched. "They treated my Mama like she was a piece of meat. We loved her, she was our world, our everything—"

A muted scream was torn from her throat, and she bent

forward as sobs wracked her body. The pain in her midsection increased and for a moment she thought she would be torn apart by the depths of her anguish. Never, in all the years since that horrible night, had she told anyone the full story. Never had she given into her anger and loss as she did now.

Strong hands took her shoulders, and then she was in Matt's arms. Syn clutched at his jacket, her sobs uncontrollable. She shook from head to toe. His grip was secure and he made soothing noises in her ear. She leaned into him, inhaling his warm, masculine scent and struggling to calm herself.

For the first time since her mother died, she felt a small measure of safety.

Syn's tears fell even faster, until she wasn't sure who or what she was crying for. Her mother? Her sisters? Herself?

Matt never said a word. His arms remained around her, and his cheek had come to rest against her hair. She couldn't remember the last time a man had held her without wanting sex in return.

Her sobs slowed, then finally stopped with a noisy hiccup. Utterly weary, she went limp, oddly comforted by the sound of his heart. She didn't want to leave the security of his arms. Who knew if she would ever have this chance again? If she closed her eyes really tight, she might be able to pretend he liked her, if only a little...

"Feeling better?" His voice destroyed her daydream.

"I'm sorry I cried all over you." She pushed out of his arms. "I didn't mean—"

"Syn, it's okay." He caught her chin and forced her gaze to meet his. "You've been carrying a heavy burden for a long time, and it's past time for someone to help you shoulder the load."

Her laugh was watery. "That would be nice."

"Solving this case won't be easy. We don't have any evidence and right now I don't even know who was on the scene that night—"

"When has anything in life ever been easy?" She gave a noisy sniff. "Sometimes I think I was born with a massive To-Do list and a chip on my shoulder. I always seem to have something to prove."

He chuckled. "Somehow I don't doubt that." Reaching around her, he opened the glove compartment and pulled out a paper towel. "Sorry, this is all I have."

"Thank you." She rubbed her cheeks with the stiff paper, wincing when it grazed the cut on her cheek.

"I had my assistant pull your mother's file. I reviewed it, then had one of my men read it over. Most of the documentation is missing, and what is there is a mixture of truth and lies. If it weren't for the photographs, whoever orchestrated this would've gotten away with murder."

Chapter Ten

"There were photos?" Syn stopped scrubbing her cheeks.

"Accident photos, mainly. They don't show much—"

Their gazes met and Syn froze. Their faces were only inches apart, and if she leaned forward, their lips would touch. Heat burned in the depths of his black eyes and she breathed in his scent. Unable to decide whether to kiss him or climb out of his lap, she licked her lips. That was all it took.

With an angry mutter, Matt took possession of her mouth in a swift, commanding kiss. Her head swam and she allowed herself to be sucked into a maelstrom of need and hunger. His hand captured the back of her head, angling it for deeper penetration. She moaned deep in her throat when his free hand moved under her sweatshirt to pluck at the hem of her T-shirt.

Releasing her grip she had on his jacket, Syn fumbled for his free hand. Guiding it under her shirt to cover her breast, he growled and pushed her bra up and out of the way.

He wanted her. He really wanted her.

They groaned simultaneously when his hand plumped her breast before zeroing in on her nipple. Her hand came down over his as he teased it into a hard peak. Hunger ripped through Syn and she was seized by the desire to shove him down on the cramped seat and take him anyway she could. Her need burned white-hot, strong enough to engulf them both.

Lost in the morass of heat and need, it wasn't until the blare of a car horn sounded that Syn regained her senses.

Breaking the kiss, she yanked his hand from her breast, mortified. With her cheeks burning, she literally vaulted to her side of the seat. With clumsy fingers she struggled to straighten her bra and shirt while a blue pickup truck cruised slowly by them.

The driver and his missus were openly staring with rapt expressions.

Matt muttered under his breath even as he waved. When they passed he put the SUV into gear and pulled onto the road with a spray of gravel. Syn peeked at him out of the corner of her eye. His jaw was hard and now his eyes were hidden behind dark sunglasses.

"What's the matter, Cowboy, lost your sense of humor?" Syn fell back into the cocky, world-weary persona that had saved her so many times before.

"Trust me, there was nothing funny about that," he gritted.

"Really? Now, I thought it was quite funny. You and I sucking face, with my tit hanging out for all the world to see—" Something inside crumbled and the fledgling sense of confidence turned to charcoal on her tongue.

"I am the police chief. I cannot afford to be caught in a compromising position on a public road in broad daylight," he growled.

"Yeah, well, it was only a kiss there, King Tut. Even the puritan residents of Salem would expect you to get your rocks off somewhere. Who better to screw than the Whore of Salem's daughter?"

"Rocks, eh?" He wrenched the wheel, and with a squeal of tires they careened into the parking lot of The Coffee Pot. Slamming the SUV into park, he killed the engine before they'd come to a complete stop. Syn had to brace her hand on the dash or she'd have smacked her head on the windshield.

"Whoa, there—"

Matt grabbed her jaw and forced her to face him. "Do you think that kiss was about me using you to get my rocks off?"

"I—"

"I'm not a fuck-em-and-leave-em kind of guy, Syn. I would hazard a guess the men you've known weren't the upstanding kind, but I am," he ground out. "Even so, if that truck hadn't come by when it did, you'd have a lot more to be worried about than a naked breast. If I'd had my way you'd have been stripped bare and I'd have been pounding into you like an animal. At that point nothing would've been able to stop me from fucking you until you'd come so many times you wouldn't have been able to walk for days."

With that he exited the car, slamming the door so hard it rocked on its axles. Syn stared after him, her mouth agape.

What had he just said?

A huge grin spread across her face. Kissing her had caused him to lose sight of what was most important to him, his career. A mad giggle broke out.

"Wow, how about that, kids? Chief Matt has the hots for me."

Grabbing the visor, she popped open the mirror then groaned. It was a wonder she hadn't scared him away with the way she looked. Her eyes were red and her mascara smudged. Her skin was pale, causing the scratch to look worse than it was and her lips had the look of a woman who'd been thoroughly kissed. There was no way she could walk around in public looking like this.

Placing her hand over her eyes, she murmured a familiar spell.

"My face is a disgrace, my pain for all to see. Please freshen me so I look more like me."

As she spoke she moved her hand down her face and the changes were nothing short of miraculous. Her eyes were bright and clear, the circles were gone. Her mascara was tidy and her cheeks rosy with good health. Her kiss-swollen lips had returned to normal with a thin coat of red gloss. Staring into the mirror, she decided one more thing was needed.

"Cat's eyes."

Eyeliner appeared beneath her lashes, giving them a more dramatic look.

"Perfect."

Satisfied she looked much better, she got out of the car and almost skipped into the café. Matt hadn't made it to the coffee bar, as an elderly couple had caught him near the door and they were deep in conversation.

Moving past him, Syn gave his butt a gentle pat before walking to the counter.

"Can I help you?" The fresh-faced boy behind the counter smiled to reveal his metal-clad teeth. "We have our Holiday Spice Chai Latte on special and it goes great with our cinnamon bread."

"Uh, no thanks." Syn made it a rule to not imbibe drinks that had more letters than her name. "I'd like a white mocha, double shot, please. Also, do you have any idea what Chief Whitefeather drinks?"

"Oh yeah, he comes in every morning. French roast, straight up."

"One of those too, please, to go."

"Sure thing." He gave her the total and she handed over the money and a generous tip.

"Sandy will have your drinks ready at the end of the counter. Have a nice day." He gave her a wide, shiny smile.

Syn murmured her thanks and strolled toward the pick-up area. In the center, two refrigerated cases were packed full of almost any kind of treat imaginable. Cheesecake, scones, muffins, Danish, cookies, fudges, biscotti, and her most favorite things in the world, snickerdoodles.

Her mouth was watering by the time she spied the pale, fat cookies sprinkled with cinnamon. Mama used to make them for the holidays. Even now she remembered the scent of the rich, buttery cookies baking in the ancient oven. The kitchen would be warm, the windows steamed up, and all the girls would be doing their chores in the hopes Mama would make their favorites, too.

"Ma'am, your drinks are ready." The girl put two disposable cups of coffee on the shelf. "I hope you have a good day."

"You, too."

Syn was putting lids on their drinks when someone slammed into her from behind. If it weren't for the fact she'd been reaching for a second lid, the coffees would've been spilled all over the counter.

"Well, boys, who do we have here?"

Steeling herself, she turned and looked into the hard eyes of Donnie Haines. His hair had grayed at the temples and his face had lost its Opie-esque look to morph into that of a grown man.

"Well, well. Synnamon Angelov in the flesh." He placed a big, meaty hand on the counter, trapping her on one side. His insolent gaze scraped over her body. "And what beautiful flesh it is. It's been a long time, babe."

"Trust me, not nearly long enough." Her gaze flicked over the two men who accompanied him. She was surprised to see they were the same guys who'd hung with him in high school. "Haven't you guys caught onto his line of crap yet?"

They looked at each other and Donnie laughed.

"That's what I always enjoyed about you, Synnamon, your wicked sense of humor."

"That's funny. The last time I saw you, I think you told me it was my rack you liked so much." She picked up the coffees. "Now if you'll excuse me, I need to get going."

"Two coffees? Are you here with a friend, babe?" He chuckled. "They must be new to Salem I guess. No honest Salem resident would befriend the daughter of a witch."

Conversation at the closest tables dwindled, then died.

"Peter Pan." Syn rolled her eyes at Donnie. "When are you going to grow up?"

"I call them like I see them." He shrugged.

"Well, you would certainly know a witch, wouldn't you? Once I saw your Mama lay into Mr. Stubbs at the grocery store for fondling her produce. She certainly resembled a witch that day."

Several people twittered and a few whispers broke out. Donnie's face grew red and he leaned forward until his nose was mere inches from hers.

"How much?" he snarled.

"How much what? To buy you a breath mint?"

"How much to make you disappear?"

"You don't have enough money to make that happen, little man." Her smile was hard. "You see, I know your Daddy had a hand in helping to cover up Mama's murder, and I suspect you know all about it." She leaned forward, ensuring he wouldn't misunderstand her. "No amount of money in the world could drag me from Salem," she hissed. "At least not until I see those responsible rotting in prison."

He reared back, a look of utter astonishment on his pink face. "You're delusional, girl. Your mama's death was an accident. Hell, everybody knows that."

"I know there are people still living here who don't buy that line of bullshit at all. Mistakes were made, lies perpetuated to protect the innocent...or the stupid," she shot back. "You see, I'm going to take all of you down, one by one. And I'll enjoy every minute of it."

"Bitch," he ground out. "I know all about you, Synnamon Angelov. How you murdered a man in Arizona, your drug addiction—"

"That's old news, little man. I paid my debt to society."

"A murderer doesn't change, no matter how much you want to cover it up—"

"Did you learn that from your daddy? And here I was thinking he was stupid," she drawled. She'd shaken him up; the stench of fear lay thick on his skin.

"You stay here in Salem and play Nancy Drew, I don't give a fuck," he growled. "But let me tell you, you're going to wish you'd taken the money and left. Nothing good will come of you p-p-poking your nose into ancient business."

"You think? Somehow I don't see it that way. I never cared much for money. It makes most people assholes, and as long as I live I'll never regret returning home." Her voice was silky soft. "But you and your friends—well, that's a different story, isn't it? I know you're going to regret my arrival, as it's time for the sons to pay for the sins of the fathers."

Cups in hand, she moved to walk around him, relieved when she saw Matt walking toward her. He had that sexy, no-nonsense look that made her want to strip naked and proclaim herself virgin territory, ripe for exploration.

Without warning, two hands struck her back and gave her a shove. The cups flew from her hands and hit the floor just seconds before she did. The hot liquid seared her palms, and without thinking, she cast a spell.

"Ice, make nice, heal my burns and then take turns."

With her palms still stinging, she sprang to her feet, unharmed.

"You're not very graceful, babe," Donnie chortled. "Come on

guys, let's go." He started to walk past her and when he stepped on the now frozen coffee, he slipped and fell flat on his back.

"What the hell?" he roared.

One of his companions stepped up to help Donnie, but he too hit the floor.

"How in the hell could this be ice?" Donnie yelled, his face even redder than before.

"Ice melt away and let them burn as I today." Syn barely moved her lips, and the ice vanished. The men began shouting as the hot liquid made contact with their skin.

"What the hell happened here?" Matt asked.

"It looks like an unfortunate accident," she said. "Old Johnny Haines was right. This can be a dangerous town."

Chapter Eleven

"You realize it's no longer safe for you to stay out here alone," Matt said.

"You don't need to worry about me. I'm a very self-sufficient woman." Syn walked up the porch steps.

"Who had dozens of rounds fired at her home last night," he shot back.

"Tell me about it. Did you see what that asshole did to my tent? The only thing it can be used for now is draining pasta."

"Syn, this is serious."

"And you think I'm not being serious?" She turned and their gazes met. "I appreciate your concern, I really do. One thing you have to know is, when I left here my childhood was over. I was shipped out to California and into the foster system in Los Angeles, the Crenshaw area to be exact. After spending six months getting beat up, I had to adapt or die." She smiled. "In case you haven't noticed, I'm not the kind of girl to roll over and play dead."

"No kidding."

His smile was slight and her heart melted a little more. His expression was so serious. This man was truly a Boy Scout.

"Just my being here is making people nervous and tongues are beginning to wag. There's no way in hell you'll ever convince me to leave Salem, not when it's taken me twenty years to come back."

"I wasn't going to ask you to leave."

"Good, at least we agree on something. My being here will make your job a little easier—"

"You think?"

She ignored his sarcasm. "—as I will be flushing out the bad guys."

"And this is supposed to make me feel better?" He crossed his arms over his chest. "I don't need nor want to use you as bait. Good old-fashioned police work will ferret out the truth, and I want you out of the line of fire. I need to know you're safe."

"I appreciate the sentiment, Matt, but this is my battle. From a legal standpoint, you have every right to try and call the shots—"

"Gee, thanks."

"Sarcasm does not suit you," she said primly. "But it wasn't your family, your mother dead in the middle of the road. Our entire lives were destroyed twenty years ago. It's my responsibility to make this right, not yours. The only way I'll leave Salem is on a slab."

"After last night, that's a definite possibility," he muttered.

She shook her head. "We don't know each other very well, but you should understand that for all my big talk I'm actually very cautious. I don't make nice with strangers and I'm fully armed at all times."

His brow shot up. "You own a gun?"

"Oh, heavens, no. I'm a convicted felon and that would be illegal." Syn gave him an impish smile. "Haven't you heard the rumors? I'm a witch, and I never go anywhere without my wand."

"Fuck," he muttered.

"Treat me right and you might get that, too." She reached for the door handle.

"I'll be back later," he bellowed.

"I'll be waiting." She wiggled her fingers at him then walked into the house with a smile threatening to split her face.

જી

Later, with her head pounding from the noise, she snuck

upstairs for a few moments of relative quiet. The door to Victoria's room was partially open and she slipped inside with Maddie at her heels.

It was an out-of-body experience to walk into this room. It was here Syn's past and present collided. She was close to her mother's age when she died, and Syn felt she'd come to a unique understanding of the woman she'd called Mama.

Victoria must've been lonely, raising four children on her own with her family so far away. It couldn't have been easy for her, but she never let her children see her worry. To them she was this big, shining force in their lives, a whirlwind of rose perfume, laughter, music and warm hugs.

Syn trailed her fingers over the foot of the dusty four-poster bed. Mama used to go out at night a lot. She'd said the peace and quiet helped her think. In hindsight, Syn realized now she was probably meeting someone. A lover, perhaps?

"Who was he, Mama?" Her voice was whisper-soft.

Mama's dressing table had been thoroughly searched, the drawers pulled out and dumped on the floor. Righting the dainty chair, Syn brushed off the seat, then sat. The mirror was tilted away and Syn pushed it up until her face was reflected back at her.

Her mother would sit here and do her makeup, polish her nails, brush her hair or write in her journal. She'd had a Chinese silk dressing gown with a dragon embroidered on the back, and she always wore it after her bath. Chloe thought the robe was wildly exotic and she'd sneak in here to try it on when Mama wasn't looking.

Staring into the eyes so much like her mother's, a sense of quiet purpose descended over her. Alone and surrounded by Victoria's things, Syn could admit the shooting had given her a serious scare. Yes, she'd run outside like an ignorant heroine from a paperback novel. The only thing that would've made it more clichéd was if she'd fallen flat on her face.

Scratch that, she did fall down.

Another giggle bubbled up. Well, she might just be too stupid to be really scared. Her mother had always told the girls, no matter what, the house would protect them.

"Were you talking about Itsy, Mama?"

It had never occurred to her to be frightened when she'd seen the man in the clearing; only when he'd started shooting had she become scared. When she'd run out the door, getting hurt simply wasn't a possibility in her mind. She sighed. Sometimes she was a complete idiot.

Without thinking, she began rearranging the scattered items on the dressing table. She found a semi-clean scrap of cloth and carefully began wiping down and arranging her mother's treasures.

A small silver hand mirror.

Syn slipped into a daydream.

જી

A music box.

She wound the key and a tinny, classic tune started playing. It was lonely living out here. There were times when the burden of being an Angelov weighed heavy on her.

Dainty glass swan.

She was hungry—

Delicate china dish.

Why were the first-born Angelov children always women? What were the odds of that?

Chunk of tourmaline.

Was she still beautiful?

Sable makeup brush.

She needed to call Bethie tonight. They had so much to get caught up on.

Silver hairbrush.

She was getting older—

Engraved silver bracelet.

Her sister had the matching one. She slipped on the bracelet.

Lipstick.

And with the winter setting in, she needed to get ready for the solstice. A celebration was in order. Her family would be coming to enjoy the holidays with the girls, and Mama and Papa were getting older. Who knew if they'd ever come back to Angelov house again?

An amethyst ring.

The gold felt strangely warm as she carefully cleaned it with the cloth. Muted rays of the sun hit the stone and the sparkle was brilliant. It was one of her favorite pieces—

He'd given this to her, Synnamon and Chloe's father. Victoria looked in the mirror, and a soft smile tugged at her lips.

She'd loved him, with all her heart and soul. He'd pledged his love and loyalty to her, though in the end it hadn't stood up to the stresses they'd faced. She slipped the ring onto her finger. Poor man, the last she'd heard he regretted the demise of their relationship very deeply.

As did she.

Reaching for the drawer, she frowned when she realized it was on the floor. Now who in the world had pulled the drawers?

Those girls—

છ

Synnamon jerked backward, overbalancing on the stool and falling to the floor. Her heart pounded like mad and her skin was sweaty.

"What the hell?" she panted.

She rose, then righted the stool again. Syn was torn between wanting to sit and see what happened next and wanting to run from the room. Curiosity got the best of her, and she chose to sit and see what would come.

With shaky hands she removed the ring and bracelet and laid them on the table. Staring at the mirror, she saw the glass was dusty and she gave it a few hasty swipes with her rag. Over her shoulder, the reflection of the room wavered. The scent of roses reached her nose and she gripped the edge of the dressing table.

"Mama?"

The reflection shifted, and the room morphed into the memory of what it had been like when Mama was alive. It was a warm, friendly place with the rich burgundies and jewel tones Victoria had adored. A fire crackled in the fireplace, and candles were lit all over the room. It was clean, though Mama's clothes were scattered about. Being orderly wasn't Victoria's strong suit.

Dressed in the red silk dressing gown, Victoria lay stretched out on the bed. Given her mother's lush figure and saucy smile, Syn understood why men found Mama desirable. Her hair was a cloud of black curls held in place with a red ribbon. Those vivid dark purple eyes held a hint of mischief, enough to cause any man to take a second look.

"Hello, kitten."

Syn slapped her hand over her mouth, a sob caught in her throat. Shaking from head to toe, she fought for calm and was unsuccessful.

"Don't cry for me, kitten." Mama's voice was soft and low, just as she'd remembered it. "I'm okay, really."

"Mama," she gasped.

"Yes, you are seeing me. Remember what I taught you about the magic of mirrors?"

Spirits can be caught in reflective surfaces such as mirrors...

"You're a reflection?" Tears were running down her face, and even though she was shaking, she'd managed to regain a modicum of control.

"Sort of." Victoria sat up, then slid to the edge of the bed. "Everything I was—my energy, my thoughts and feelings—are saved in the mirror. But I'm not really here. You can think of it as a recording of the real me."

"Oh," Syn sniffed. "I have so much I want to ask you—"

"Synnamon, we have so little time." Victoria looked sad. "You're in danger."

"I know."

"They're biding their time, hoping to scare you into leaving."

"It won't happen." Syn scrubbed at her cheeks.

"I want you to leave, kitten."

She gaped at her mother's image. "Why would you say

that?"

"They've taken enough, and I don't want them to have any more of my family. Your sisters need you, and staying here is too dangerous. You don't know what you're dealing with—"

"Then tell me!"

"I can't." Victoria shook her dark head. "A plan is in place for you already. The universe has already put things into motion, and you're the only one who can alter it. I'm no longer on this plane of existence, and I cannot interfere."

"Mama, what were the police looking for the night you died? Why did they tear the house apart?"

"I can't tell you that, kitten, not in words anyway." A peculiar light gleamed in her dark eyes. "Close your eyes and think back, Syn, back to the day we were working in the sunroom and I'd taught you how to make a broom dance. Do you remember?"

"Yes, ma'am."

"That day, I told you if anything happened to me you had one specific job to carry out. Do you remember?"

She frowned. "You asked me to retrieve the grimoire and keep it safe. But I don't know where it is—"

"Wake daughter, someone is coming."

ॐ

Syn blinked and her mother was gone and the room was back to normal. Dust and cobwebs littered every surface imaginable. For a moment, she panicked. There was so much more she wanted to say and she'd lost her chance.

"Ms. Synnamon?" Jorge's voice sounded in the hall.

"Yes, Jorge! I'll be down in a minute."

"Okay!"

Shocked, Syn let her head drop into her hands. How could she have forgotten the spell book?

The grimoire was hundreds of years old and had been passed down through the first-born Angelov daughters. Every morning Victoria had studied it while she drank her tea. She'd record any new incantations she'd created and memorize others.

As children, Syn and her sisters had looked forward to those special moments when they were allowed to use the book for themselves. Every birthday was commemorated by learning a new spell and spending a few hours alone reading the wonders inside the grimoire. Victoria had been extremely careful with the tome, never leaving it out in the open for anyone to see.

Syn had always felt her mother had been a little over the top when it came to protecting the book. It was useless to anyone who wasn't a witch, and in Salem witches had been few and far between.

ॐ

Pen in hand, Matt read through the Angelov file. With the attention of a skilled surgeon, he culled every scrap of information the paltry pages contained.

Reopening this case would not be easy. What little evidence might've once existed was probably missing. He'd already looked in CAD, and the sequential case list skipped the number assigned to this one. It was becoming clear someone didn't want anyone looking into this particular case.

A knock sounded.

"Come in."

Mary walked in, carrying a handful of papers and a fresh cup of coffee.

"I thought these might interest you." She laid the pages on the desk. "I went through the archives at the newspaper offices and copied every article mentioning the Angelov family, starting from the time Victoria took ownership of the house. As you can see, there isn't much there."

He scanned the titles, stopping when he found one that mentioned the accident. It was barely even four lines, the gist of which was that the death had been ruled an accident and the children were sent to Boston to live with family. Case closed.

But they hadn't been sent to Boston, now had they?

"Thanks, Mary. These just might be helpful, and I appreciate the extra time you took to do this."

"Yeah, you appreciate it now; just wait until you see my timesheet." She gave him the coffee and headed for the door. As she was about to leave, she stopped. "Almost forgot. According to the historical weather data website, it was a clear night on October 12. Is that what you're looking for?"

"Yes, Mary. Thanks for your help."

"Don't get too used to it; I'm on vacation next week."

"What will the department do without you? Salem will be awash with crime." He smothered a grin.

"I believe it. Just may have to call in the guard to hold down the fort for me."

Matt was chuckling when she shut the door. Scanning the article headlines, he saw there was a Halloween piece about the history of Angelov house. He put that one aside. Next was a short blurb about the accident.

Since living in Salem he'd noticed when locals died, the paper did a nice write-up about their life and usually included a photograph. Why had Victoria's death received only a few lines in the back of the newspaper?

He was about to drop the page on his desk when he noticed there was another one stuck behind it. Pulling them apart, he saw it was a gossip column, and the highlighted text stunned him.

Salem resident Daniel Crane has been seen around town asking questions about the night Victoria Angelov was killed. This reporter would like to know if Mr. Crane has any new evidence to share, or if he is yet another victim of Ms. Angelov's witchy ways.

Witchy ways?

What was it with this town and its witchcraft issues? Why were they so intent upon painting this woman as being evil?

Some things in life defied explanation, but nothing or no one would ever be able to convince Matt that witches, real witches, roamed Salem casting spells.

Chapter Twelve

The intercom buzzed as Matt was shutting down his computer. It took him a moment to remember which button to push, as Mary never used the thing. If she needed his attention she was more likely to bellow through the open door instead.

"Yes, Mary?"

"Chief, uh, Mr. McNutt is here to see you, sir."

"Send him in."

Ah, that explained it. When McNutt had run the place, he was all formality and starch. The admin staff had been required to wear skirts, which was sexist, and it was the first rule Matt had changed when he came on board.

He rose when the door opened and Chester McNutt filled the doorway. McNutt was a big, hulking man who moved with impressive speed and agility. Looking at him now, it was no wonder the Angelov girls had been so terrified of him. To a child, this man would be a giant.

"Chester, good to see you." Matt shook the other man's hand.

"And you, Whitefeather." Chester looked around the office. "Place hasn't changed a bit."

"Well, it is difficult to make piles of reports, catalogs and other odds and ends more welcoming." Matt waved the man to a leather chair in front of his desk. "Coffee?"

"No thanks, the wife won't let me touch it." He settled his bulk into the chair. "Seems I developed an ulcer and it's something I'll never be rid of. I can't imagine why, what with this job." He chuckled. "No stress involved with police work, none at all."

Matt smiled at the level of sarcasm in the other man's voice. "I hear you."

"I thought I'd drop in and talk to you about something I heard this morning." He reached into his pocket and withdrew a fat cigar. "I decided you might need a heads-up on a situation that's brewing."

"Sorry, Chester, this building is non-smoking now. All of the city buildings are."

"No shit?" He shoved the cigar back into his pocket. "Damned Democrats, pretty soon they'll require tree hugging and feeding the birds."

Actually it has to do with paying painters a great deal of overtime to scrape thirty years of tar and nicotine off the walls of the police department.

"So what can I do for you?" Matt resumed his seat.

"I heard one of the Angelov girls returned to that old wreck of a house on the hill. Seems she was in town stirring up trouble last night." Chester met Matt's gaze dead-on. "Hear anything about this?"

"Actually, I did." Matt leaned back in his chair.

"And there was a shooting at the house last night?"

"You have good sources. Seems some hunter mistook her property for a big white deer. Shot it all full of holes."

McNutt's eyes narrowed. "Which girl is it? Synnamon?"

Curious. This man could remember the name of a fourteen-year-old girl who'd been gone from Salem for twenty years, when most officers couldn't remember a case from two years back. McNutt was playing with him, and Matt was curious as to where this would lead.

"I believe that's her name." Matt propped his heels on the desk, adopting a casual posture. "As for causing trouble, she was alone in her home, that's hardly cause for someone to aerate the place."

"Nonsense," McNutt barked. "Them Angelovs are bad people, Matthew. You don't know what it was like when their mama was alive. That woman sprang from the loins of the Devil himself."

Nutcase.

"Chester—"

"You have no idea what it was like in Salem with that woman and her offspring running wild. Haines had those bastard girls in his office probably once or twice a week; they were always up to no good."

Matt was beginning to enjoy himself. With every word, McNutt sealed his fate. It was fast becoming clear something bad had happened while this man was in charge of the investigation.

"What do you mean, no good?" Matt steepled his fingers and adopted a concerned expression.

"Their mama ran around with half of the town's married men, which meant their wives were none too happy with the situation." McNutt settled back in his chair, getting comfortable for the tale to come. "This is a good, moral town and we enjoy our strong, homespun ideals."

"Some in the town can't be too moral, or they wouldn't have run around with Ms. Angelov in the first place," Matt said.

"Well." The other man shrugged. "Some men can't help their natural urges, especially with a woman that beautiful in our midst."

No, he did not just say that...

"What happened back then is ancient history, Whitefeather. Salem is a different town now; we've learned from our mistakes and we don't aim to repeat them." His gaze turned sharp. "We don't abide trashy women, especially witches."

Matt had to struggle to keep from laughing out loud. In the last three years, two new stores had opened and they were both pagan-oriented. For a town this size, to have two pagan stores said a great deal about those living here.

"Witches?" he asked.

"Yes, sir. Ms. Angelov was a witch and she raised her daughters to follow in her footsteps."

"Witch. As in flying brooms, eye of newt and pointy hats?"

"No, Matthew." Chester was starting to look a little irritated. "Witch as in casting spells, making potions and ruining people's lives. That kind of witch."

Do you even hear yourself?

"And she told you she was a witch?"

"Not in so many words. On several occasions we received calls from people on the hill who'd seen her running naked through the woods or dancing under the moon." McNutt shook his head. "You should've seen her. She had the kind of sexual power that could turn a man against his family."

"I'm sorry, Chester, but I find all of this hard to believe. I've met the woman living up there, and trust me, there is nothing remotely supernatural about her."

"That's what she wants you to think." Chester's eyes narrowed. "Mark my words, Matthew, that woman is up to no good. We don't need her kind around here, and if she stays the trouble will start up again."

"Chester, I can't just roust her out of her home. I have no legal reason to do so. I checked her out thoroughly, she's the owner of the property and her background is clean. She has every right to move here if that's her wish."

"Her mama brought a lot of heartache to this town with her loose and devious ways. I'm warning you, son, that woman is here to cause trouble."

Well, as long as she didn't wear them new fangled ear bobs and start lacquering her mouth...

"Just what did this woman do that was so bad, Chester? She seduced a few men and had her children without the fathers? Maybe she ended up with men who treated her like dirt and had the good sense to not marry them." Matt sat up and braced his arms on the desk. "We're not in the Dark Ages anymore. Single women have children all the time."

"Any woman who held as much power over men as she did has the devil in her blood."

"So you were also affected by her 'powers'?"

For a moment the mask slipped, and Matt caught a glimpse of steel determination. For some reason it was incredibly important to Chester that Matt buy his ridiculous story.

Looked like McNutt was out of luck.

"Of course not, Matthew!" he blustered. "I've been married to my beautiful wife for many, many years. She's the mother of my children, and there's no way I'd dishonor her by running around with loose women."

"But other married men dated Victoria, took her out."

"They'd come running like dogs in heat and fall over themselves to buy her gifts, dinners—as well as her services." The mask was firmly back in place. "Not in Salem of course; their wives would've found out. They'd take her down to Montrose and when they got under her skirts they'd hit that old motel on Crescent just outside of town."

"Hmm, I'll bet that got the women riled up, their men running after this woman."

"Hell yes, it did." His expression turned indignant. "Several of them came to me and asked me to speak to their men, and Lord knows I tried." He shook his head and the sunlight caught on the threads of silver in his hair. "They were bewitched by her. I never managed to sway any of them, not a one."

"So the women in town hated her."

"They weren't the only ones. Most of the townspeople wanted nothing to do with the family. Everyone knew what they were—"

Thanks to their friendly police department.

"—older kids, they took to tormenting her girls at school. Finally Victoria pulled them from the school system and taught them at home. Things settled down a little bit after that."

"Who else in town was suspicious of this family?"

"I don't know of a family that wasn't wary of them. Ms. Thatcher over at Patti's bakery almost lost her daughter because of that family. Child was choking and Victoria came out of nowhere. All the witnesses in the bakery swore she was trying to kill the child. She might've succeeded if Brittany hadn't managed to cough it up herself."

"I don't know, Chester." He shook his head. "It's pretty hard to believe that a woman would try to kill a child in broad daylight with witnesses."

"Victoria knew they wouldn't try to stop her. All the women-folk were afraid of her."

"But what do you think she was trying to gain from killing this child?"

"Keeping everyone afraid—"

"So the whole town was basically held hostage by this family and their supposed witchcraft?"

"Hell, yes. There wasn't a person in town that wanted anything to do with them. Her dying like that was the best thing she'd ever done."

Okay asshole, party's over...

"Is that why you closed her death as an accident?"

Chester blinked and for a moment Matt saw utter shock in the other man's gaze. He waved a hand as if to blow off the question.

"Personal feelings aside, it was an accident. It was late and you know how bad those curves are up there. Bam, someone took her out."

"And you never caught the driver."

"Nope, never had any idea who struck her. No witness ever came forward. We didn't have any cars come into the repair shops with heavy front-end damage." Chester chuckled. "I always thought maybe it was the Devil himself, come to take his handmaiden to hell with him."

Bastard.

"I'm pretty sure whoever was driving that car was all too human. The devil might have problems steering, with hooves instead of hands."

The other man chuckled again. "You just might be right, Matthew." McNutt pushed himself out of the chair. "I just wanted to let you know it might be wise to keep an eye on that girl. I'm telling you now, she's nothing but trouble."

"I'll take your comments under advisement." Matt rose. "So far she's been pretty quiet up there."

"Except for the shooting."

"She wasn't the one doing the shooting."

McNutt shrugged. "Mark my words, Matthew, you're gonna have some trouble on your hands."

"Thanks for the warning, Chester. You take care now."

"That I will." He reached for the doorknob and was about to leave when Matt stopped him.

"Before you leave, I have a quick question for you."

McNutt turned, and again the good-ole-boy expression was in place. "Sure thing, shoot."

"Where are the missing pages from the Angelov accident file?"

⋈

Mad as hell didn't even begin to describe Chester McNutt when he left Matt's office. By the skin of his teeth, he managed to keep his plastic smile in place all the way through a short conversation with Ms. Peabody, who'd caught him on the street to complain about stray cats in her neighborhood.

Now, headed to his car, he finally let the façade dissolve like snow on a warm car hood.

"Old biddy probably doesn't even realize I'm not chief anymore," he muttered. "Fuck, its cold out here."

Cranking the engine of his restored 1959 Ford Truck, it started without a hitch. Carefully, he backed out of his parking spot and headed around the square. Before he made the first turn he had his cell phone in hand.

He punched a speed dial number, and a man answered on the first ring.

"It's me," McNutt said. "We need to meet."

"For what?"

"I spoke to Whitefeather."

The other man chuckled. "And what did the red man have to say?"

"He knows more than we thought."

"Than *you* thought. I told you not to underestimate the man."

"Somehow he got into the case file and some of the contents are missing."

"What?" The man's voice was deadly calm.

"Someone found the file and removed some of the contents, and now we have that bastard on the hunt for the missing pages."

"How could you be so fucking sloppy?" the voice ground out.

"Hey, I buried that fucking file. How was I supposed to know someone would find it?" Chester snapped.

"Because you were the chief, you idiot." The other man took a deep breath then expelled it slowly. "It was your job to take care of that file. Instead, you were hopping from one retirement party to the next, living the good life, weren't you?"

"I—"

"Shut the fuck up," the voice snapped. "Before you left the department I gave you one final job, to kill the file and the evidence. You blew it."

"The evidence has been destroyed."

"Hopefully with more efficiency than the case file."

Chester kept quiet though he longed to curse the bastard into next week. Weeks of torment were not worth the five minutes of relief the act would bring him.

"I think we need to call a meeting," Chester said.

"I know that," the voice snapped. "One of the problems we have now is that you continue to think. I'm in charge and I'll call the meeting, the sooner the better. In the meantime, you keep an eye on Whitefeather and the Angelov girl. The less time they spend together, the better off we'll be."

The line went dead and Chester stared at the phone.

"Well, fuck you too, shithead," he muttered.

Hitting another speed dial entry, he put the phone to his ear, more than ready to tear someone a new asshole.

"Where the hell have you been?" The voice on the end sounded like a whiny, petulant child.

"So much for your bright idea, jackass. You shoot a rifle like a pussy," he snarled.

"That damned dog of hers almost killed me. It took a chunk of meat straight outta my ass."

"You've got more than enough to spare," McNutt said. "Your plan didn't work, so we have to come up with something else."

"Like what?"

"I don't know yet, but it's your ass on the line so you'd better straighten up and devise something. That woman is a danger to all of us."

"Damn straight."

"The Man-in-Charge is calling a meeting, so you'd better have something solid and foolproof to put on the table," McNutt snapped. "I'm telling you and your family right now, I'm not going to hang because you couldn't keep your dick in your pants. I've stuck my neck out for you long enough."

"Calm down, McNutt. You can't abandon ship now, we're all in it for the long haul," the other man's tone was harsh. "If one goes down, we all go down, and you know it."

"Fuck."

"I will come up with something and The Brotherhood will agree to my plan. Just keep your mouth shut and carry on like everything is normal."

"Fine."

McNutt closed the call, then threw his cell phone onto the passenger seat. It had been so long since he'd experienced "normal", he wasn't even sure what it was anymore.

ಐ

The sun sank in the west and the last worker had left for the night. Thrilled to be free, Syn grabbed her jacket and headed outside with her dog. Maddie took off for the clearing, barking madly all the way.

Skipping down the steps, Syn had to admit she felt better, lighter than she had in years. Was it because she finally had electricity and a working fireplace in one room? Or could it be the toe-curling kiss from this morning?

"Either one will do."

She laughed and tilted her head back, then twirled around until she was dizzy. As she stopped, her gaze fell on the house and she couldn't help but wince at the sight of the holes made by the shooter.

Poor house. No matter why that idiot had decided to shoot

up her property, this house didn't deserve that kind of abuse. She was tempted to use a spell to fix it, but it would be hard to explain later.

Turning, she headed in the direction of the cemetery. The path was no longer visible but it didn't matter as Syn knew exactly where to go. At least a million times she'd followed this path in her mind in the past twenty years. Sometimes her memories were the only thing that kept her sane during her darkest hours.

Approaching the barn, she couldn't help but notice how well tended it was. Nowhere could she detect any peeling paint, nor did it have the air of general neglect the house did. Why had the caretaker spent so much time keeping up the barn but letting the house go to pot?

Victoria had used the barn to store the gardening equipment, and they'd kept a few chickens for eggs. They'd also had some stray cats that lived there. When it rained, the girls would climb into the loft to work on spells, read or simply daydream. Once Chloe had set the hay on fire when she was practicing levitation spells. Lucky for her Syn had learned the water spell, or the barn would be but a memory now.

Behind the barn was a large, open field. It was here they'd play kickball, baseball and run races. Even though winter had taken a firm hold on the land, Syn imagined she could smell the fresh grass and turned soil heated by the sun. She couldn't wait to plant a vegetable garden this spring, and roses. Lots and lots of roses.

She could only hope they survived her ministrations.

A low stone wall with a rusty iron gate marked the end of the field. For centuries, the Angelov families had been buried in this cemetery and Mama was one of the few exceptions. Once things settled down and her sisters were home, Syn was determined to move Mama from the Salem cemetery to this place. It was only right she spend eternity on the land she loved so much.

Ignoring the gate, Syn sat on the low wall, then slung her legs over to the other side. The caretaker had done an excellent job keeping the plots in good order, and everything was clean and well tended.

She didn't have to read the stones to know who was where.

As children, they'd memorized the layout of the cemetery, and she'd spent many hours making up fantastic stories about how her ancestors had lived. Chloe would make fun of her daydreams, but since Chloe could communicate with spirits, she alone knew the truth of their lives.

Syn took care to avoid walking over the graves that had sunk into the ground. Even though she knew the bodies would be long gone, it still seemed disrespectful to just walk over them as if they didn't exist.

Angelina, the first Angelov wife, was called "The Bride" by the family. She'd been buried with her bridal veil and the dried flowers she'd carried down the aisle. Her husband, Pieter, was laid to rest next to her, and he'd been buried in the same suit he'd worn on their wedding day. As children Syn and her sisters had thought the story unbearably romantic, and they'd parade around wearing white T-shirts on their heads like veils while carrying handfuls of weeds as their bouquets.

Her smile was bittersweet. It seemed like a lifetime ago.

In the far corner of the cemetery was a lone oak tree. Syn had vague memories of the day they'd planted it. The twins were but babies in diapers and Mama had put them in a wagon to bring them all the way out here.

All of them took turns digging the hole, though the twins had been in the way more than anything else. The sapling was miniscule when it had been planted, and now it was a beautiful tree with wide branches. This was where Mama should be laid to rest, under the branches of the tree she and her daughters had planted.

Syn sank to her knees on the hard, unforgiving ground.

"I'm trying to be so strong," she whispered. "Now that I'm home, I'm missing all of you so much that sometimes I can't breathe."

A low breeze sprang up and sent a few dried leaves scuttling across the ground.

"I know the answers are here, and I promise I'll do whatever it takes to find them, Mama. Someone will pay for what they did to you, to us."

The breeze tugged at her hair and for a moment she thought she smelled roses. If only Chloe were here, she'd know what happened to Mama. Syn's lips twisted. It was really too bad her own gift was so limited.

Chapter Thirteen

It was late by the time Matt headed home. Salem was quiet, but it would be a different story tomorrow. The forecasters were calling for snow to begin just after midnight and if they received the predicted amount, traffic would be a nightmare in the morning. The only ones who'd benefit from the coming storm were the tow truck drivers and the salt crews.

Welcome to winter in northern Ohio.

After McNutt left, the rest of the afternoon was uneventful. Whether the other man knew it or not, he'd given up valuable information in his conversation with Matt.

Not only was it highly suspicious McNutt remembered the name of a fourteen-year-old girl from twenty years ago, he'd called her mother by her first name.

His instincts were telling him McNutt knew Victoria much better than he'd let on. Was he one of her boyfriends or did he fall into the column of spurned suitor? Ending up in either position was enough to add the former police chief's name to the list of suspects, not that he wasn't there already.

Matt had been hoping McNutt would give a hint as to the location of the missing pages from the Angelov file. Unfortunately the man's face had gone blank, and his response had been less than helpful.

When I left the office, everything should've been there, so it must have been lost on your watch.

Not likely.

If he wasn't mistaken, McNutt had been taken aback by Matt's question. It was possible the ex-chief hadn't known the file had been looted. The burning question was, why would someone remove some pages, but not the entire file?

If the file was missing, almost anyone would label it as misplaced and that would be the end of it. In the basement there had to be at least ten thousand archived files; losing one would not be unusual. But losing a few pages, that was enough to cause suspicion.

Someone wanted the theft to be noticed.

He slammed the heel of his hand into the steering wheel. It was the only logical explanation. Taking the entire file would've been too easy. So who had access to the archives?

Anyone with a building pass.

He groaned. The list of possible suspects was huge. Officers, administrative staff, dispatchers, maintenance crew, temporary staff, interns and any repair contractors, all had the run of the building.

As of today the only obvious suspect was McNutt. He was the chief at the time of the incident and it was he and Lieutenant Pine whose names had appeared on the outside of the file. So what about the lieutenant? He was not a stupid man. Surely he knew the Angelov case was no accident.

Making a mental note to speak to him in the morning, Matt turned onto Winding Oak. His condo was in the opposite direction, but he'd told Syn he'd drop in and since he was already heading in that direction...

"Crazy bastard."

All day he'd deliberately kept himself busy if only to keep his mind off their scorching kiss. He hadn't been exaggerating when he'd told her if they hadn't been interrupted, he'd have stripped her bare and taken her on the front seat. Never had he felt such an immediate, fiery reaction to a woman.

Matt knew he was attractive to the opposite sex, and for his adult life, sex had been easy. Women were always been attracted by the badge and the color of his skin. Serial dating just wasn't his style. He and his brothers had been brought up to respect women, and it was rare he indulged in a one-night stand. Since coming to Salem, he'd dated around, but none of the women came close to capturing his imagination the way Syn did. Though he'd be damned if he knew why. The woman was a pain in the ass through and through.

"Mouthy," he muttered.

Intelligent.

"Back-talking." He pulled into her driveway.

Confident.

"Argumentative."

Strong-willed.

"Stubborn."

Like a goat...

"Sexy."

Hell, yes!

Matt made it a practice to be attracted to a woman's mind before her body came into play, but he couldn't deny he'd had an immediate physical reaction to Syn. When he'd searched her on that first afternoon—if it hadn't been for Bryan watching them, he might've disgraced himself on the spot.

She was also wickedly funny and had a wit that turned him inside-out. The fact she was beautiful and possessed a body built for sin was an added bonus.

It would be unethical to get involved with her...

Matt's jaw tightened. Unethical, maybe; but once the case was closed, all bets were off.

Emerging from the woods, he was surprised to see a bright light spilling from the living room window. Pulling up near the steps, he parked and turned off the headlights.

The large window had been broken last night, and someone had repaired it with duct tape. Through the lines of tape, the room looked much better than it had only two days before.

The fireplace sported a cheery fire, and a few feet away was a pallet with an inflatable mattress on the floor. Sound asleep, Maddie lay in the middle of the sleeping bags with all four feet in the air. It looked cozy to Matt. A bedstead had been assembled, though it didn't have any mattresses.

Syn walked in from the dining room with a towel in one hand. Taking the handle of a metal bucket hanging over the fire, she poured steaming water into a large iron tub on the far side of the fireplace.

Before he could even register that she was going to bathe,

139

she'd stripped off her jacket and thermal shirt, leaving her clothed in a skimpy red bra that exposed more than it concealed.

"Pervert," he muttered. What kind of man would watch an unsuspecting woman take a bath?

A very horny one...

Syn stepped out of her pants to reveal matching red panties. He groaned when she bent to pick up her discarded clothing. She had the perfect ass. Big and firm, it was just the right size to hang onto while fucking against a wall, in a shower, or any other vertical position.

Syn shed her underclothes and, fully nude, stepped into the miniscule tub. The firelight bathed her skin in a warm reddish glow, accentuating her curves and the perfect violin shape of her figure. Her long dark hair was in its customary braid and the end licked at her waist. What he wouldn't give to see her hair loose and spread across his pillows.

Bending, she wetted a cloth, then used a bar of soap to work it into a lather. Raising her arm, she began washing. In profile, her breasts were perfection, the nipples taut and the globes more than enough to fill a man's hands.

She drew the cloth across one breast and he groaned again. Streams of soapy water ran over her stomach and thighs. A flash of metal caught his attention.

Damn! The woman had a belly-button ring.

Searing heat swept his groin and had him reaching for the window control. Cold air. He needed cold air, now.

The sweet patch of dark hair between her thighs was soon covered in lather, and his only thought was of busting into the room and offering to help her rinse off. His throat was tight and sweat broke out on his forehead despite the dropping temperatures.

It seemed like her bath lasted for hours, when in reality it was only ten minutes or so. By the time the washcloth slipped between her thighs, he would've eaten his badge to be that scrap of cloth right now.

Finally, just when he'd decided he couldn't take it anymore, she rinsed the cloth and set it aside. Taking a bucket of clean water, she poured it over her body, rinsing away the soap bubbles.

Her body gleamed with water, turning her from flesh-and-blood woman into any man's most erotic fantasy. His teeth gritted as the need for release pounded at his crotch, but he couldn't, wouldn't give into it. The only time he'd come in his pants he was fourteen, and that had been in his bathing suit at the swimming pool.

With her bath completed, Syn stepped from the tub and reached for a towel. She made quick work of drying off before donning thermal long johns and fat socks. Turning off the light, she sat in front of the fire for a few moments then stretched out in her pallet.

Maddie stirred, then got up for a leisurely stretch. Once Syn settled, the dog lay beside her with her head on her mistress' shoulder.

Matt envied the dog. Maddie had an established place in Syn's life. Given how prickly the woman was, it would take some work to convince her to trust him.

Luckily, he was a patient man.

୪

Syn couldn't say what it was that woke her. The fire had burned to embers and the room was chilly. Outside, the wind howled, and the house creaked with each blast. Maddie grumbled in her sleep when Syn got to her feet. Grabbing her jacket, she hustled over to the window.

It was snowing.

Flakes danced and darted through the air, riding the air currents in a magical dance that transfixed her. Winter was her favorite time of year, and living in the South, she'd forgotten how beautiful it could be. The snow was barely sticking to the grass, but she'd bet by morning—

"What the hell?"

When she saw the vehicle parked next to the steps she thought her heart would stop—until she realized it was Matt's departmental SUV. Her breath left in a noisy huff, and warmth spread through her belly.

He'd been worried about her.

Something shifted in her chest and she was struck by the urge to cry. In her life it was a rare occurrence to come across someone who genuinely cared what happened to her. With the exception of her family, most of the people she'd known were shallow, pleasure-seeking and superficial. While she understood most of this was due to not wanting people to get close to her, she also knew that at some point she'd have to let someone in.

No one is an island...or a rock, however that saying went.

A huge grin spread across her face and she placed her hand against the cold glass. Now who would've thought she'd get tangled up with a man like this? He was so patient, caring and yet wasn't about to put up with any of her crap. She'd always thought when she made the decision to let someone into her heart, he'd have to be extraordinarily strong and as patient as a saint, but never would she have guessed he'd carry a gun, legitimately.

Clapping a hand over her mouth, she stifled a laugh. While in prison she'd decided the days of messing around with bad boys were in the past. No longer did she want to have a man in her life that she was forced to prop up due to a weakness in his character. Bad boys might be a turn-on, but the serious ones would be in for the long haul.

And that man could kiss...

After their sexually charged minutes in his car, she'd been surprised her panties hadn't caught fire. She'd never, ever gone from zero to sixty that fast before.

Before becoming celibate, sex was something she could take or leave. While she liked the closeness of being with another person, she still wasn't sure what all the fuss was about. It was nice to be held, and she loved just cuddling on the couch and kissing for hours, but the actual act of sex left her cold.

Maybe she was frigid?

Her shoulders slumped. She'd like to think it wasn't true, but the facts didn't bear out the evidence. The bottom line was that she'd never experienced an orgasm with a partner.

But Matt isn't one of your bad boys...

No, he wasn't. He's the first man who genuinely cared about her without wanting her in the sack after saying hello. He was smart, funny and when he smiled, her mind went right into the gutter. In one word, that man was smoking.

Without even thinking about it, she turned away from the window and headed for the front door. When her fingers curled around the cold doorknob, she stopped.

What the hell do you think you're doing?

Syn released the knob as if burned. Now was not the time to bring someone into her life, especially with her sisters still missing and someone using her home for target practice. It wasn't sensible or safe to be tangled up with Matt, not when she needed to keep her wits about her. She'd waited twenty years to make her return to Salem and she couldn't let the sudden arrival of a handsome man cause her to deviate from her plans. Too much was riding on her to make a mistake now.

Reluctantly, she turned away from the door. She had three lives depending on her, and that was the bottom line. Walking back to her bed, she couldn't help but sneak one more look out the window at Matt's truck.

It was humbling to know someone cared.

Chapter Fourteen

It was early when Matt arrived at the station the next morning. Night shift was still on duty and wouldn't be signing off for another half-hour. The building was quiet and there was no coffee to be had on any floor.

There was something to be said for coming in later in the day.

Stopping by his office, he signed on to his computer and checked CAD to see where his officers were. Everyone was listed as available, and it was only because they'd dodged a bullet last night. At the last minute the storm had shifted north, leaving only a dusting of snow behind.

Scanning the list of officers, he noted Lieutenant Pine was in the shooting range. Now was the perfect time for a conversation.

Jogging down the steps, he heard the gunfire long before he neared the range. Checking the door to the archived record room, he was pleased to see it was locked tight. There was no way he was going to let any more of the files grow legs and walk away.

Per policy, the door to the range was locked at all times. Pulling out his key ring, he opened the door and stepped into the control room. A wall of windows overlooked the shooting range, and Matt took a spot near the control panel.

Pine was the only one on the range, and in his hands he held a Beretta nine-millimeter pistol. Down range was a line of bowling pins, and many were already lying on their sides. With impressive precision, Pine took out the rest, one after another.

Matt was impressed with Pine's accuracy. As a paper-pusher, he wasn't required to have the accuracy of a trained marksman. Snipers spent thousands of hours training in the hopes that when they received the call, they'd make the shot. Most police officers were lucky to maintain twenty-percent accuracy with their shooting.

The range logbook sat next to the console, and Matt began to leaf through it. All officers were required to sign in and out of the range whenever they used it. As an incentive to keep his men on mark, they were permitted to bring in a family member. Most officers had multiple guns in the house, and Matt figured one way to prevent accidental shootings was through education.

Automatically, his gaze ran down the list of names, and he wasn't surprised to see Pine was a frequent visitor. Pulling the book closer, he scanned the dates and times. His lieutenant's sign-ins were easily twice Matt's own and most were at early hours before his shift.

Flipping through the pages, he was surprised to see Bryan Haines spent a lot of time on the range, though usually with company. On the majority of his entries was the notation "brother". Seeing that Haines had several brothers, Matt was curious as to which one it was.

On the range, Pine stopped to reload and Matt hit the intercom switch.

"Hey, Eagle-eye, if I come out there do you promise not to shoot me?"

Pine gave him a wide grin and waved him out. Matt walked into the large, cellar-like room. The scent of gunpowder and hot brass was thick.

"What brings you in this early, Chief?" George Pine got to his feet, leaving the gun on the floor.

They shook hands.

"Paperwork. It's never-ending torture."

"Tell me about it. Paperwork is the bane of my career." Pine picked up the gun, careful to keep it pointed down-range. "When I was a kid, all I ever wanted to be was a cop. When we played cops and robbers, I was always the one with the badge. I think it was in my blood even then."

"Mine, too."

"I was due to retire three years ago and I can honestly say I regret climbing the ranks. The moment I left the streets, I ceased to feel like a cop anymore."

"After retirement you're welcome to stay on as a reserve officer."

George laughed. "What? Be unpaid and put up with your shit? Who are you kidding?"

"Yeah, but if you're unpaid you can talk back to me." Matt grinned. "I don't regret moving into administration, but I need to make an effort to be on the streets more just to keep my sanity."

"Yeah." Pine's eyes took on a faraway look. "I hear you."

Matt was surprised the lieutenant had made such a personal statement. Normally, the man kept everyone in the department at arm's length.

"I'd like to talk to you about a case you worked on years ago, Pine," Matt said.

"Sure thing, Chief. Let me take care of my gun, and I'll meet you in your office."

"Works for me. I'll put the coffee on."

"Sounds like a plan."

Matt left the range and headed upstairs. Officers were gathering their gear as they readied themselves for roll call. Sidestepping the mayhem, he headed for his office, pleased when he caught the scent of fresh coffee.

Mary stood by her desk, chatting with one of the evening-shift officers, and her brow arched when she saw him.

"What's the matter, did your coffee maker break?" she called.

"Nope, just couldn't wait another minute to see your smiling face." Matt nodded at the officer.

"About time you started to appreciate me," Mary said.

"I'd appreciate you more if you'd put your considerable talents to work for me. When a case is disposed, at what point does the evidence get purged?"

She shrugged. "We purge twice a year."

"What about film, photos?"

"They're in cabinets in one of the old workrooms

downstairs. After case disposition, the negatives are cataloged and filed. I don't know how many years we have, but there's a lot of them."

"Can you take a look and see if you can locate the negatives from the case we were talking about yesterday?"

"Sure thing, but it's going to cost you. Nobody gets in there anymore since we moved to digital photos. The only living things in that cabinet have at least six legs."

"You can take a gun. Only a small one, though."

"Do I get bullets, too?" She was grinning.

"Hell no, I'm not that crazy."

Mary and the officer started laughing, and Matt headed for the coffee machine. By the time he got two cups of coffee and made it back to his office, Pine had arrived. The other man had changed into his normal work attire, a standard police uniform *sans* gun belt.

"Nectar of the gods." Pine dropped into the chair and reached for the cup.

"I agree." Matt took his seat. "I was thinking of putting coffee pots at all the building entrances, so when the officers are coming and going they would never have to do without."

He chuckled. "You might make officer of the year if you do that."

Matt unlocked a desk drawer and withdrew the Angelov file, careful to remove the accident photographs before putting it on the desk.

"I need some information about this case you worked on twenty years ago." It only took a quick glance to see Pine knew which file Matt had. The lieutenant's gaze was glued to the red sticker on the front. Matt pushed the file toward him. "I have quite a few questions about it."

"That was a long time ago." Pine made no effort to pick it up. "Anymore I'm lucky to remember my middle name."

Matt wasn't fooled; Lieutenant Pine had one of the sharpest minds in the department.

"That's too bad. I was reading what little information this file contained and it seems there were some serious mistakes made."

Pine shrugged. "I don't remember much about that case. I was called in after taking my wife to dinner and I'd had a few glasses of wine. I probably shouldn't have come in at all that night."

"You didn't even look at the file; how do you even know which case it is?" Matt's gaze remained focused on his lieutenant's. He was fascinated by the officer's obvious discomfort.

With reluctance, Pine put down his coffee and reached for the file. Opening it, the man blanched. Matt had deliberately left the portrait of Victoria on top.

"Oh yeah," the other man's voice was faint. "I remember this one now. Hit and run on the hill. Young woman was struck from behind on one of those blind curves up there, killed on impact." He shut the folder and handed it back to Matt. "There wasn't much to it; pretty open and closed case, in my opinion."

"Can you tell me what happened that night?"

He shrugged again. "Not really. Like I said, it was a long time ago. I was called in to act as the forensics officer. We didn't have that kind of staffing back in the Dark Ages. I arrived on the scene around twenty-three hundred hours and the corpse—"

"Ms. Angelov," Matt interjected.

"Uh, Ms. Angelov was lying on the pavement about twenty yards from the bend. We determined the accident happened at the curve. I believe someone found a shawl or something in the area. She was struck from behind and killed instantly, case closed."

Matt wasn't impressed. George Pine was a career officer and even after thirty-three years on the force, he was as sharp as a newbie. This man could recall crime statistics from twenty-five years ago, and there was no way he'd have forgotten facts from this case.

"So she was dead at the scene?"

"I believe so." He shook his head. "She was a mess. One look at her skull, and we knew she was a goner. No one could've survived the impact."

"The car was never found, correct?"

"Correct. There were no witnesses, no leads. I believe a

neighbor called in the accident, but I can't even tell you who it was. There aren't many houses up there and someone might've heard the impact, but I can't really say for sure."

"Can you tell me why Chief McNutt signed off on this as an accident? Under normal circumstances, especially in the case of an accidental death without a suspect, this case should've been left open and labeled as a cold case."

"We didn't have a cold case detective back then." Pine was looking more uncomfortable with each question. "Without any leads, we had nowhere to look, so I guess the chief closed the case as an accident and that was the end of it."

"Did you look into Ms. Angelov's background?"

"Not that I recall."

"It didn't occur to you maybe this could've been an intentional crime?"

"No, why would we think that?" His grip tightened on his coffee cup. "She was walking along the road, a speeding driver didn't see her and took her out."

"So you didn't think to see if she had been dating anyone or had broken up recently?"

"No, sir."

"If there was any kind of unusual upheaval or disturbance surrounding her?"

"No, sir."

"It's my understanding neither Ms. Angelov nor her daughters were particularly popular among the residents of Salem." Matt leaned back in his chair. "Do you know anything about this?"

"Not that I remember." Pine shrugged again. "There was a lot of gossip going around, but I don't pay any attention to gossip. That's women's stuff."

And a good officer's secret weapon.

"So you have no idea what was being said about the victim?"

"I don't rightly recall."

Liar.

"Any idea why the bulk of the file contents are missing?"

149

Pine frowned and leaned forward. "No idea at all."

Matt opened the file. "No coroner's report, no incident paperwork, no photographs other than this one." He pointed to the portrait. "No measurements, sketches, witness statement from the caller or officer notes."

"I really have no idea where the information would be, Whitefeather. I would've assumed it would all be there."

If Matt didn't know any better, he'd say Pine was telling the truth about the file. It was obvious he was as taken aback as Matt had been upon finding the file almost empty.

"I'm reopening this case, Pine."

Their gazes met and the lieutenant's was troubled. Was he concerned because of the obvious misconduct or was there something more sinister going on?

"Sir, if you don't mind me asking, why are you pursuing this?"

"I believe Victoria Angelov was murdered."

"Murdered?" Pine spluttered, shock written on his coarse features.

"In my mind, this is a clear case of murder." Matt withdrew the other photos and tossed them into Pine's lap. "Take a good look at her, George, or what's left of her."

The blood drained from the other man's face, and his mouth opened and closed a few times. When Pine picked up the photos, Matt couldn't help but notice the other man's hands trembled. He said nothing, just stared in horror at the once-beautiful face of Synnamon's mother.

"Do those jog your memory?"

The other man swallowed hard, and for a second Matt thought Pine might throw up. Still silent, he shook his head and laid the photographs down on the desk, slowly, almost reverently.

"Those images tell quite a story, and I believe this case was a murder," Matt said. "It's possible she was struck by a car, and it's probable she was still alive when someone tied her to the back of a vehicle and dragged her along the road. I hope she was spared that much, but I don't know. What I intend to do is find out why this happened to an innocent woman."

"I don't know what to say—"

"What happened to her four daughters, George?"

The man swallowed hard again. "Child services—"

"Children's services weren't called, were they, Lieutenant? Instead the daughters were divvied up and taken away, without the family ever being contacted. Any idea why that would've happened?"

Pine remained silent and simply shook his head.

"There were any number of standard procedures violated in the course of this investigation. Lines of command not called into play, mishandling of paperwork that we, as a department, are legally bound to retain. Someone made the decision to throw the departmental standards in the toilet and flush them down on this one. You were a corporal at the time; you would've been one of the commanding officers on the scene. Who made that decision, you or McNutt?"

That question seemed to shake Pine out of his stupor. "I'm not sure what you're implying, sir." His tone was tense.

"I'm not implying anything. I'm telling you there was serious misconduct on your part and McNutt's. The two of you stood by and directed this investigation to an erroneous conclusion."

Pine's eyes narrowed. "It's because that woman came to town, isn't it?"

"Who are you referring to?"

"The daughter. I'd heard she was back and stirring up trouble about her mama." Pine's gaze turned sharp. "Got to you, didn't she? I guess she thought the easiest way to resurrect the ghosts would be to grab you by the balls and twist. Her mama was like that too, used sex to get whatever she wanted, to cloud the minds of men."

"You're out of line," Matt ground out.

"And you'd better have some concrete proof before you come at me again with any accusation of misdeeds with regards to this or any other case." Pine rose. "I've worked hard for the citizens of Salem, and my record stands for itself." He turned to leave.

"You told me you didn't recall any of the gossip connected

with Ms. Angelov. How do you know she used her sexuality to get her way?"

The other man didn't respond. Instead, he walked out and slammed the door so hard the windows shook.

A rush of adrenaline hit Matt's system. His instincts had been spot-on with this one, and Pine was in up to his eyeballs, as was McNutt. Just how many current and previous department employees were involved?

Matt grabbed his phone and called upstairs to the Dispatch supervisor.

"Dispatch, Crystal Boudreaux," a woman's voice answered.

"It's Matt. I need you to monitor any and all phone calls to and from this department for the next twenty-four hours."

"O-o-okay."

"That includes cell phones."

"Oh my." He heard her scribbling some notes. "Would you like the raw data, or do you want me to compile some kind of report?"

"Raw data on my desk first thing in the morning."

"I can do this if you okay the overtime."

"Consider it done. And Crystal, this needs to be confidential."

"Of course, sir. I'll take care of it personally."

"Thank you."

Matt hung up. It was time to head up the hill and talk with the residents. Most of them had lived there many years, and one of them had called in the accident.

৪০

George's knuckles were white by the time Chester answered the phone.

"We've got trouble," Pine hissed.

"No kidding. What now?" Chester sounded bored.

"Whitefeather has the Angelov file and he's reopening the case."

"What?"

"He called me into his office and started asking me all kinds of questions. He especially wanted to know what compelled us to close the case as an accident."

"Fuck."

"He has some of the photographs."

"Some?"

"The file was almost empty when he found it. Only the most superficial things were still in there. The accident and incident reports had been removed."

"Damn," McNutt hissed.

"He told me he's opening the case. He saw enough to realize this was no accident."

"Did he say anything else?"

"No but he seems to have a superficial understanding of what happened out there. Some pieces are missing, but if anyone, and I mean anyone, talks, those missing pieces will be sorted out pretty quickly."

"We'll just have to make sure that doesn't happen," McNutt growled. "Meeting tonight, eleven p.m. at our usual spot. Be there."

"I will."

Hands trembling, Pine hung up the phone. He hadn't been kidding when he'd told Matt he'd wanted to be a cop since childhood. It was all he'd ever dreamed of, and when he'd been offered the job, it had been the chance of a lifetime. For a while it had been perfect—until October 12th twenty years ago, the night Victoria had been run down like a rabid raccoon.

He should've retired three years ago when he'd had the option. Instead he'd stayed because his marriage was a wreck, his kids hated him and it was easier to bury his head at the office than go home and face the ticking bomb his life had become.

When he'd taken the oath to protect the citizens of Salem, he'd never dreamed thirty-three years later his hands would be covered with the blood of an innocent woman. He'd have to watch every word he spoke. His career might be over, but if he screwed up, The Brotherhood would see to it his life was cut short as well.

Chapter Fifteen

Syn was in the midst of the produce section of the grocery store before she realized people were staring at her. Reaching for a bag of carrots, she looked around, her face partially camouflaged by her baseball cap.

Two women stood by the apples, whispering furiously to one another. Every few moments they'd look at her. One woman appeared fascinated, while the other was furious. Two others stood by a display of cranberries, and they too were whispering back and forth while another woman stood with a cucumber in her hand, openly gawking.

Thank you for tuning in to the Salem freak show, everyone. I'll be back tomorrow, same bat time, same bat channel.

She tossed the carrots into her cart and headed for the apples just to see how fast the two women would move. They scrambled to the side, as if by being near her they might catch something.

Humming under her breath, she picked through the apples. The two women had moved only a foot away and they were still whispering back and forth. Syn was struck by the desire to drop her pants and flash them. That would give the bitches something to talk about.

"I'm thinking of making a pie. My mother just adored apple pie." She spoke to no one in particular, and the two women hushed. "There's something about cold weather and the smell of pie in the oven. It brings back such happy childhood memories."

"You should be ashamed of yourself," the older woman hissed.

"Why would I be ashamed?" Syn gave her a wide, welcoming smile. "I'm not the one wearing white pants after Labor Day."

The cucumber woman let out a bark of laughter, then tried to stifle her mirth by covering her mouth. Her shaking shoulders gave her away.

"Listen here, you little slut, your kind isn't welcome here," the woman snarled.

"My kind? You mean human? Black-haired? Tall?"

"A witch," she crowed.

"Edina." The younger blonde began tugging on the older woman's arm. "You're causing a scene."

"Like I care—"

"Edina? Edina Haines?" Syn's gaze traveled over the woman, and she had to admit, Edina looked pretty good for her age. "Imagine meeting you here. I would've thought you'd be dead by now."

"If you know what's good for you, you'll shut up." The older woman bristled. "It's about time someone in this town dealt with those damned Angelovs once and for all."

Their gazes met and Syn was taken aback by the level of malevolence there.

"Your mama was the town whore, we all knew it," she taunted. "None of the good families here would have anything to do with your kind. The best thing your mama ever did was to get run over like the dog she was."

By now Edina was screaming. Anyone within earshot had given up the pretense of shopping and now gathered close so they wouldn't miss anything good.

"Mama was a good woman who sought to raise her daughters and live on her own land, but y'all couldn't let her be, could you?" Syn spat. "I remember how the so-called good families would shun us when we came into town. They'd cross the street just to avoid us. I can't help but wonder how many children of those families are now closet alcoholics or caught a disease in the backseat of the quarterback's car—"

"Your damn mama had her legs so far apart every man in town fell between them—"

"Your husband included?"

Edina looked as if she'd been struck.

"Oh, I see how it works." Syn dropped the apple and approached the woman slowly. "Your husband told you he had an affair with Mama because he wanted to put you in your place, didn't he? What, you got a little too uppity with your white bread, tight-assed ways, did you?"

"You bitch—"

The woman's face was so red, she looked as if she were about to have a heart attack. Syn wasn't sure if it was the accusation or being called a tight-ass in public that Edina found more distressing.

"I remember you, Edina Mayhew Haines. Your husband worked at the elementary school—" Syn began.

"He did. He's retired now," the younger woman hissed.

"Shut up, Jessica," Edina snapped.

"It must've been mighty embarrassing for you when your husband was caught playing hide-and-go-seek with Ms. Sargeant, the kindergarten teacher. I never did understand how he thought hiding his head under her dress would work." Syn tapped her finger against her chin as if she were contemplating it further. "Nope, just not very smart. Anybody coulda seen his big ass stickin' out from under there—"

"You diseased, murdering whore!"

Like a bull, Edina lowered her head and charged. Syn was caught off guard and the woman plowed into her. Syn's breath left in a rush and together they fell backward into the cardboard apple bin and it broke beneath the combined weight of their bodies. Fruit flew every which way and Edina landed on top of Syn. Even though the other woman was a good deal older, she was also thirty pounds heavier. Edina grabbed Syn by the collar and began slamming her head against the floor.

"Why can't you stay dead, bitch? You ruined everything, everything!"

Syn was so shocked by what the woman was screaming, it didn't occur to her to fight back. She was dimly aware of other customers calling for help and Jessica was trying to pull the enraged Edina off, to no avail.

157

Beneath her head, the apples were getting smashed, and her only thought was she was going to die in a puddle of apple juice with no one to mourn her.

Two stock boys came out of nowhere and forcibly pulled Edina away. She fought, kicking and screaming, and they had to drag her across the floor. Slowly, Syn sat up. Her head ached and shock had made her body go numb.

The store manager came running, and for a second Syn thought he might actually help her up. Instead, he ran to Edina, who was sobbing wildly on Jessica's shoulder. He patted her arm, then turned on Syn. "What the hell did you do to her, girl?"

"Oh, for crying out loud." Syn rose, aware her clothing was covered with smashed apples. "Any one of these people can tell you she attacked me, not the other way around."

"Is that the way of it?" The manager spoke in a loud voice. "Did anyone see what happened here? Was Ms. Edina provoked in any way?"

Syn rolled her eyes and people looked away from her. Those on the edges of the crowd began slinking back into the aisles.

Cowards, all of them.

"Looks like they don't see it your way." The manager's smile was unpleasant. "Josh, call the police."

"You do that, as I need to file an assault report," Syn snapped. "I was attacked in your crappy store, and if there was any resident of Salem who didn't have their head shoved so far up their ass they could barely breathe, they'd tell you that."

A few people gasped and others turned away.

"The nerve—"

"Who does she think she is?"

"Look at her, coming in here—"

"Spitting image of her trashy mama—"

The manager got closer to Syn. "Now you listen to me, girl—"

"Oh shut up, Tate." The cucumber woman walked toward them. "Edina done lost her mind years ago, but none of her friends could be counted on to rein the poor woman in. They just let her go spouting craziness around town and now she's attacking people. It ain't right."

"M-m-ms. Summers, I didn't see you there."

"Yeah, I'll bet." She gave Syn a kind smile. "Come on child, let's get you cleaned up."

"I can take care of myself, thank you."

"Ohh, prickly like your mama. You have to be her eldest, Synnamon. Am I right?"

Startled, Syn nodded. "Did you know—"

"Course I did." She took Syn's arm and helped her out of the mashed apples. "Everyone in this town knew your mama, they just won't admit it. Come with me and we'll get you cleaned up right quick."

The woman kept hold of her arm and Syn allowed her to take charge. When they started for the door, the manager spoke up.

"Hey now, you can't just leave. The police are coming, and who's going to pay for this mess?" he bellowed.

"Call Edina's husband, Tate. The man's as rich as Moses," the woman called over her shoulder.

"What about the police? She needs to talk to them. I'm pressing charges—"

"You haven't pressed anything in years other than your toupee. The officers know where my shop is, and that's where we're headed. If you send them over, tell them to run past the diner. I'm hungry."

By the time they left the store, Syn was laughing, feeling welcome in Salem for the first time ever.

∽

"Your mama and I were really good friends at one time."

Carolyn Summers sat across the table from Syn. The woman had given her a pair of sweat pants and a sweater to wear, as her apple-juice-soaked clothing was in a plastic bag in the back of her car.

"I'm sorry, I don't remember you—"

"You wouldn't, hon. It was many years ago, and I was such a fool back then. Newly married, just had my first child, and I was terrified anyone would find out about our friendship." She chuckled and the hint of bitterness was unmistakable. "We would talk on the phone for hours late at night, get together when we could, but it wasn't very often. Last time your mama and I spent any time together was shortly after the twins were born."

"What happened between you? Why didn't you see her again?"

Carolyn's expression grew weary. "It's all water under the bridge now, and I regret my foolishness with all of my heart. I wasn't there when Vic needed me the most, and I live with that knowledge every day." A soft smile lightened her features. "She was a wonderful woman and I loved her so."

"She was." Syn smiled. "I miss her every day of my life."

"I'll bet you do, child." Carolyn's hand covered hers. "Sometimes, when I'm about to fall asleep, I think I hear her laugh. I'll go out shopping and sometimes I swear I see her out of the corner of my eye."

"The wall between this world and the next is very thin." Syn gave her hand a squeeze. "Sometimes those who have passed will come back for a visit."

Carolyn's smile was wry. "Samhain?"

"According to pagans, the line between the worlds is thinnest on that day."

"I believe it." Carolyn leaned back in her chair. "I opened this store two years ago and I think your mama's spirit was pushing me into it." She laughed, her eyes shiny with tears. "Imagine, opening a pagan store in the midst of Salem. People were shocked, and my kids wouldn't talk to me for weeks."

"I don't know. Salem should have witches, don't you think?" Syn took a drink of the hot, spicy tea. The shop was cozy and warm, and Maddie lay at her feet, snoozing in utter doggie bliss.

"Thanks to the college this town is filled with quite a few wannabes. Some of them are serious, lifelong pagans and others are curious about the craft." Her gaze sharpened. "But your family, the Angelovs, they're the real deal, aren't they?"

160

"Yes."

"And Vic passed it on to you girls?"

Syn nodded.

Carolyn smiled. "It's good you received the gift from her. Authentic power is so rare anymore."

Uncomfortable, Syn stirred her tea. She did not like speaking of the craft to anyone outside her family. "People keep saying Mama was a whore, Carolyn. I don't remember her being around any men at all."

"Darling, your mama wasn't a whore, so don't you even waste a moment's thought about that." Her tone was firm. "There was a time when Vic was a little freer than some at that time. Your grandparents had left her the house and moved to Massachusetts, and Bethany finished college, then she took that job in Boston. When she left, your mama was alone. I think she went through a period where she longed for companionship and she looked in all the wrong places. Vic was a very lonely woman at times."

"I..." Syn frowned. "I don't remember her being sad or lonely."

"In the eyes of a child, our parents are just that, our parents, and they're bigger than life. Your mama died when you girls were so young, and none of you got to know her as an adult. She had a good heart but like everyone, there were times her fears overruled her head."

"What was she like, as a friend, as a person?"

"We had such fun together." Carolyn's grin grew wide. "She loved to laugh, dance and play her guitar. Before you were born we'd hang and be girls. We'd go shopping in Montrose and then hit the Russian Tea Room for lunch. Every time we went, she'd order cheesecake for dessert."

"It was her favorite."

"We'd go to the fabric stores and she taught me how to sew. We..." She shrugged. "...had fun. Talked about our dreams, fantasies, what we wanted out of life."

"What did Mama want?"

"Love. Isn't that what we all look for?" Carolyn reached for her tea. "I met and married my love, and your mama...Well, I

161

don't think she ever found hers, or if she did, she never told me. One thing I know for sure, she loved her girls more than anything else in the world."

"She told us everyday how much she loved us." Tears stung Syn's eyes. It felt alien to be talking to a stranger about her mother.

"I'll never forget when she told me she was pregnant with you, Syn. I never saw a woman so happy in my life."

"Did she ever tell you who my Daddy was?"

Carolyn's eyes shifted. "No baby, she never would talk about that."

℃℃

Carolyn had lied to her.

The other woman knew her biological father's identity, and Syn had seen the unease in her eyes. Why would she lie about it?

Darkness had fallen by the time Syn turned onto Winding Oak. The wind had picked up and a sleet-and-rain mix began to fall. The thought of returning to a cold, empty house was daunting. Now more than ever, she was acutely aware how far removed she was from her family.

Was this what her mother had gone through?

Matt's handsome face came to mind and she couldn't help but smile. The poor man had spent the night in his truck, and she couldn't deny she'd slept better knowing he was watching out for her. In the morning she'd awakened to find the driveway empty, the only evidence of his presence the tire tracks in the snow-dusted grass.

Maybe if he showed up tonight she'd invite him in and share what she'd learned today. It would be nice to sit in front of the fireplace, sipping chocolate, sharing a conversation and maybe, just maybe, a kiss—

Without warning, a car came flying down the road well over both the speed limit and center line. Caught by surprise, Syn wrenched the wheel, and her tires caught on the gravel. After a few more heart-stopping twists and turns, the Jeep came to a stop on the shoulder.

"Holy shit!"

Maddie started barking.

The black car was yards away, sitting diagonally across the road. Her windshield was beginning to freeze and all Syn could make out was a shadowed figure behind the wheel.

"There are some really stupid people in this county," she muttered.

Releasing the brake, she maneuvered her car around the reckless driver. Maddie whined deep in her throat.

"Its okay, baby, we'll be home in a few minutes."

Shooting a glare in the direction of the driver, she concentrated on making her way around the car. She released a deep breath when her front wheels reached the safety of the asphalt, so the sound of a powerful engine revving startled her. Maddie began barking madly, and the car plowed into the side of her Jeep. Tires squealed and her car was pushed sideways until the passenger-side wheels were shoved off the shoulder.

"Oh my Goddess." Syn grabbed her barking dog and hugged her close. "Fleet of feet and light as air, give us wings and—"

With a final push from the other car, the Jeep tipped over the edge. Syn, still clinging to Maddie, began to scream.

ॐ

Matt drove along Winding Oak slowly. The sleet was playing hell with the road conditions, and even in good weather, this was a treacherous drive.

He'd just finished speaking to Walter Reed, the man who'd called in Victoria's accident. Unfortunately he'd had nothing to add to help Matt. He'd heard the crash, a woman's screams, and then he'd called in the accident. No one from the police department had approached him about making a statement.

Matt was not surprised.

He'd read articles about corruption within various departments and almost every case was triggered by money. So far he hadn't come up with any possible motive for the crime. The burning question in his mind was, how many of his officers were involved?

McNutt and Pine were a given, but it would've taken more than them to literally erase the case from existence. Then there was the case file. No matter how much he chewed on the issue, he couldn't shake the feeling that whoever had messed with the file had wanted it to be noticed.

It had to have been someone within the department.

Deep in thought, Matt was shocked by the sudden appearance of a woman standing in the middle of the road. Her dress was blue, and her long black hair and beautiful face were as familiar as his own.

Victoria Angelov.

Their gazes met and ice water trickled down his spine. Matt wrenched the wheel, sending the SUV into a skid on the icy road. The gravel shoulder slowed the spin and the rear tire struck something hard, bringing him to an abrupt stop.

Without hesitation, he hit the switch to turn on the beacons. The red-and-blue strobes would warn drivers to slow down and hopefully not hit him.

Jumping out of the car, he looked around for the woman. Sleet was still falling and the dark hampered his search, but try as he might, he couldn't find any sign of her. Walking back to his car, he realized this was the same curve where Syn's mother had been killed.

Standing in the freezing cold with every sense on alert, he wondered if he'd really seen Victoria in the middle of the road.

"That's just crazy, Whitefeather," he muttered.

In the distance he heard a dog barking. This wasn't the bark of a dog frolicking in its yard; it was the strident, repetitive bark of an animal in distress. As if his feet had taken control of his body, Matt jogged toward the opposite side of the road. Fresh skid marks caught his attention, as did the marks where the gravel had been scraped to the dirt beneath it.

Something big had gone over the side.

Running back to his car, he grabbed a flashlight then hotfooted it back. Shining the light into the ravine, he was shocked when he saw Syn's Jeep about thirty feet down. Some trees had prevented the car from falling into the river, but the Jeep didn't look too stable to him. Maddie was half out of the car, baying for all she was worth, and there was no sign of Syn.

Grabbing his mike, he keyed it.

"Four-ten."

"Four-ten," dispatch responded.

"I have a ten-five-A out on Winding Oak. I need every available officer, medic, engine, heavy rescue and a battalion chief out here, now."

"Copy that."

"Tell them to run hot, but be careful. The roads are crap."

Matt ran for his SUV, aware of the chatter on the radio as officers and fire department personnel scrambled to respond. Opening the back, he grabbed a handful of flares. After lighting them, he dropped them in a line across the road.

A raincoat was superfluous at this point, as he was wearing a leather jacket and his head was already soaked. Going back to the car, he grabbed a length of rope, heavy gloves and a rappel harness. Hauling his gear to the side of the road, he made quick work of donning the harness and securing his rope to a railing support.

Matt attached the rope to his harness, then tossed the rest of the rope over the edge. Checking his gear one more time, he stepped over the edge and dropped into the ravine.

The grass and brush was half-frozen, and his feet slid no matter how hard he tried to remain upright. Matt grit his teeth and his mind went blank as he worked his way down. Emotions would only get in the way right now. All he could concentrate on was putting one foot behind the other and working his way down to the car.

Maddie saw him, and her barking turned to excited whimpers.

In the distance the wail of sirens sounded. Several times, his feet slid, causing him to slam into the hillside. By the time he reached the Jeep, Matt was bruised, soaked and more concerned about Syn than he'd have ever thought possible.

Maddie went wild and leapt at him, forcing him to stop and give her a quick rub before he could do anything else. Pulling out the flashlight, he noticed the old tree supporting the weight of the car looked even worse up close. If the tree shifted even an inch, the Jeep and Syn would fall another twenty feet or so into the river below.

Climbing onto the side of the Jeep, he flashed his light into the interior. Thanks to her seat belt, Syn was still in the driver's seat, though she was leaning far to the right, away from him. He wrenched open the door.

Reaching in, he took her arm and felt for a pulse. It was there. She was still with him. The only injuries he could detect visually were an egg-sized knot on her forehead and a small amount of blood at the corner of her mouth. Her breathing was even, though her color wasn't too good.

Beneath his feet, the car shifted, and the harness was the only thing that kept him from falling. Time was running out; he had to get her out of the Jeep now. Overhead, the shouts of men signaled the arrival of his backup.

He grabbed his radio.

"Four-ten to anyone on Winding Oak."

"Three ninety-seven to four-ten, I'm here."

"We're on the south side of the road about thirty feet into the ravine. Driver is unconscious and the car is going to go any minute."

"Copy that. Fire is gearing up and the basket is almost ready. I have on my harness and I'm on the way down."

"Copy that."

Energized by the knowledge that help was on its way, Matt cut Syn's seatbelt, trying to ignore the pelting sleet and shifting car. Gently, he managed to extricate her from the car, though now they both sat on the side of the car. Maddie was practically in his lap, making whining noises in her throat.

A small shower of rocks and debris signaled Bryan's arrival.

"What do you need, Chief?" He was panting.

"Get the dog down, she's in the way."

Bryan grabbed Maddie and maneuvered her to a safe spot near another tree. The dog was none too happy about being separated from her mistress.

166

"Brace yourself on the edge there and take her arms. We can maneuver away from the car easier this way."

"Gotcha."

Like a monkey, the officer climbed onto the side of the Jeep by Matt. Bryan took Syn's shoulders, and together they maneuvered her limp body off the car. Hampered by their ropes and the icy rain, it took a few minutes before they were all huddled next to a tree waiting for help to arrive.

The ground was at an uncomfortable angle and Matt braced his foot against the tree, Syn in his arms. He buried his nose in her hair and inhaled her soft, fragrant scent. She was alive; that was all that mattered. Bryan sat near him with a very nervous Maddie in his lap.

"Battalion Chief Rose to four-ten."

Matt keyed his mike. "Four-ten."

"Do you need the litter down there?"

"Litter, paramedic, and cervical spine gear. I had to move her out of immediate danger, but she has a knot on her forehead."

"Copy that; they're coming down."

Matt closed his eyes and let his forehead come to a rest against her hair. There was no doubt in his mind that Victoria had caused him to stop. If she hadn't, Syn might not have been found for another day or so. By then, it would've been too late.

Chapter Sixteen

"What do you mean, I have to stay here?"

Syn sat cross-legged in the narrow bed, glaring at the emergency room doctor. She'd been here for hours, and she was about to come out of her skin. Staying in the hospital overnight simply wasn't an option.

It was when she'd entered prison she'd realized she had serious issues with being confined. Just knowing she wasn't able to come and go as she pleased was enough to bring on a panic attack, something she struggled to avoid. She didn't want anyone to see her in such a vulnerable state, especially not in Salem. The less these people knew about her, the better.

"You suffered a minor concussion and lost consciousness for approximately forty-five minutes. We'd like to keep you here overnight to ensure you don't have any serious damage."

"I would know if I was hurt—"

"So you can tell if you have an internal bleed in your brain? Fascinating." The sarcasm wasn't lost on Syn.

"Look, I need to get home. I have a dog to worry about, and I need to find out how much damage was done to my car—"

"And these things are worth more than your life? Well, I can't keep you here against your will, so go ahead and leave. Take your chances with a bleed or any number of other possible complications," the doctor said. "Your dog will be the one to find your body should you hemorrhage in your sleep."

Syn opened her mouth to object and never got the chance to do so.

"You don't have to worry about her, Doc. She's got a head

like granite and nothing short of dynamite can penetrate it."

Matt walked into the small trauma room, bringing with him a breath of cold air. He looked big and sturdy and when he smiled, the edge of her panic receded. Taking a deep breath, she willed the shakiness to subside.

"That may be true, but she really needs to stay here under observation for the rest of the night," the doctor said. "In good conscience, I can't release her with no one to look after her."

"I don't need anyone to look after me." She sounded like a spoiled child, but Syn didn't care. She needed to be free of this place.

"Honey," Matt chuckled. "You need a platoon of special forces to keep an eye on you." He leaned over and kissed her gently on the forehead. "You're being foolish."

"I don't care."

"Doc, what if she has someone to keep an eye on her?" Matt sat on the edge of the bed and took her hand. If he noticed it was sweaty and trembling, he gave no sign.

"Her caregiver would need to wake her up every hour, hour-and-a-half to ensure she hasn't lost consciousness."

"For how long?"

"Roughly twelve hours. She was unconscious, and bleeding in the brain is a serious concern. We did an MRI, and it came back fine, but just in case, someone needs to keep an eye on her."

"Will you consider releasing her into my care? I could take her back to my place and keep an eye on her for the night."

"I'm not sleeping with you."

The words were out of her mouth before she could stop them. Both men turned toward her. The doctor appeared shocked, while Matt was amused. Her cheeks burned.

"Darling, it's a little late to protest your innocence, don't you think?"

Matt's intimate tone and teasing look were enough to glue her tongue to the roof of her mouth.

"Especially after last night."

He looked away and it was all Syn could do to keep from launching herself at him. What the hell did he mean by that

169

little remark? She snatched her hand away from his as her gaze darted from Matt to the doctor then back again. He wanted the doctor to think they were...were...having sex?

"...if you'll come out to the desk, I'll sign the discharge papers and give you some instructions on helping your patient through the night." The doctor was speaking. "I'll meet you out there."

The doctor left, and Syn turned on Matt.

"I'm not going home with you," she spluttered. "How dare you presume I'd—"

"Suck it up, kid. I just got you sprung." Matt rose. "Get dressed so we can get out of here."

Syn glared at his back as he walked out of the room. How dare he just come in here and take over her life. It was her choice—

Matt's handsome face reappeared in the doorway, and with an impish smile, he said, "You're welcome."

With that, she was goaded into action. Rising, she had to hold onto the bed when the room swam around her. Closing her eyes, she remained still until the swirling feeling dissipated. Moving slowly, she opened her eyes and managed to retrieve the bag with her clothing. She groaned when she saw they'd cut her sweater and bra. Luckily she'd been wearing sweatpants and someone had taken mercy on her, as those were undamaged.

Thankful for small things, she pulled on the pants and tucked in her hospital gown to serve as a shirt. In-style she wasn't, but it would do for now. It took a while to get her shoes on because bending over triggered pains in her head. By the time she was ready, Syn felt as if she'd run a marathon. Already she was utterly exhausted and would've given her left arm to be at home and in bed.

A nurse came into the room and Syn signed the form the other woman handed to her. As she left, Matt strode into the room with a handful of papers and his sharp gaze fell on Syn.

"How are you feeling?"

"Okay, I guess."

"Liar." He stuffed the paperwork in the hospital's version of a suitcase, a white plastic bag with PATIENT NAME emblazoned on the side.

"Pig."

"Your jacket's a mess." Matt held the battered garment in one hand. "It's soaked all the way through. I guess you'll have to wear mine instead."

"What about you?" she protested. "It's cold out there."

"I'm a man, and we men don't need coats. We're tough."

Syn rolled her eyes. He was such a guy.

"Are you ready, miss?" An orderly pushing a wheelchair stopped at the door.

"I have to go downstairs in that?"

"Yes, miss, hospital orders." He gave her a wide, cheerful smile. "Don't worry, my name is James and I make a great chauffer. We can even take the scenic route, if you feel up to it."

Syn had to smile. Matt took her arm, then assisted her into the chair. Once she was settled, he removed his leather jacket and wrapped it around her shoulders. Immediately heat, accompanied by the scent of leather and Matthew Whitefeather, enveloped her. Already she was feeling better.

"I'm going to run out and start the car." Matt spoke to the orderly.

"Fine, sir. We'll see you in a few minutes."

Matt left with Syn's bag, and the orderly wheeled her out into the hall.

"I heard you were in a car accident, miss," James said. "Was it very bad?"

"Bad enough," Syn said. "I suspect my car was totaled."

"But you're okay, that's what counts." His voice was soothing. "Do you remember what happened?"

"Not really."

The police had quizzed her, and she hadn't been able to recall anything useful. She remembered making the turn onto Winding Oak and that was it. She couldn't remember anything else until she woke up in the emergency room.

"That's probably a good thing, miss."

When they approached the entrance to the waiting room, the mechanical doors opened.

"Maybe they could've caught the person who caused the

accident."

Who said someone else was involved?

"Yeah," she said.

No doubt about it, she was becoming paranoid. Not everyone in the town knew who she was and what she was doing here.

The walk down the hall was silent, and with each passing minute Syn felt more uneasy. Why, she couldn't say for sure but she felt as if darkness was slowly enveloping her. Automatically she invoked the protection spell.

White light, seal and protect me against darkness.

By the time she'd said it the third time, the dark edginess had eased and she was feeling centered. What had triggered the darkness to surround her like that? Was it James?

Pulling inside of herself, she gathered her flagging energy and gave him what could only be described as a poke. It was the way witches felt each other out, sort of a magical shoving match to see who was the strongest.

The orderly had no outward reaction, and she wasn't surprised when she received a stronger poke back.

He was one of them.

An image of Mama's face appeared, and her lips were moving.

Stay away from them, girls, they're bad people.

Who were they, and why were they bad?

Syn breathed a sigh of relief when they rounded a corner and were headed toward the exit. Beyond the glass doors Matt's SUV was idling. Never had she been so happy to hitch a ride in a police car.

"Here we are, miss."

Matt exited the car, and Syn literally leapt out of the wheelchair. He opened the passenger door for her and she was about to get in when James spoke again.

"You be careful, miss. There are many dangerous people in this town, and it's pretty easy to rub them the wrong way. You wouldn't want to have another wreck, now would you? Next time you might not be so lucky."

Syn's gaze met James' and the threat was unmistakable. Always one to have the last word, she sent him a blast of energy that literally rocked him on his feet. If he hadn't been holding onto the wheelchair, he'd have ended up on his butt. The man's eyes widened, and the threat was replaced with an emotion she knew all too well.

Fear.

ဢ

Matt couldn't deny he enjoyed the sight of Syn wearing his jacket. Granted, it was an official Salem Police garment, which made it illegal for her to wear, but he couldn't help but think she looked sexy as hell.

"Are we really going to your house?" Syn's voice was small.

"Yes."

"Where's Maddie?"

"Corporal Jacks is picking her up from the vet and he'll meet us at the house."

"Was she hurt?"

"Not a scratch. According to Doc Lee, she's in excellent health, though she's missing you really bad."

Her smile was weary. "We've rarely ever separated for more than an hour or two."

"Which explains her anxiety." Matt cast a cautious look in her direction. "So what was going on between you and James back there at the hospital?"

"What do you mean?"

"It sounded like he was speaking in code. What did he mean by 'it's easy to rub them the wrong way'?"

"Just a friendly warning, I guess." Clearly uncomfortable, Syn hunched her shoulders and slid down in the seat until only her eyes and the top of her head were visible over the jacket collar.

"I don't believe you, Syn."

"Look." She sat up. "I can't explain it to you; you'd never believe me."

"So you won't even try?" He was disappointed.

"And have you drive me back to the hospital for another MRI? I don't think so."

"I'm not going to drive you back to the hospital for an MRI. I'm surprised your head fit in the machine the first time." Matt chuckled.

"Yeah, look who's talking. They'd have to use a jackhammer to open up your skull," she muttered.

"Nothing that hard. When I was a kid, my twin threw an ashtray at my head and opened up my scalp. My mother heard bloodcurdling screams and came running in. She thought my brains were coming out of my head." He grinned. "I might be hard-headed, but you set a new standard."

"Uh huh."

Syn stared out the window, her arms crossed over her chest in a "don't talk or touch me" position. The mental distance between them was gargantuan.

"My father is career law enforcement, as is my twin, Micah, and siblings. My parents met when Dad was in the academy and Mom was still in high school. We've always said police work was in our blood, and so far it's held true.

"My father is a disciple of truth. He always maintained that hard facts and the evidence tell the story. He tried to instill that concept into all of his kids, and he partially succeeded. Then there was my mother. In some ways she agrees with him, but she also thinks we'd be ignorant to ignore the other, not-so-concrete methods of detective work."

"Like what?"

"Your instincts. A well-trained officer will listen to his gut as much as he does the evidence; both are equally significant."

"Intuition."

"Exactly. Dinners at home can be an interesting show when my mother and father start haggling over the old ways versus scientific methods used in police work. My mother is a true daughter of her people. She follows the old ways, and our grandmother believes she walks the line between the living and dead."

"She's a nightwalker?"

174

"You know the term?" Matt was surprised.

"Yes, my sister Chloe had...has the same talent. She can communicate with the dead."

He shot her a funny look.

"Well, supposedly," she said.

"When relatives passed on, Mom always said they'd come back and give her some kind of a sign. I don't know if she was right or not, but she always knew when something was going on or if we were up to no good. There was no fooling her."

Syn smiled. "Mama was the same way."

"I think there's a switch that gets thrown the moment women get pregnant. They develop eyes in the back of their head and a super-long rubber arm that can spank you from across the room."

She chuckled.

"We grew up treading lightly between both worlds, that of my father and my mother. Over the years I leaned toward physical reality, like my father. Evidence always points to the criminal, and everything in life is black and white. My brother is the opposite. He's very much rooted in his origins and relies on his gut nine times out of ten. His instincts are amazing."

"And it works for him?"

"Like a charm. He's fearless. For years now, he's been telling me to let go and open myself up to the possibility of something else out there."

"And why didn't you?"

"Fear. I can't control what I can't see or understand, so it takes the power out of my hands." He shrugged.

"And you hate that."

"About as much as you do."

"You have an incorrect perception of me." She laughed. "I can embrace reality or retreat into the shadow realm. I live in both places peacefully and I walk between both worlds, Matt."

"But you hate not being in control," he pointed out.

"Don't we all?" She shrugged. "Try opening your brain to this concept. In reality, no matter what plane of existence we're on, we're never in control. There isn't a single minute in any day we're truly in control of our destiny."

"Oh, come on now—"

"I'm serious. You do everything you can to remain in control—you exercise, eat right and do all you can to live a long and healthy life. Then one day you're out jogging, and wham, your life is ended because someone didn't put on the parking brake and their car rolls over you and you're dead. Was that something you could control?"

"No, but—"

"There is no 'but', Matt. There are more things in this world we don't understand than things we do. There are instances that cannot be explained away with logic and evidence. Sometimes things simply are what they are."

"Like seeing your mother standing in the middle of the road tonight." He held his breath for her response.

"What did you say?"

"That's how I found you, Syn. I was driving along Winding Oak, and out of nowhere I saw a woman standing in the middle of the road. I swerved to avoid hitting her and I ended up on the shoulder. "

"And you think it was my mother?" Doubt was thick in her tone.

"It was."

"How do you know this?"

"She led me straight to you, Syn. I never would've found you in the ravine if your mother hadn't caused me to stop. Given the fact we're expecting a sizable snow tonight, you might not have been found until the spring thaw."

"Dead?" Her eyes were wide.

"Dead." He glanced at her. "You look like her, you know."

"Everyone says that."

"The resemblance is uncanny. I'd seen her photo, but seeing her in, uh, person...you could easily pass for her."

"Matt, did someone try to kill me?" Her voice was steady, low.

"It's possible," he said. "The driver's side was crushed in, and about ten yards from where you went over we found pieces of grill from another car. We're still working on the evidence, but it looks as if someone hit you from the side and shoved you over the edge."

Her head tipped forward and she began rubbing her forehead.

"Are you okay?"

"It's a lot to take in," she whispered. "Someone trying to kill me and my mother's ghost saving my life."

"We're almost to the house. Just close your eyes and before you know it we'll have you home and tucked into bed."

To his disappointment, she turned away from him. Pulling up her legs in a near-fetal position, she leaned her head against the back of the seat. The air of loneliness was palpable, and he had no idea how to bridge the gap.

Chapter Seventeen

"It's time to wake up."

Warm in slumber, Syn didn't want to get up. The sun on her face was soothing and the plush summer grass served as the perfect cushion. She couldn't remember ever being more comfortable.

"Princess Synnamon, your subjects await your pleasure."

Opening her eyes, she blinked several times against the brilliant sunlight. Overhead the limbs of her favorite oak shielded her from the worst of the rays. Rolling onto her side, she stretched her body until every little kink was gone. Sitting up, she saw her sisters were near the barn playing a rambunctious game of tag.

Home.

Birds chattered as her gaze drank in every nuance of her childhood home. The house looked marvelous, with a fresh coat of white paint and the windows open to catch the summer breeze. Climbing roses wound their way up the trellis and their scent was intoxicating. Lilacs and honeysuckle dueled for supremacy, while a small crowd of hummingbirds took delicate sips of their nectar.

"Synnamon, are you awake, darlin'?"

Mama stood on the edge of the porch wearing a huge smile and a wide-brimmed hat. She looked so beautiful, Syn simply couldn't respond. Her long black hair hung loose around her shoulders in thick waves. Her pale skin glowed with good health and her violet eyes gleamed with amusement.

"Yes, Mama," Syn whispered.

"Come on now, baby. I don't want you sleeping outside any longer, you'll get a sunburn."

"Yes, Mama."

Syn struggled to her feet, confused by the long gangly legs and scabbed knees. How old was she?

"Baby, can you watch your sisters for a little while?" Mama straightened the low cut bodice of her dress. "Mista and I are going into Montrose to do a little shopping."

Mista?

"Of course, Mama." Syn walked toward her Mama, wanting to touch her, inhale her rose-scented perfume. "What are you going to buy?"

"The twins need some new shoes." She laughed, and it was a merry sound that made Syn feel all the better for just hearing it. "Those girls just grow right through everything. I swear, I need to tie bricks on their heads to keep them small for a while longer."

How many times had Mama made that very joke? She'd threatened to put Syn's feet in wooden boxes to keep them from getting any larger, too.

"I miss you so much, Mama."

Victoria gave her a puzzled look, her head tipped slightly to the side. "Whatever do you mean, Syn?"

"I've missed you."

Her smile returned in full force. "Darling girl, you should know by now, no matter how far apart we are I'll always watch over my girls."

But you don't know what happened—

"Those sisters of yours are playing down by the barn and Chloe is in the cemetery again. I really don't think she needs to spend so much time down there, seems disrespectful somehow."

"I'll get them, Mama."

"You're such a good girl, Synnamon."

Victoria brushed her hand over her daughter's chin, and Syn wanted to cry. She couldn't feel her mother's touch, just a faint caress of air where it should've been.

"You're always the strong one, aren't you?"

"Yes, ma'am."

"I'm depending on you to keep your sisters safe." Mama's expression grew uncharacteristically solemn. "There are many dangers I've sheltered all of you from and there isn't much time. You are my weakness and my strength, my beautiful daughters."

A shout drew Syn's attention to her sisters. Coming from the direction of the cemetery, Chloe jogged toward the house. As usual, her red hair was askew and her knee socks had fallen around her ankles. When the twins saw her, they ran shrieking toward their beloved older sister.

"They'll be fine, Mama, they're very smart girls."

Syn looked over at Victoria, and in the blink of an eye the world wasn't as welcoming as before. The colors had faded to gray, and the wind turned icy cold.

Mama was still on the porch watching her daughters, though now a large figure stood behind her, hidden in the shadow of the door. She couldn't see him well, but somehow she knew it was a man. A very big man.

"Synnamon, make sure you get your book from under the tree. You don't want to forget it. Do you?" Mama asked.

Beneath the oak was the book she'd been reading when she'd fallen asleep. The wind ruffled the pages, flicking through them like an invisible hand.

"No, ma'am, I'll get it."

Syn dashed off to grab it, and when she picked it up, she smiled when she saw the title. It had been her favorite book the summer before Mama died. Holding it securely in her arms, she ran back to the porch.

Victoria stood on the top step leading to the driveway and her expression was distant. A large black car idled in the drive, and a man sat behind the wheel, but Syn couldn't see his face.

"You'll take good care of your sisters, won't you?"

"Yes, Mama. I already said I would."

"Don't let them forget me. Never let them forget me."

"Mama, how could you ever think they'd forget you?" She stared hard at her mother's face, but there was no emotion there. It was like staring at a mask.

"And most of all, don't forget the book."

Their gazes met and the energy that was Victoria Angelov's life-force tore through Syn's body, rocking her on her feet. Her breathing turned ragged, and for the first time ever, she was afraid of her mother.

"I have it right here." Syn looked down, her eyes widening when she realized her favorite book had been replaced with Victoria's grimoire.

"It's all in there, Synnamon. Remember that."

When she looked up, Mama, Mista and the car were gone. Around her, the house sank into disrepair and the paint peeled before her eyes. Her sisters stood together on the path leading to the cemetery. The three of them held hands, and to her horror, their eyes were gone, leaving only black holes where they should've been.

"You didn't take care of us," Chloe called.

Syn's knees gave out and she fell.

"They separated us and we're forever lost." Summer spoke, her high voice heartbreaking to hear.

"I never wanted this," Syn whispered.

"And you forgot the book," Autumn accused. "By forgetting, you've endangered us all."

"But I have the book now!" Looking down, she realized her hands were empty. Crumbling to the porch, she began to cry.

છ

Syn woke with a jerk and a sob lodged in her throat. The unfamiliar room threatened to throw her into a panic, and she kicked her legs in order to free them from the blankets. Too late, she realized Maddie was part of the bulk trapping her legs. The dog groaned and reluctantly climbed off Syn's feet, giving her a dirty look in the process.

Sitting up, Syn was gasping for air and her head throbbed. She'd finally managed to free herself when Matt walked in half-dressed, his hair disheveled.

"What's going on?" he asked.

"I n-n-need to go home."

"Home? It's the middle of the night."

"You don't understand, I need to go now." She scrambled to her feet and began looking for her shoes.

"Synnamon, can you tell me what's wrong?" He stepped closer.

"I had this dream and Mama was there and I was supposed to take care of my sisters. She'd made me promise her again and again I'd look out for them and I forgot the book and that's a big problem." She ran a trembling hand through her hair. "I need that book."

"Baby, hush." He caught her hands. "It's the middle of the night, and you've had a rough day. I don't think it's a good idea to go barreling off in the middle of the night to your place."

"You don't understand, I promised her. I promised her and I fucked up—"

"Syn, you were a child—"

"Doesn't matter. They were depending on me and I blew it."

She leaned forward, her forehead coming to rest on their clasped hands. Her heart was pounding so hard, she was afraid it would burst from her chest.

"Slow down, Syn," Matt was speaking. "You're about to hyperventilate."

She nodded but couldn't speak.

"It's okay, just listen to the sound of my voice." He took her hands and steered her toward the bed. "Can you hear me?"

Nodding, she sat, grateful to be off her wobbly legs.

"Good. Remember when I told you how my heritage and analytical side were constantly warring?" He chuckled. "I don't think it will ever end. I've been in Salem for six years, and I'm plagued with more doubts than ever. I've seen too many things that are out of the ordinary and I can't just kick them to the curb. There has to be something to this occult thing, but I can't quite come to an understanding."

"Why do you think it was here this h-happened to you?" Her voice sounded winded, as if she'd just sprinted a mile.

"Geographical location maybe? Or it could be the pagan shops that have opened in the past few years. They bring in a certain element I find interesting." Matt sat next to her. "One thing I know is, ever since you set foot in my town, all sorts of strange things have been happening."

"I'll bet you say that to all the girls," she whispered.

"Did it work on you?" He chuckled.

"Not yet." Slowly the pain in her head eased, as did her breathing. "So what things have you experienced since I've been here?"

"Ghosts."

"They're not particular to Salem." Syn forced herself to relax her death-grip on his hands.

"Maybe they aren't, but I've never seen them before now."

"Fair enough."

"Around town they say your mother was a witch."

"Yes." Chilled, Syn reached for a blanket. "That's what they say."

"My knee-jerk reaction is, I don't believe in witches and witchcraft."

Her smile was shaky. "You didn't believe in ghosts either, and now look at you."

"True. Do you think your mother was a witch?"

"It doesn't matter what I think. You need to use your experiences and draw your own conclusions. Do you agree there are many things in this world that we don't even begin to understand?"

"Yes."

"Then why would witchcraft be so hard to believe? Wiccans have been around since the beginning of time. Their religion predates Christianity by thousands of years."

"You're talking about the tree-huggers?"

She couldn't help but smile. "If that's what you want to call them."

"They're witches?"

"Well, some Pagans are. My mother believed that true witches are born, not made."

"So one can't call herself a witch and it be true?"

"No, most of the so-called witches are wannabes. I think if you were to ask the college kids, most of them fall into that category. They think wearing gothic clothing and dying their hair black will make them a witch."

"And your mother?"

"Was a wonderful woman and I loved her dearly." Syn smiled. "Just because you don't believe in witchcraft doesn't mean it can't exist."

"What about you, Synnamon Angelov?" Matt took her hand. "Are you a good witch, or a bad witch?"

"You're laughing at me," she said.

"Well you have to admit, this is a lot to tangle with in one night."

"I'd imagine it is." Matt draped an arm around her shoulders and she snuggled into his side, enjoying the warmth and security he provided. "My mother, her family, my sisters and I were raised with witchcraft in our lives."

"So you're a witch."

"As was my mother."

He was silent for a moment.

"So, are we talking about the TV witch who wiggles her nose and things happen, or dancing in the moonlight naked?"

"Yes."

"You're not answering my question," he growled.

"Matt, what do you want? Do you want me to perform for you? I'm not pulling your leg."

"I know, I just—"

Syn heaved a sigh and pushed out of his arms. "Pay attention, King Tut, you're about to get a lesson in witchcraft one-oh-one."

"I'm waiting with bated breath."

Concentrating her strength, she directed it toward the fireplace. She exhaled and simultaneously released the energy. The neatly laid tinder and wood burst into flames in a WOOSH of power.

"How was that?"

Matt seemed both shocked and disturbed at the same time. "Interesting." His tone was faint.

"What an underwhelming statement."

"I'm having a little difficulty in processing this."

"I'd be more concerned if you weren't. Running into a witch isn't something one does everyday. Well, unless you're me."

"And you said your mother also was a witch."

"She was much more powerful than I," Syn said.

"Why is that?"

"My training was never finished. When Mama died, that was the end of it. I didn't receive any more lessons, so my skills are somewhat crude and rudimentary."

"Could you train yourself?"

"I guess so." She shrugged. "With great power comes a certain level of responsibility. I can do what I need to do, and that's fine with me. My sister Chloe, she's the one who's truly gifted. I can only hope she's learned to master her skills. As a child she ran around with her hands over her ears to block out the voices of the dead. It was really hard on her."

"I can imagine." Matt pulled her back into his arms and Syn went willingly. "If your mother was a witch, and people knew about it, do you think it could've been a reason to kill her?"

"Very few people outside the family knew. The townspeople might've suspected, but I seriously doubt any of them had evidence. Now, I think most of them are repeating the stories they've heard all these years. In reality we were very secretive about our powers, and we never spoke of it to anyone outside the family."

"Are there others like you?"

Syn yawned. "Tons."

"Really? Any locals?"

"A few. There was the Mischou family, who lived on the other side of town. The mother was a genuine Transylvanian witch. They're rare, you know."

She yawned again, this one threatening to split her face wide open. She was feeling much calmer and becoming sleepy again. It was amazing what a little conversation could accomplish.

"Was there anyone else?"

"Only a few more locally, but we didn't socialize with them much. There was a man, but I can't remember his name. We called him Mista."

"Mista?"

"I don't know his real name, I barely remember him. He and Mama were friends."

ೞ

Matt couldn't sleep.

After Syn passed out mid-sentence, he'd put her to bed and this time he'd joined her. Even though his body was exhausted, his mind would give him no rest. A myriad of questions were bouncing around his brain and very few answers were forthcoming.

The funny thing was, he couldn't tell if his sleeplessness was due to Syn's tricks or the knowledge that Victoria had a man in her life and her daughter knew about him. Just how did one go about finding a man called Mista?

He rubbed a hand over his face. Everything about this case was convoluted. A flesh and blood woman who was a witch, a real one, found dead on the roadway. Her children deliberately split up and sent to far flung destinations, and it appeared there was a massive cover-up by the officials in charge. If he were a writer, he'd make millions with this story.

Scratch that, no one would believe him.

Victoria Angelov was a witch.

A witch.

What did it mean to be a witch? What kind of powers did a witch possess? Syn claimed she wasn't as powerful as her mother, but could she conjure money out of thin air? Could she cast a spell and force someone to do something out of the ordinary such as rob a bank?

While the idea was leagues away from anything he'd ever dealt with before, it sounded like a plausible motive for murder to him.

Chapter Eighteen

"I want to know which of you tried to kill that Angelov girl last night." Harlan White, little-league coach and the lieutenant mayor of Salem, stood at the podium.

The Brotherhood lodge was only half-full, but they didn't need or want the entire assembly there; only key members were needed to get things back on track.

"Wasn't me, but the little bitch deserves whatever she got," Donnie Haines yelled.

"She might be a pretty piece of ass, but that isn't enough to keep her safe," someone else called from the back.

Most of the men chuckled and Harlan felt his blood pressure rise. With every passing week Donnie was becoming more and more of a threat to The Brotherhood, much more so than any of the Angelov girls. His drinking was out of hand, and when the man got drunk, it was impossible to keep his mouth shut.

Harlan gave John Haines, Donnie's father, a hard look, silently willing the man to take his son in hand. With reluctance, John rose.

"You're out of order, son," he said. "You don't have the floor."

"Shit, Dad." Donnie waved away his father's words.

"Whoever made that boneheaded move last night has endangered all of us." Chester McNutt spoke up. "We do not do anything without consulting the group first."

"But what if she finds the book before we do?" Tate, the grocery store manager, spoke up.

"We've looked for that damned book for twenty years. If we can't find it, how do you think she can in just a few days?" Chester snapped. "Hell, she doesn't even have running water yet."

"She'll find it because she's Victoria's daughter," Donnie said. "Who would know her mother's secrets better than her eldest daughter?"

A few grumbles of agreement rang out.

"She was a child when her mama was killed," Harlan said. "We questioned that girl for several days and got nothing useful out of her."

"Well, there are other methods," Donnie leered and reached for his crotch. "Just make her scream like a cat."

Some of the men started laughing, and for the first time in Harlan's life, he wanted to strike someone down with a thunderbolt.

"You're out of order again, Donnie. One more time and I'll deal with you myself." Harlan let the words sink in, and the room settled. He knew most of the members were afraid of him, and this time it worked in his favor.

"From here on out, no one, and I mean no one"—he nailed Donnie with a hard glance—"touches or approaches that woman, do you understand?"

A few whispered "aye's" were uttered and Donnie glared at him.

"This is a sensitive issue, and one wrong move could leave us vulnerable." Harlan's gaze moved over the twenty or so men in the room. "We've been looking for that grimoire for twenty years, and have seen neither hide nor hair of it yet. The right thing to do just might be letting the girl find it for us." His gaze flicked over the crowd, coming to land on George Pine. "George, I hear Whitefeather is looking into Victoria's accident. Do we have anything to be worried about?"

George stood, and Harlan couldn't help but notice the lieutenant wasn't looking too good this evening.

"We might. Somehow he found the accident file, but there wasn't much there. A few photos and some half-assed notes."

"And who in the hell messed with that damned file?" McNutt spoke up. "Whitefeather has already questioned me about it and he isn't done yet."

"Why didn't you destroy it in the first place?" Pine shot back. "I thought you'd have had enough sense to destroy everything when it was safe."

"Now you just wait one minute—" McNutt rose.

"Gentlemen, this is not helping. Please take your seats." Harlan spoke over their raised voices. "McNutt, you and Pine look into this file business. Question other members who are or were affiliated with the police department and see if they know anything about it."

Both men fell silent, though they continued to shoot evil looks at each other.

"We need to determine what this woman is up to. It is very possible she's returned to her home to live in peace—" Harlan started.

"Maybe she's here to make sure the town pays for the death of her mother," someone called out from the back.

"I'll be happy to get close to her..." Donnie laughed.

"You are not to get within a hundred yards of that woman," Harlan ordered. He took note of the stubborn look on the other man's face.

"She's not going to let anyone in on what she has in mind—" John started.

"Gentlemen, I have just the person in mind." Harlan gave them a reassuring smile. "In just a few short days we'll have a good grasp on what the Angelov girl knows and what she's thinking." He picked up the gavel. "If we have no objections, this meeting is adjourned. We'll be calling another meeting when our President returns, so everyone please make yourselves available."

Harlan rapped the gavel on the podium. The men began to disburse, most of them headed for the pots of coffee and pastry trays set up on one side of the room. He motioned for John to join him.

"John, can I have a word with you, sir?"

"Of course, Harlan." The other man's smile was nervous, though he came willingly enough.

"How is your lovely wife doing, John?"

"Fine, fine, much better actually. Almost like her old self again."

"Good. Is she still under a doctor's care?"

"She is, but she's doing so well the doctor feels Edina is ready to go into maintenance mode now. She's on the correct medications and her moods are excellent."

"That is wonderful news, Haines. I'm glad to hear it." Harlan maneuvered the man over toward a quiet corner. "I heard about her little breakdown at the grocery store the other day—"

"That was an unusual circumstance," John spoke rather quickly. "My daughter-in-law said the Angelov girl provoked my wife into a confrontation—"

"It doesn't matter, John." Harlan placed his hand on John's shoulder, using a tiny amount of power to bring him to heel. "We can't have that kind of behavior, because the moment Whitefeather gets wind of it, he'll start asking questions that are better left unasked."

"Yes, I understand." John's skin was starting to pale.

"And I'm sure you won't be surprised if I tell you it's past time to take your son in hand."

"I know he's been a little rambunctious lately—"

"John." Harlan's grip tightened and the other man's eyes widened. "Your oldest son is a drunk and he can't keep his mouth shut. For the sake of The Brotherhood, you need to bring your family in line." He smiled. "It would be far more kind coming from you, and I'm sure you don't want us to deal with your loved ones, do you?"

"N-n-no."

"I knew you'd understand." Harlan gave his shoulder a final squeeze then released him. "I saw Bryan last night; he was on patrol. Is he enjoying his job?"

"V-v-very much, he enjoys it very much."

"He was directing traffic out on Winding Oak." He shook his head. "Dangerous job, that. Did you know more officers are injured working traffic detail than doing anything else?"

"No, I didn't know that."

"It's true, read it on the Internet. Your boy was out there in the cold and dark directing traffic as the Perkins boys were hauling a car out of the ravine. Hell John, anyone could have come around that corner and hit Bryan." He shook his head. "Damned dangerous job that one has, and we'd all really hate to see that boy get hurt."

Their gazes met, and Harlan saw John had gotten the message.

"Yes, sir, surely would hate to see that boy hurt." Harlan released John and headed for the pastry trays. His job was done.

∾

Synnamon's headache had moved to her shoulders by the time she'd hung up the phone. It was barely noon and she was ready to go back to bed any minute now.

Matt had dropped her off at the house early this morning, just as the sky had begun to cloud over. Now, a few hours later, snow was falling and the temperature was dropping. Living on the east side of the lake guaranteed an abundance of lake-effect snow, and that was fine with her. She could use a day of peace and quiet.

Due to the weather, the workmen were off, but they'd fixed the bathroom yesterday and now she had running water. Not that she had hot water yet, but having running water in the house was a great luxury. Now she wouldn't have to use the old hand pump out back.

Right now her biggest issue was not having a car. She hated being stranded, not that she had anywhere to be. It was just knowing if she wanted to go somewhere, she couldn't. She'd only been here a few hours and she grew more restless with every passing minute.

Outside, a gust of wind wailed past the house, sending the windows dancing in their frames. This was the kind of day she'd love to spend in bed with a good book and some hot chocolate. Thanks to the snow, her mattresses wouldn't be here anytime soon.

"I hate waiting on other people," she muttered.

Climbing over her sleeping dog, Syn picked up a fresh log for the fire. Once the house was in working order, adding central heating was the top item on her to-do list. She didn't remember noticing the cold when she was a kid. They'd always worn layers and run around playing like wild Indians—

Upstairs, something fell over.

Startled, she looked up at the ceiling, and Maddie's head came up from the pallet where she'd been snoozing. Syn held her breath, waiting to see if anything else would happen. The dog growled, and Syn rose from her crouched position.

The growls continued and the hair rose on Maddie's back. A softer thud sounded overhead, then all hell broke loose. Syn jumped and the dog, barking like a crazed beast, took off like a shot for the stairs.

"No, girl, no!"

Syn was hot on Maddie's heels, but the dog was too fast. She was up the steps and out of sight before Syn made it to the first step. Overhead, Maddie's furious barking was interspersed with the thud of her paws on the floor. She dashed up the steps as fast as she could. By the time she reached the attic, her breath was coming in pants and her head hurt enough to blur her vision.

"Maddie-girl!"

The bare room was ice cold, as the French doors stood wide open and snow was blowing in.

"Well, hell, no wonder this house is freezing."

Gritting her teeth against the icy blast, she hustled to the doors and secured them. Was this the cause of the noises, the doors flying open and hitting the wall?

Turning around, Maddie sat in the center of the room with a pleased expression and her stump of a tail wiggling madly.

"Proud of yourself, aren't you?" Syn laughed when the dog made a throaty noise then smashed her muscular body against her mistress' leg. "Yes, you're my good, brave girl. Thank you for saving me from the wind."

It was the first time she'd been up here since returning home. The cleaning crews had been through here to remove the big dirt, as they called it, though the room needed a lot more attention. This had been the girls' bedroom. It was a huge space with quasi-gothic-style columns supporting the ceiling and tons of nooks and crannies to play in. Both the east and west sides featured spacious balconies, perfect for watching the sun rise and set. In the far corner was a ladder leading up to the roof and the widow's walk.

The once-white floors had grayed in the intervening years, as had the walls. Their beds had been dismantled and now leaned against one wall; the mattresses had been thrown out only yesterday.

All of their childhood possessions had been boxed and stacked in a corner, each one neatly labeled. The bookshelves were bare, festooned with cobwebs and the remains of dead bugs. The dressers were also gone.

Overhead, all sorts of creatures hung from the beams. Wooden butterflies, caterpillars, birds, dragons and other mythical beings dangled from the ceiling, which had been painted to resemble a tree.

It had been a magical experience to sleep in the boughs of a tree. At night when the storms came in, the shadows danced over the walls while they slept, safe in their tree. A childhood of memories rushed Syn and she began to walk around the room. They would sit on a hand-woven rug in the middle of the floor, playing marbles and learning how to cast glamour spells, Syn's specialty. Even though she wasn't supposed to teach them those spells, not yet anyway, she had and they'd had great fun with them.

Mama had been appalled when Chloe turned her hair grass-green when a spell turned horribly wrong. In the end she'd decided to make Chloe keep it that way until her daughter finally perfected the spell to turn it back to red.

Autumn and Summer would push their beds together and create a fort for themselves with blankets and rugs. They would sneak away with a favorite book or some other treasure and spend hours in their "hiding" place. Syn had never had the heart to tell them both she and Chloe knew exactly where they were playing.

In each corner of the room was a door, and each led to another room. The two in front led to the turret rooms, while the other two were unused. Well, by the family at least. Itsy's chamber was on the right, and Syn couldn't remember ever seeing the door open, not once.

On leaden feet, she moved toward the closed door. Evidence of the police department's determination to enter the room was still visible. The entire frame around the door had been replaced, though the original door was still intact. There were numerous gouges on the floor, probably from when they had tried to pry open the door. Three locks had been added, one at the top, one at the bottom and one just above the handle.

No one would be getting in here without the key.

Bethany had to have been the one to order the repairs. Did her aunt know what secrets were still locked inside?

Syn pressed her palm against the door, surprised to discover it was warm despite the brisk chill up here. Closing her eyes, she sent out a gentle pulse of energy, only to have it returned within seconds.

Her eyes flew open and she backed away. Even after all these years, Itsy was still in residence.

ೞ

When Matt got close to his office, Mary came out of the copy room to shove an interoffice envelope in his hands.

"This is from Dispatch, and here," she slapped a typed sheet of paper on top, "is the list of officers who were on duty the night of the Angelov accident. Your coffee is on your desk and the lieutenant mayor would like you to return his call as soon as possible."

"Good morning, Mary."

"No, not yet." She hustled off toward the steps.

Walking into his office, he scanned the handwritten list of officers' names. Nine of them had been on the scene that night. Considering the size of the department then, that was roughly one-third of the sworn officers. Sitting at his desk, he grabbed a pen and began checking them off the list as he muttered to himself.

"Pine, Whitney, Sebring and Travis are still working here. McNutt, Wells, Strider and Johnson, retired and still living in Salem. Summers, died in three years ago and that leaves, Doug

Davidson." He dropped the pen. "Now who in the hell is Doug Davidson?"

Reaching for his keyboard, Matt logged into the city database and then into the employment files. It took only seconds to locate Doug Davidson. His gaze scanned the information. Took early retirement eight years ago...highly decorated officer...was a field training officer...his address was just a few miles from Matt's.

Bingo.

Armed with the envelope from Dispatch and the list of officer names, he escaped his office.

"I'm going to be out for the morning, Mary." He headed for the back door.

"Did you call the lieutenant mayor?" she yelled.

"No."

"He's gonna be mad, Matthew."

"He can just get in line with the rest of the town."

Chapter Nineteen

Twenty minutes later, Matt pulled up at the Davidson residence. The falling snow had slowed more than enough for Matt to see the house was in sad shape.

The gray paint was peeling off the siding and more shutters leaned against the garage than were on the house. Weeds and bramble had grown up along the porch, and the yard was strewn with junk such as car parts and a broken refrigerator. It was obvious the place hadn't been cleared up in years. This kind of neglect indicated either a sick mind or a sick body. He hoped for the latter.

Matt exited his SUV, then walked up the creaking porch steps to knock on the door. Hearing no sound, he knocked again and this time a voice shouted through the closed door.

"Go away, don't want any!"

"Mr. Davidson, this is Police Chief Whitefeather, and I'd like to speak to you for a few moments."

There were a few seconds of silence, then cursing. Matt stepped away from the door when it sounded as if something large was being scooted across the floor on the other side. As was his habit, he flicked off the holster release, then his palm came to rest on his gun.

The door opened with a screech of long-unused hinges, reminding him of the B horror movies he and his siblings enjoyed as children. Inside, the house was dark and Matt could barely see the bearded face peering at him through the torn screen door. Judging from the stench wafting out, the man hadn't bathed in weeks.

"Chief Whitefeather?" Despite his frail appearance, the man

had the confident tone of a police officer.

"Yes."

His gaze flicked from the car back to Matt. "I was wondering when you were going to pay me a visit." He unhooked the screen door and held it open, his gaze coming to rest on Matt's hand still on his gun. "Ain't no need for that, Chief. I ain't crazy, I just don't like people much."

"That's funny, me either." Matt removed his hand, then allowed the holster safety to flip back into place.

"Come on in. My house ain't pretty, but it'll do."

Matt followed the man into the house, surprised to see it was very orderly. Worn blankets covered the couch and next to that was a leather armchair with a crater in the center. This was obviously where Doug spent a great deal of his time. Beside the chair was a jug of whiskey.

"Mr. Davidson, why were you expecting me to pay you a visit?" Matt asked.

"Call me Doug, and have a seat." He gestured toward the couch. Despite the scruffy facial hair, his gaze was bright and direct.

"We both know why you're here, Chief. I heard one of the Angelov girls was back in Salem stirring up trouble. I figured you to be a smart man, and if she poked hard enough I knew you'd probably take a look at that case." He picked up a glass of whiskey. "Can I get you one?"

"No, thanks. On duty."

Doug's smile was nostalgic. "Yeah, I remember them days. Wearing the blue. Back then my life was worth something." He looked into his glass. "Damned waste, if you ask me."

"What is a waste?"

"Victoria being murdered like she was." He took a deep drink. "Wasn't a bad woman, just got tangled up with the wrong people, I guess. It sure as hell didn't end well for her, that's for sure."

"You were there that night." Matt sat on the edge of the couch.

"Sure was. I'd been on the force about four years, I guess. Back then the department wasn't like it is now, it was more like a frat house." He stared into the bottom of his glass. "Sexism, racism, officers liberating drugs from the evidence room." He sighed. "There wasn't a damned thing I could do about it; it was the way it was. Back then I was the new kid, and the first time I saw it happen I filed a complaint with the chief and got my ass kicked, hard."

"By Chief McNutt?"

"Old bastard, that's him. Never happened again, though. From then on, I was careful to keep my nose clean and my eyes on my work."

"The night of October 12th, can you tell me what you observed?"

"It wasn't real late, around just after twenty-two hundred hours or so. Call came in that there'd been an accident up on Winding Oak." He shrugged. "Accidents up there are a weekly event. Them blind curves claimed a lot of cars and drivers over the years. Seemed like every other month we were peeling someone off the rocks down in the ravine.

"I got there about three, four minutes after the call came in. Officer Travis was already on scene when I got there. The victim was lying in the road about an eighth of a mile above that first curve."

"Do you believe she was hit on the curve?"

"No, sir. She was hit below that first curve near the entrance to the subdivision. Even at night any fool paying attention woulda seen her. It was a clear night and that section of the road was lit. There wasn't no reason to hit her, unless they were aiming or very drunk."

"What makes you believe she was hit at the bottom of the hill?" Matt pulled out a notepad and pen.

"That's where I found her shawl. It was cool that night and she'd been wearing a wool wrap. It was lying in the road and there was blood splatter on one side."

"Then what happened?"

"She was moaning. I could tell she was in real bad shape. Her head was bleeding, and blood was coming out of her mouth. I asked Travis if he'd called an ambulance already and he said he had.

"The funny thing is, I didn't hear any sirens, but the next

thing I knew, half the department had arrived on scene, including the chief. I think she was losing consciousness. She wasn't trying to move, but I heard her breathing ten, fifteen feet away."

"Did the ambulance ever make it on scene?"

"That bastard Travis never called for one." Doug reached for the bottle. "The moment McNutt hit the scene, I was put on traffic detail and moved about a quarter-mile closer to town to block the road. Hell, there weren't no traffic that night. It was a school night, Tuesday, and most people were already home and in bed."

"So what happened next?"

"I set up barriers at St. Francis, and on the radio I heard Summers was sent up the hill to do the same."

"Could you see the scene from where you were?"

"Barely. I took out the binoculars to see what was going on. Pine arrived on scene and made an attempt at playing Forensics Boy." He snorted. "He was drunk and didn't know one end of a fingerprint brush from the other. Finally McNutt shoved a camera at him and he took photos."

"Did he take a lot of photos?"

"Sure seemed like it. I was far enough away that I couldn't hear anything, but I could watch. Dispatch kept calling out to see if we needed assistance from Montrose and no one answered them for the longest time.

"At one point McNutt and Pine were standing over her, and I coulda sworn they were laughing. McNutt bent down and picked her head up by the hair and just let it hit the road like she was trash." Davidson shook his head. "She was a nice woman, always polite to me. A dog didn't deserve that treatment."

Matt was perturbed. With every word it was becoming harder and harder to imagine men sworn to uphold the law acting this way. It went against everything in him.

"What happened next?"

"Strider brought out the wagon. I figured at that point she must be dead and maybe the coroner couldn't come out to pick her up. Looking back, I realize I was pretty stupid. If the M.E. was delayed, they should've just covered her up and waited for them but they didn't." He took another long drink of the whiskey, this time straight from the bottle.

"Strider got some kind of rope from the van. I couldn't see what happened after that because I got busy. By the time I was free, the officers were getting in their cruisers, and one officer—Sebring, I believe—was collecting evidence from the road.

"The next thing I heard was someone gunning an engine. The van took off and the chief and Pine were right behind it."

"Did you see what they were doing?"

"No. Summers hailed me on the radio and all he said was, 'Are you seeing what I'm seeing?' At the time I didn't know what he was talking about. I found out later they finished off what someone else had started."

"They killed her?"

"Yes, sir."

"What led you to that conclusion?"

"When they left, Corporal Pine got on the radio and ordered Summers and me back to the streets. I never saw anything illegal that night, but I had sense enough to know something wasn't right. The next day I checked the radio log and found Travis hadn't requested an ambulance, as he'd reported her dead on the scene. He waited until McNutt and Pine hit the scene, then they killed her."

"What did you do then?"

"I went to Summers and asked him what he saw that night. He played dumb. Told me I was hearing things and he'd give me no more. I went to Corporal Pine and demanded some answers to my questions. He held a gun to my head and said if I valued my life I'd keep my mouth shut and my head down. If anyone asked, I was never on the scene and I didn't know anything about the case."

"And that's what you've done for the past twenty years, kept your head down and your mouth shut," Matt said.

"Just like a cowardly dog. It makes me sick to think about what I allowed those bastards to do." Doug's voice was haunted. "That poor defenseless woman couldn't help herself. I was her only hope and I blew it. She was in bad shape, but maybe with proper treatment she coulda been saved."

"What is your hunch?" Matt closed the notebook. "Why do you think she was killed, Doug?"

"No idea. She was a lovely, kind woman and I never heard a mean word from her. All she wanted was to raise those girls of hers."

"Did you ever see the car that struck her?"

"No, sir. It wasn't on the scene when I got there. I did see some broken pieces of grill and glass on the road, I assume someone retrieved it as evidence. There was some black and red paint on the railing and I can only assume the driver hit that just before hitting the victim. So the car was either red or black."

"So you have no idea who could've been driving the car?"

"None. I don't remember much about the grill either."

"Would you be willing to testify in court as to what you saw that night?"

He laughed. "Hell, man, if anyone gets wind I've spoken to you, I won't be around long enough to testify. They'll come get me first."

"What do you mean?"

"Them, up on that hill. They're called The Brotherhood, and if you cross them..." He sighed. "Let's just say a few people have ended up dead lately."

"The Brotherhood? Who are they? What do they—"

"I've said enough." Doug rose. "You go talk to John Haines if you want information on The Brotherhood." He headed for the door. "If I'm around and if this case comes to trial, yes I will testify. It's about time I stand up for Victoria. I only wish I'd done it twenty years ago."

Matt rose. "Thank you, Doug."

He shrugged. "You're welcome."

"I might have some more questions later. Can I call you?"

"Nope, don't have no phone. I don't much like the outside world," he said. "That night changed me forever, Chief Whitefeather. I don't trust anyone anymore. The men who should've put their lives on the line for that woman killed her instead. How am I supposed to come to terms with that?"

"You don't. Betrayal is a bitter pill to stomach, especially when it strikes at what you hold dear." Matt left the house and stepped into the storm. "Oh, before I forget, do you have any idea where the investigation file would be? I found the folder and it's been emptied."

Matt watched the other man closely, but if Doug was faking his surprise, he was doing a damned fine job of it.

"No idea. Only saw that file one time and it was on McNutt's desk. Who knows what that slimy bastard did to cover his own ass?" He frowned. "You know, it suddenly occurred to me that you might want to talk to Donnie Haines. That summer he was going around town telling everyone he and Victoria were hot an' heavy. From what I hear she publicly slammed him and he ended up trying to rape her daughter."

Matt froze. "Which one?"

"Synnamon, I believe. She was young, but the girl looked just like her mama. I guess old Donnie figured if he couldn't have Victoria, her daughter was just as good."

"Thanks for telling me this, Doug. I will certainly look into it."

"You met this girl?"

"Yes."

"Is she okay? I mean, right in the head?"

"She seems to be. She's been through a lot in her short life and there's a lot more yet to come."

Doug nodded and looked sad. "If I were you, I'd be keeping a close eye on her. The hatred of her family didn't end with Victoria's death, and I wouldn't be surprised if her daughter was next."

Chapter Twenty

Deeply disturbed, Matt drove toward the diner. Syn had mentioned Donnie messing with her but she'd never hinted it was anything more than a randy teenager trying to get under a pretty girl's skirts. Was this an oversight or had it been deliberate? Ever since he'd left Doug's place he'd tried to call her, but her voice mail had picked up each time.

Enough snow had fallen to slow things down around town. The plows had been out since daybreak and they were keeping up, but just barely. According to the forecast, Salem was in for a rough couple of days and just in time for the weekend, too.

He didn't like the thought of Syn alone on the hill with only a cell phone and her dog. The conversation with Doug had been eye-opening, and after reviewing the events of the past few days, Matt was more convinced than ever she was in danger.

The only question was what to do about it. He couldn't just assign someone to sit on her. Not only would she argue the issue to death, but if the City Council were to get wind of it, his tail would be chewed off.

Pulling into a parking spot, he reached for the radio.

"Four-ten."

"Four-ten." Angie was on duty and her sunny voice made him smile.

"I'll be on a five-seven at the diner."

"Copy that. I hear the chicken and noodles are real good today."

"Thank you for your input, Tech twenty-seven." Matt chuckled. "I'll pass your compliments to the cook."

The dispatchers were well aware anything other than business-related chatter on the radio was a write-up offense. In his view, as long as the work got done and calls were answered efficiently, he didn't care if they threw in a comment here and there. Some days the officers' jobs were so boring, a smile was more than welcome.

Grabbing the envelope from Dispatch, he headed into the diner. The crowd was unusually light for a Friday as the weather prevented some of the regulars from coming in.

Behind the counter was Mamie, a rail-thin woman with the voice of a garbage disposal, serving up her homemade pies in her usual sarcastic style. Sitting in front of her was Cyrus, the man who kept the city buildings in spotless condition.

Matt nodded at people who waved or called out to him, but he didn't stop to chat. Instead he headed for his favorite spot in the corner of the dining room. From this vantage point, he could see the village square and the comings and goings of the diner's patrons.

Opening the envelope, he began sorting through the printouts. Damn, who knew the department made this many phone calls in one day?

"Boy, you're the talk of the town today." Mamie placed a large mug of coffee in front of him.

"Well, I was voted Mr. Congeniality in college," he quipped. "The ladies just love me."

Mamie rolled her eyes. "I'm surprised your eyes aren't brown, boy, you're so full of shit."

He chuckled. "So why am I the topic of conversation?"

"That damned Angelov case. There's a lot of people around here who don't like what you're doing." She pulled out her order pad.

"Well, life isn't a popularity contest, Mamie." He closed the pages so she wouldn't be tempted to take a peek.

"Boy, I ain't trying to tell you your job, but you be careful. That Angelov woman is a sore subject in this town, and some people are getting all stirred up again."

"Now Mamie, why would someone get in a twist over my reopening a twenty-year-old case?"

"Most people 'round here think she got what she deserved."

"You know, for a town with this many churches, that's hardly a godly point of view."

"Shit, Matthew. Half the people in this damned town are God-fearing only one day of the week. The rest of the time they compound their sins just like everyone else, I suspect."

"You've been around here for a long time. Did you know Victoria Angelov?"

Mamie shrugged "A little. Seemed like a nice enough sort. Kids were well-mannered, clean and polite. No matter what the idjits in this town say, the way her children behaved says a great deal more about her than some wagging tongues."

"Then why did this town hate her so much?"

"Hell boy, all you have to do is look at a picture of her. That woman was drop-dead gorgeous." She snorted. "Every man in town, married, single, divorced—it didn't matter, they wanted her. Because she was beautiful every woman hated her."

"So the women felt threatened by her?"

"How could they not be? The funny thing is, I don't ever remember Victoria trying to get the attention of the men. She certainly didn't court it, but she got it anyway."

"Did you ever see her with anyone, say, out to dinner?"

"Only her kids and her sister from time to time. Never saw her out except in the daytime, and one or more of those girls were always with her. Once a week in the summer, she'd bring the girls in and they'd have ice cream sundaes with all the trimmings." Mamie smiled. "That woman just loved to laugh and so did her girls. It always was a pleasure to see them, they were always so happy—"

"Hey, Mamie," Donnie Haines bellowed from the end of the counter. "I need some more coffee."

"Don't you dare yell at me across my own diner," Mamie shot back. "I'll tell your wife you been in here sucking down coffee and pancakes, and she'll kick your ass to next week."

The patrons laughed.

"Chicken and noodles?" she asked.

"That sounds good, Mamie."

"Be right back."

Matt returned his attention to the phone pages, leafing through them until he found Pine's office number. Yesterday morning, within minutes of meeting with Matt, he'd called several phone numbers. One he recognized as Chester McNutt and the other was the lieutenant mayor of Salem.

Interesting.

"Chief Whitefeather, there you are," a loud voice boomed across the diner.

Well, speak of the devil.

Harlan White walked toward him with a determined stride. The usual good-ole-boy smile was firmly in place, but behind the façade was a thread of steely determination.

"Didn't your mama teach you to return calls, boy?" His tone was jovial but Matt wasn't fooled. The man was pissed.

"In case it's escaped your notice, Harlan, it's snowing like the devil out there and I have cars sliding into each other all over town." He reached for his coffee mug. "You'll have to excuse me if returning calls is low on my list of priorities right now."

Harlan's smile slipped, but he recovered quickly enough. "Anyone get hurt?" Without waiting for an invitation, he seated himself on the opposite side of the booth.

"No, just a bunch of fender-benders and a few cars off the road." Scooping up the pages of phone calls, he tucked them back into the folder. "What can I do for you, Harlan?"

"I just wanted to take a few minutes to catch up with you, that's all. As the acting mayor of Salem, I wanted to make sure everything was going well, crime rates are down, you know, the usual."

"Mayor still out of town?"

"Yep. Won't be back until after the new year."

Smiling into his cup, Matt took a healthy drink. Mamie did make some good coffee. He set the cup on the table.

He couldn't ever remember Harlan wanting an update on the status of the city before now. If he had, Matt would've told him to wait for his end of the month report like everyone else on the Council.

"What would you like to know?"

"I hear that Angelov girl was involved in an accident on the hill." He began to unbutton his coat. "Any idea what happened?"

"Someone forced her off the road."

Harlan feigned surprise. "Surely you're mistaken."

"I don't make mistakes, Harlan. I can tell an accident from a murder attempt."

"Murder? Who said anything about murder?" he spluttered.

"Let's cut the shit, shall we?" Matt braced his arms on the table and leaned forward. "You want to know why I'm reopening the Angelov case. That seems to be the gossip around town."

"Well, now you mention it, I have to admit I'm curious as to why you'd reopen that case," Harlan said. "It's ancient, and the woman would be bones by now."

"Is that an adequate reason to allow a woman's murderer to go unpunished?"

"Murder?" Harlan laughed. "What nonsense are you talking about, son? That woman was hit by a car in the dark while walking home. That was no murder, it was an accident, plain and simple."

"You think?" Matt reached for his coffee cup again.

"I do. I lived in this town when the accident occurred. Chief McNutt thoroughly investigated the situation and closed the case as an accident."

"Your statement is partially true. McNutt did close the case as an accident, but he was...mistaken."

"That's a pretty heavy accusation for you to make, Whitefeather." Harlan's brows drew together. "That man put his life on the line for this town day after day for thirty years and I'll not have the likes of you running him down?"

"The likes of me?" Matt's smile was thin. "Do you mean my being an Indian bothers you?"

"Uh, no. Lord, no, boy." He laughed and several heads turned toward them. "That doesn't matter to me, son. The Council hired you, didn't they?"

"Yes." Matt's tone was dry. "But I'm still reopening the Angelov case, because this woman was grievously wronged by my department."

"It's a waste of taxpayer money. You have no evidence, and from what I heard that damned case file is empty."

Bingo.

Matt leaned forward, his gaze direct. "And what would you know about the file, Harlan?"

"Me, uh...nothing, boy." His chuckle was hard. "What would I know about police work? The only thing I understand is that you're reopening a twenty-year-old case and squandering tax dollars—"

"To uphold the law? This is a waste of taxpayer money? Well hell, Harlan, why doesn't the Council dissolve the department and then the town can just run amuck? That would surely save some cash."

"Now, son—"

"Harlan, I'm not your son. My father is the Sheriff in Logan, Ohio, and even he doesn't call me 'son'."

Matt didn't miss the glint of anger in Harlan's eyes. The other man was neck-deep in this mess, and seeing that Harlan wasn't terribly bright, he was the perfect person to unknowingly drop a few hints.

"Matt, I think we've gotten off on the wrong foot here." Harlan held up his hands as if to placate him.

"No, I don't think so. I think we both have our feet firmly beneath us," Matt said.

Harlan looked at him for a few moments, his gaze assessing. "You're a hard man, Matthew Whitefeather."

"For damned good reason."

"Salem is a nice little town, Chief. We, the Council, aim to keep it that way. That Angelov woman was trash of the nastiest sort. She and her daughters brought a lot of heartache to this town—"

"And she deserved to die for this?"

"Now quit interrupting me, damn it. It took several years after Victoria was laid to rest for this town to settle down and return to normal." Harlan looked out the window, his steel-gray gaze moving over the square. "I love Salem, and I won't see it torn apart again because you're reopening that case. McNutt declared her death an unfortunate accident, and I'd like to see it stay that way."

I'll just bet you would.

"But since you're determined to go ahead and reopen that case, you go right ahead and do what you feel is necessary." Their gazes met. "Just keep in mind I'll have to bring it up at the next council meeting. Me and the boys will take a good look into your funding while we're at it. Weren't you thinking of buying some new radios for your officers?"

Matt's jaw clenched, though his gaze didn't waver. "Are you threatening me, Harlan?"

"Not at all. That would be unpleasant, now wouldn't it? You can just consider that a promise from me to you." His smile returned in full force. "I must be going. I promised my wife I'd be home for lunch, and I'm running a little late."

"You do that. Something you should keep in mind is, I'm not a man who takes threats very well."

"Yeah, I suspected as much, but it doesn't worry me." Harlan hauled his big body from the booth, then slapped his hat on his head. "Oh and Chief, you be careful out there in this weather. I hear them cruisers don't handle very well in the ice and snow."

As he turned away, Harlan's public mask was firmly in place. He strolled through the diner, stopping to shake hands here and chat there. He was the consummate politician, as phony as they come.

Donnie Haines was still sitting at the lunch counter, and he was watching Harlan with a queer little smile on his face.

Whether they realized it or not, Matt would tear this town apart if it meant bringing a murderer to justice.

Chapter Twenty-One

Syn stared at the list of missed calls on her cell phone. So much for better living through technology. Then again, it was highly probable the phone had rung and she simply hadn't heard it. This house was far too large for the phone to be heard in every room. Obviously she needed to get a regular telephone line.

"Yeah, right after I get central heat and a Jacuzzi for ten," she muttered.

Checking the time on her phone, she saw Matt's final call had been around nine fifteen, almost two hours ago. Damn, she'd been outside with Maddie for her final potty break before bed. Of course the dog had found a fascinating scent, and the outing had lasted close to a half-hour.

Seeing that it was too late to call him now, she'd have to wait until morning. What with the snow and all, he'd probably had a long, hard day and was fast asleep.

She put down the phone.

"He needs his sleep more than I need to hear his voice."

Picking up the phone again, she ran her finger over the keys.

"Then again, if he is awake, I could just let it ring once and hang up. He could call me back if he wants or ignore me until morning."

She put down the phone.

"I'm being selfish."

Maddie's head came up, cocked to one side, and she gave her mistress a curious look.

"Yeah, you agree with me, don't you Maddie?" Her shoulders slumped. "Being a good girl is highly overrated, especially when I already know the bad girls have all the fun."

And drugs, men that beat you, throwing up your guts in dark alleys and your friend dying in your arms...

"Never mind, strike that," she said. "I have no intentions of ever going down that road again." Shaking her head, she looked down at Maddie. "Do you realize your mama is sitting here talking to herself like a complete fool?"

The large teakettle on the stove began to whistle and Syn left the cell phone on the table.

"Ah, saved from my own inane conversation!"

She'd already set up the bathtub near the hot stove, looking forward to a bath. The tub was filled with several gallons of cool water and there were six large pots of water on the stove. After dumping three of them into the tub, she tested it and decided it was the perfect temperature for a bath.

Stripping off layers of clothing, Syn stepped into the tub with a delighted sigh. She sank into the water to sit in a cramped, cross-legged position. It really was too bad the water only reached a few inches above her waist.

Picking up a washcloth, she couldn't help but wonder if Matt were here, what would she be doing now? She grinned. If she was lucky, probably not washing up alone.

A soft heat awakened in her lower belly at the thought of his big, strong hands on her flesh. Moving over her breasts, her hips and thighs. Syn dragged the soapy cloth over her breasts and her nipples hardened.

She'd never considered herself a sexual person. Men had always told her she was beautiful and they looked at her as a prize to be won. They'd all wanted the same thing from her, a beautiful woman on their arm and free pussy at all times of the day or night. There were only a select few who'd managed to talk their way into her bed, and every one of them took her for all she was worth and left her with a broken heart.

Luckily for her, she'd caught on quickly to their games and learned how to turn the tables on them. With her smart mouth and irreverent ways, men pursued her but she'd made sure to get what she needed before they hurt her.

After leaving prison, she'd yet to meet a man worth shaving her legs for...until Matthew.

A slow smile crept across her face. He was the kind of man she'd always steered clear of. What use would a good man have for a woman like her? He was intelligent, strong, funny, protective, good-looking and moral.

Moral, what a concept.

McNutt had been the chief of police for many years, though she'd never seen anything remotely moral about him. Then there were his officers. In her heart she knew some of them had witnessed or participated in her mother's death. Who was there to trust, when the police took four orphaned children and deliberately lied to them, then shipped them off to different parts of the United States?

Reaching for her shampoo, she poured some into her hand then began lathering her hair.

So far he'd been more than helpful and, if it wasn't too much of a cliché, went above and beyond his duty. Even though he hadn't believed her story about Mama at first, he'd taken a look at the case and changed his mind. The fact that he believed her suspicions was icing on the cake. It was when he took the first step she realized this was a man she could trust.

Trust.

It was a concept she wasn't familiar with. She trusted her family and Ms. Raines, the English teacher at the prison, but that was about it. Trust was hard to come by when it seemed like everyone around you wanted something from you.

The fact that she'd trusted Matt enough to share her talents with him was nothing short of miraculous.

Spectacular.

Life-altering.

Rising, Syn took one of the buckets from the stove and rinsed her hair.

In fact, knowing Matt was out there somewhere with the knowledge she was a witch made her very nervous. Her mind was torn between two scenarios. One was him showing up on the lawn with half the town bearing torches and pitchforks, screaming, "Burn the witch."

The other, far more pleasurable, image was him with a broomstick asking her to sweep him off his feet.

Unable to help herself, Syn began to laugh. It wasn't just an easy chuckle of amusement, this was a bend-double, grab-your-belly laugh that threatened to have her on the floor. She made quick work of rinsing off and was reaching for a robe when she heard the front door fly open with a crash.

Maddie went from sleep to attack in less than a second and she raced for the door, her bark sounding particularly vicious.

"Damn it to hell, woman. Don't you know how to lock a door?" Matt's voice sounded from the hall. The dog stopped barking and began whining in her, "I'm so cute, play with me" voice.

Oh, hell.

On wet feet, Syn grabbed the robe and threw it on over her wet skin. She grimaced when it stuck like glue.

"Where are you, woman?" he called.

Holding the front of the robe together, she scrambled to find the tie that would keep the two halves together. It was nowhere in the kitchen.

"Oh, no!"

"Syn?" Matt called. "Do I need to draw my gun?"

"No, I'm in the kitchen." She clutched at the front of the robe. "I'm bathing."

Maybe her belt was in the front room?

"Do you need your back scrubbed?" He sounded quite pleased with himself.

His boots sounded in the front room and panic took over. With her cheeks burning, she fled through the family room, howling when she stubbed her toe in the dark. Once she made it to the front hall, she dashed to her clothing and began scrabbling through the basket to find something, anything to hold the robe together.

Maddie started barking again and Matt's voice sounded behind her.

"Who are you running from, Syn?"

Her heart beat double time and slowly she turned, still clutching at her robe. Matt stood in the dining room entrance,

214

his gaze focused on her. His cheeks were ruddy from the cold and his dark eyes held a look she recognized well.

Lust.

"M-my belt. I think it left it here."

"Your belt, eh?" He started toward her, each movement slow and deliberate. He pulled off his gloves and carelessly dropped them on the floor. "What do you need a belt for?" He tossed his coat over a sawhorse.

"My robe...I'm wet," she stammered. "I was—" With each step he took, her knees grew weak, and the urge to throw him to the floor and have her way with him increased. "Bathing."

"Bathing is good. I like bathing." He continued advancing, removing his shirt as he came closer. "So you're wet? That sounds...promising."

"I was in the bath." She stepped away, every hair on her body standing at attention. "When you came, bathing." Her voice faded. "I was bathing when you came, uh...arrived. I mean arrived."

"This is a new side of you, Syn." Matt dropped his shirt on the floor. "You're really beautiful with your hair loose and damp. You look scared, but you keep licking your lips and that tells me you're excited."

She wasn't able to respond. Her throat was so thick her breathing was impaired. Syn took another step backward and her buttocks connected with the wall.

"So tell me, Synnamon," Matt removed his bulletproof vest with a few rips of Velcro, and it hit the floor with a solid thud. "Just how wet are you?"

"I, well..." She had nowhere to go, as her back was to the wall, literally. "I told you I was in the bath," she whispered.

"Mmm, I'm really sorry I missed it." He braced his hands on either side of her head. "Really sorry." He leaned forward, his lips only a breath from hers. "If I'd been here, you'd be even wetter than you are now."

With shaky fingers, Syn released her grip on the robe, allowing it to gape ever so slightly. "Somehow, I don't doubt it."

His gaze dropped to her breasts and she made her move. Seizing his neck, she took possession of his mouth. His immediate response was gratifying and within seconds she lost control of the kiss. Their lips became fused and his teeth grazed her tongue. She responded with a gentle suck and Matt moaned deep in this throat.

His big hands landed on her shoulders and he pulled the robe away from her body. She didn't even realize it was happening until the damp cloth landed at her feet. Nude, she leaned into him, the press of his gun belt incredibly erotic against her bare skin. His hands skimmed her sides, coming to rest on her hips. Syn wrapped her arms around his neck and he picked her up.

She twined her legs around his waist. When the contents of his gun belt jabbed her legs, the sensual spell was broken.

She broke the kiss and nipped at his earlobe. "Matt, your belt."

"What?" His voice was muffled against her throat.

"Your belt. Is anything going to blow up or explode if I fuck your brains out with your belt on?"

He chuckled. "Not my belt, just a little lower."

She laughed and unwound her legs to slide down his body. Leaning against the wall, she watched him disrobe through slitted eyes. His mouth was shiny from her kiss and his jaw was hard, tight. The gun belt hit the floor with a heavy thud, taking his pants with them.

"They're attached?" she asked.

"My gun belt is attached to my regular belt. If they weren't, cops all over the world would be losing their drawers."

She giggled, and he stripped down to his long johns only to realize his boots were not going to allow him to get naked.

"Allow me."

Sinking to the floor, Syn ran her one hand down the back of his calf until she came to his boots. Slipping her free hand under the pants, she unlaced the heavy boot and assisted him out of it before moving to the next. His breathing was as heavy as hers by the time she'd removed his other shoe. Syn was dizzy with lust; the smell of his skin, hot male and healthy sweat, made her hungry. With clumsy fingers, she tossed the boot out of the way.

Still on her knees, Syn allowed herself a leisurely look at his long body. Covered in rich, coppery skin, his legs were firmly muscled and almost hairless. His hips were narrow, and his cock...his cock was nothing short of a work of art. Jutting from a thatch of black hair, his cock was long and thick, the head broad, and as she checked him out, a drop of clear liquid appeared at the tiny slit at the end. Without conscious thought she reached for him, her hand clasping his thick rod. Licking her lips, she wanted to taste him—

"Are you done?" His tone was tense.

"Do I look done to—"

He grabbed her under the armpits and she squealed. Matt lifted her off her feet and she twined her legs around his waist and her arms around his shoulders. The sensation of his hot skin against her thighs was enough to make her feel faint.

"My bed is over there," she hissed.

"We won't make it."

Before she could guess what he was going to do, he'd pressed her against the wall, his cock tight against her pussy. Pressing forward, he guided the head to her most sensitive flesh.

"I'm sorry, Syn," he panted. "I can't wait any longer."

He caught her mouth in a scorching kiss just as his hips thrust forward. Her nails dug into his shoulders and she screamed into his mouth. He broke the kiss and with each thrust of his hips, his cock moved deeper inside until she felt full, stretched and completely at this man's mercy.

His grip tightened, bringing her body closer until he surrounded her. His hips began to move and the sensations were so incredible, so mind-altering that it was all she could do to just hang on. Sensations spiraled higher and higher until the only thing that existed was this man inside her. Matt's hips hammered against hers, and she gasped and begged for release.

His hands moved to her hips, holding her in place, and his thrusts became shorter and more contained. Her fingers clawed at his shoulders as she came apart with a sharp cry. Every muscle and tendon in her body went rigid as wave after wave of pleasure swamped her. Greedy for every second of sensation, she rode it out like a horseback rider. Her eyes closed and bright lights and colors swirled against her eyelids.

Matt came hard, his hips nailing hers to the wall. With his head thrown back, he growled like an animal as his cock spasmed in her pussy. With her nerve endings jangling, Syn let her head fall forward onto his shoulder. Their breathing was ragged as they each struggled to regain control.

Without saying a word, Matt pushed away from the wall. Syn was still wrapped around him, his cock still buried inside her, and with each step the rub of his flesh reawakened nerves that had just been expended. He lowered her to the pallet, then covered her. She loved the feeling of his big body covering her, his cock inside her. She squirmed, enjoying the drag of her clit over his hardening flesh.

"Mmm, who said there's never a policeman around when you need one," she whispered.

"Have you tried calling nine-one-one, ma'am?" He started kissing her throat.

"They kept trying to send me an ambulance." She arched her throat to give him better access. "I gave them my symptoms. I was hot."

He bit her neck.

"And shivering."

He suckled her earlobe and her eyes rolled back in her head.

"I have this itch I just can't seem to scratch on my own," she whispered.

"Mmm, sounds serious." He dragged his teeth along her jaw and she shivered. "I think I might need some help, maybe some backup."

"Trust me, Chief Whitefeather." She caught his face and pulled it up to look in his eyes. "I think you're the man for the job."

"That's good." A slow gleam lit his eyes. "I think I feel a second wind coming on."

છ૭

The house was quiet when Bryan entered through the basement door. He knew he was taking a chance, as his father slept with two guns within arm's length. Then again, his father didn't see well without his contact lenses, so maybe Bryan's luck would hold.

The reality was, if John Haines knew what his youngest son was up to, he'd happily shoot him.

He left the door open a crack because he knew it would make more noise to shut it. His mother had been after his father for years to get it fixed, but he never had.

Bryan and his family had spent many happy hours in the basement. When they were kids, his dad had finished it with paneling, carpeting and a bar. In the back was a pool table and two pinball machines.

The front half was a television room decorated in his father's favorite football team's colors. Big-screen TV, comfy leather couches—this was men's territory. Mother always said she'd come down to the basement when someone held a gun to her head. As far as he knew, she'd never made it lower than the top step.

Bryan didn't need any light to find his way around. Walking behind the bar, he headed for the door which led to the storage room. It was a long, narrow space with shelves filling one side. They were crammed with dozens of boxes, each neatly labeled, thanks to his mother. Most of them contained Christmas decorations and childhood memorabilia. On the bottom in the far corner were some boxes of his grandmother's that Father received upon her death.

Boxes he'd never touched.

Pulling his flashlight from his belt, Bryan turned it on and headed for the boxes on the bottom shelves. Dropping to a crouch, there were three large boxes labeled linens. He pulled out the middle one. Reaching behind the box, Bryan withdrew a fat, catalog-sized brown envelope.

Opening it, he pulled out a handful of yellowing pages. There were quite a few photographs, and the one on top was of Chief McNutt laughing as he stood over the mangled corpse of Victoria Angelov.

Shoving the pages back into the envelope, he carefully

replaced the box and headed for the door. To this day he couldn't say what possessed him to steal the bulk of the Angelov file. He'd been seven-years-old when the murder occurred and the only thing he knew for certain was that his parents and older brother were somehow involved. After the murder, it had seemed like everyone was frightened, and he remembered his parents fighting constantly. Donnie had been shipped off to college within weeks and his family had been torn apart.

His oldest brother had never lived in this house again. He'd returned six years later and thirty pounds heavier, with a drinking problem that rivaled their mother's. In spite of his obvious drawbacks, he'd managed to marry his high-school sweetheart, Jessica, and together they'd had three kids.

It didn't take a detective to realize neither of them were happy, and if Bryan's hunch was correct, Victoria played a role in their unhappiness even though she was long dead.

Turning off the flashlight, he tucked it into his belt before unzipping his uniform shirt. Tucking the envelope inside, he zipped it shut.

For as long as he could remember, his parents had slept in separate bedrooms. His mother had gone from a happy, fun-loving woman to unsmiling, stern character with a bottomless drink in her hand. For the past twenty years she'd gone from one psychiatrist to the next to treat her so-called depression.

For many years, his father had walked around with a long face, as if he'd lost his best friend. He'd turned his focus from his family to work and went on to become a big success in the real estate market. Bryan had seen those quiet moments when that lost look came into his eyes again.

He'd read the file over and over again, trying to piece together how deeply his family was involved. It galled him to know his parents and older brother were in it up to their necks.

What was the connection between the Haines and Angelov families?

Bryan slipped out the door, taking care to lock it behind him.

Screw the Angelovs. They might believe Salem had destroyed their family, but Bryan knew damn good and well, those women devastated his.

Chapter Twenty-Two

Matt woke when a warm, wet tongue started licking his cock. A silken female sigh sounded as gentle fingers cupped his balls. Her tongue swirled around the head of his cock to concentrate on the sensitive skin underneath. He moaned, and his hips gave an involuntary thrust when her mouth covered him. The gentle suction, coupled with the twin temptations of her tongue and fingers, was bringing him too close to the edge. He didn't want it to end like this, lightning fast with the finesse of a speeding train. He wanted to be inside her when he came.

When he opened his eyes, he noticed the fire had been replenished and Syn was wearing only his uniform shirt. Her long hair was a glossy tangle on her shoulders, and the firelight gave her bare skin a warm glow.

Syn was any cop's hottest fantasy come to life.

The little throaty noises she made, combined with the noisy sucking, caused his eyes to roll back into his head. Never had he seen a woman put so much gusto into giving head. He tangled his fingers in her hair.

"Baby, stop," he whispered.

"Mmm," she mumbled. "You taste good and I want more."

She took him deep and his grip tightened. Desperate to stop his release, he caught her head and shifted his body so her mouth couldn't reach him.

"You're not going to let me play, are you?" Her pouting lips were slick with moisture and he burned to taste them.

"I'm thinking about arresting you."

Tangling his legs with hers, he rolled her onto her back and disturbed the dog. Maddie gave them a dirty look, then headed for the clothes basket to make a bed.

"Why would you want to arrest me?" Her dark eyes gleamed with amusement.

"You know, it's illegal to impersonate a police officer." He flicked his finger against the badge. "I might have to break out my cuffs."

She laughed and rolled him onto his back again. Rising, she straddled his hips and lowered her body over his. Air hissed through his teeth when her wet flesh scraped along his cock.

"Sounds like fun to me." She dipped her head and licked his nipple, sending a bolt of arousal straight to his groin.

"Are you familiar with Sigmund Freud's theory of child development?" Matt asked through gritted teeth.

She chuckled. "What? I'm about to screw your brains out, and you want to talk about Freud?"

"Freud believed as a child develops he goes through various stages. If something traumatic occurs to stop the progression, the child grows into an adult with a fixation based on that stage."

She propped her arms on his chest, her skin warm and fragrant against his. "I took psychology in college. So tell me, Whitefeather, what is your fixation?"

"Oral."

He caught her by the waist and lifted her up toward his face. She squealed and struggled to find her balance. Her thighs bracketed his head when he slid between her thighs and claim her flesh.

"Oh!"

His tongue moved along her damp, salty-sweet flesh. Her hips began to move, a slow rocking motion as his tongue savored her aroused flesh. He insinuated a hand between her legs until his fingers could touch her pussy. From his vantage point, she looked like a goddess.

Syn's head tipped back and the tips of her hair tickled his chest. Her magnetic eyes were half-closed and a dreamy smile played across her mouth. Her pink tongue darted out to dampen her lips and the image sent a rush of lust to his lower belly.

Her movements became more focused, and all he had to do was keep licking and enjoy the view. Her body was lithe, and the firelight gleamed on her gold belly-button ring. Her breasts swung with each movement, causing his shirt to open and close.

Cupping her buttocks with both hands, he gave them a firm squeeze, pressing down so that her clitoris became locked against his tongue. Her cries grew louder, her movements more urgent, and within seconds she climaxed, bearing down on his mouth as she wailed out her release.

He didn't want to give her time to catch her breath, so he eased her down onto her back. Her drowsy gaze met his and she gave him a sexy, sleepy smile.

"What are you waiting for, Chief? Don't you need to...subdue me?"

With a low growl, he parted her thighs, then entered her with a swift thrust. The sheer sensation of being joined so intimately rendered them both speechless. For seconds they stared into each other's eyes, stunned by the overwhelming experience of being locked together.

All sense of play had vanished, and it was just the two of them, heart to heart, groin to groin. They were as close as two human beings could be without climbing into each other's skin. Slowly he moved, his cock sliding in and out of her damp flesh, and their gazes never wavered. Their lips touched in soft, reverent kisses. He tasted her mouth, licked her chin and nipped at her neck. Syn made silken little noises of approval and her thighs tightened around him.

All too soon, the gnawing heat in his belly swamped his brain and he began to thrust harder. Locking his arms under her shoulders, he moved quickly. Her body arched and her cries of completion brought his arousal to a painful level. His mind and body were on fire and release was the only possible option. Her body vibrated around his and he came, hard. Stars sparked before his eyes and every ounce of energy was sucked from his body through his cock.

As gracefully as he could, he rolled to his side, taking Syn with him. Still buried inside her, his last thought was that he'd forgotten to tell her about his conversation with Doug Davidson.

ॐ

Long years of experience had Matt reaching for his pager when the first beep sounded. He winced when his bare flesh came into contact with the cold wood floor.

Damn house needed central heating.

Luckily his belt was close, and he quickly located his pager. The green LED screen read 10-47, 10-18 followed by a familiar address.

Doug Davidson's house.

He fell back onto the pallet, feeling as if someone had sucker-punched him. Someone at Davidson's residence had committed suicide. Seeing that the man lived alone, the chances were good it was Davidson himself.

"Fuck!"

He rolled to his feet and began dressing as quickly as he could. It was still dark outside, and he had to take a few moments to build up the fire so he could see where his clothing had ended up. Showing up on scene with his boots on the wrong feet would not be a good thing. He made quick work of his clothes and when he strapped on his vest, Syn woke.

"What's wrong, Matt?"

He loved it when she said his name in that sleepy, sexy voice.

"I have a call out, possible suicide." He took a deep breath then readjusted the vest. "I need my shirt back."

"Sure thing."

He checked his utility belt to make sure nothing important had fallen out. The worst thing he could imagine would be to show up on scene without a gun or handcuffs.

"Here you are."

Syn was sitting in the middle of the pallet with only a sheet covering her breasts. She held out his shirt. "I'm afraid it's a little wrinkled, and it probably smells like me."

"If I'm lucky." He smiled.

Putting on the shirt, he zipped the front and began tucking

it in. She was right; it smelled of sex and Syn. At some point he'd need to run home and change. If he didn't, he'd be walking around all day with a hard-on.

"Does this happen often, your getting called out so early?" She drew up her knees and wrapped her arms around them.

"At least few times a month, though in the summer it's more prevalent. Dispatch will page me when it's something serious, such as a suicide, fatality accident, that kind of thing. A good chief always knows what is going on in his town."

"That makes sense." She tilted her head and a soft smile danced across her face. "You're one of those good guys, aren't you, Matthew Whitefeather?"

Looking at her, he knew she wanted some kind of reassurance from him. He'd learned enough about her past to understand she'd been hurt by those closest to her, so she was feeling him out to see if he'd do the same.

"Yeah." He held his hand out toward her. "I'm the real deal, babe."

Taking his hand, he pulled her to her feet. She came into his arms willingly, her warm, nude body pressed close to his.

"I'm glad," she whispered.

He held her for a moment, enjoying the simple pleasure of having Syn in his arms again. Did she know his heart was in her hands?

"I'll be back as soon as I can." He buried his nose in her fragrant hair.

"You'd better." She gave him a noisy, smacking kiss. "I was going to make my world famous, kick-ass Grand Marnier French toast. And sausages." She nipped his lower lip. "Lots and lots of...meat. Big meat."

Matt took possession of her mouth and gave her a kiss that was both swift and sexy. His hand landed on her butt cheek and he gave her a firm squeeze.

"I'll look forward to it," he said. "Keep your cell with you at all times today."

"Am I to be your beck-and-call-girl?" One silken brow rose.

"Yeah, well, I never know when I might need to call and talk dirty to you."

Laughing, she released him. "Go, Chief Whitefeather. Someone out there needs you."

"Be careful today, Syn."

She gave him an odd look. "I will."

"And lock the door behind me."

"Yes, sir." She gave him a mock salute. "When I was a kid, we never locked the door."

"It's a different world now, and that door needs to be locked at all times."

"We'll see about that."

Matt pushed the button to lock the door behind him then left the house with a silly grin on his face. Syn was one hell of a woman, and even though they didn't know each other very well, he had the feeling he'd be a fool to ever let her go.

∓

Syn was in the process of calling for a cab when a knock sounded on the front door. Cell phone in hand, she opened it to find Carolyn Summers on the porch with a large basket of muffins.

"Honey, are you okay?" The other woman pushed past her and into the house, bringing with her the scent of snow and the chill of winter. "I heard about your accident and wanted to make sure you were all right."

"Good morning, Carolyn. I'm fine, thanks for thinking of me." Syn started to move away when the redhead grabbed her in a bone-crushing hug.

"I was so worried about you, up here all alone—"

"Really, it's fine, Carolyn." Syn smiled.

"I made you some muffins." She shoved the basket at Syn, then walked past her into the living room. "Wow, it takes me back to be here again."

"It must be strange, like walking into a time capsule for you." Syn put the basket on a table near the door.

"It is. This house doesn't change, but we do." She stared at the mirror over the fireplace. "Boy do we ever." She gave a self-deprecating laugh. "There are mornings I feel like five miles of rough road."

Syn smiled.

"So what are you up to today?" Carolyn tore her gaze from the mirror and looked at Syn.

"I was calling for a cab. I have a rental waiting for me in Salem and—"

"You don't need a cab, girl. You can call me anytime, I'm in the book." Carolyn laughed. "Grab your coat and purse and I'll drop you off at the car place. I have a hair appointment this afternoon. It's all about the touchups, you know."

"Well, I'll have to take your word on that," Syn reached for her coat.

"You have your mother's coloring and that makes you very lucky." Carolyn was fluffing her hair in the mirror again. "I'll bet Victoria would've aged gracefully, like her mama."

Syn paused in picking up her wallet. Her grandmother had been a beautiful woman, but how would Carolyn know how she'd aged, especially in the years since Victoria died?

"I can't thank you enough for giving me a ride into town, Carolyn." Syn stepped behind the woman and her image appeared beside Carolyn's.

The other woman's eyes widened and the shock was evident. She spun around with her hand on her chest and she gave a shaky laugh.

"My God, I thought you were your mama for a second." Her hand was shaking. "Gave me a scare, you did."

"Sorry about that," Syn murmured.

Carolyn's gaze turned sharp, and for a second Syn felt as if the other woman was about to say something unpleasant. Instead, the moment passed and her bright smile was back in place.

"Are we ready?" She looked at her watch. "I don't want to miss my appointment. I always feel so good when I'm done."

The other woman headed for the door, and Syn met her mother's gaze in the mirror. Victoria's expression was serene, though there was the gleam of mischief in her eyes. She pointed after Carolyn then held up her bare left hand and pointed to her ring finger. Her smile grew wide and she tugged on her earlobe then placed her finger across her lips.

Syn nodded. Her mother was telling her there was something about Carolyn's husband that was important to know and Syn should listen to what the other woman had to say. Turning away from the mirror, she followed Carolyn, curious to see what would happen next.

Chapter Twenty-Three

"If you needed a ride into town, why didn't you give that sexy police chief a call?" Carolyn's laugh was overly loud. "I'll bet that man knows how to give a ride."

"Now why would I call the Chief?" Syn started digging in her jacket pockets, more than a little disconcerted Carolyn had connected her name to Matt's.

"Darling, you forget you're in Salem. Sooner or later everyone knows everybody's secrets." She laughed. "You can't hide anything around here."

Unless it's about my mother's murder.

"So I've noticed." Syn found her sunglasses in the inside pocket. She slipped them on.

"So dish, Synnamon. Is that man amazing in bed or what? He's built like a gladiator—"

"Carolyn, no offense, but I really don't know you. I also don't feel it's right to discuss Chief Whitefeather with you like this." She slid her hands into her pockets to hide her fists. For the first time, she wished she didn't live quite so far out of town.

"Girl, you need to lighten up."

Carolyn took the turn at the bottom of the hill way too fast, and the rear tires skidded. Syn thought her heart would stop, but the other woman seemed oblivious to her tension.

"Every single woman and a few of the not-so-single women have been after that man. He's dated quite a bit around town, and I hear he's just amazing in bed." She laughed again. "I just wanted to hear it from you as some women can be such braggarts."

"Yeah, well..."

"He dated Amanda Forrester for quite a while. You know Amanda, don't you?"

The image of a blonde girl dressed in top-of-the-line clothing came to mind. Her hair was always neat, and her mother had been constantly entering her in beauty pageants.

"Yes, I think we were in fourth grade together," Syn said. "Didn't she participate in beauty pageants?"

"That's her. Matt dated her for about a year or so. They looked good together, both athletic, the chief so dark and Amanda so fair." Carolyn sighed. "I guess it wasn't to be. Come to think of it, I thought he was seeing her again when you came to town."

"Is that so?" Syn schooled her features into a calm mask. Carolyn was trying to goad her into getting personal, and it wasn't going to happen.

"I hope if you are in a sexual relationship with him that you're not his rebound woman," Carolyn was saying. "I'd really hate to see you get hurt."

Syn made a noncommittal sound, staring straight ahead. She hated that she immediately felt jealous at the thought of Matt with Amanda. Would he really jump from one woman's bed to another just like that? It made her sick to her stomach to think what Carolyn said might be true.

Synnamon...

No, she was not going to be a girl about this. Women who jumped to conclusions, usually the wrong ones, gave mature, intelligent women a bad name. When Matt came to the house tonight, she'd simply ask him if it was true.

If he came to the house.

Her mouth twisted. He'd given her no indication of his plans, but then again, he'd left in a rush—

You're doing it again, Syn...

"You're looking serious all of a sudden." Carolyn's words broke into Syn's thoughts.

"Oh, you know how it is. I was thinking about what I need to do once I pick up the rental car," Syn lied. "I don't want to forget anything."

"Boy do I ever. Anymore I have a mind like a steel trap, usually closed." Carolyn chuckled. "That reminds me, I've been meaning to ask you something and I just wasn't sure how to bring it up. It's sort of personal."

More personal than discussing my sex life?

"Okay, spit it out." Syn was relieved to see they were less than two minutes from the car-rental place.

"Do you know what happened to your mother's grimoire?"

Syn froze, and the hair on her arms stood at attention when Victoria's words sounded in her head.

That book is your safety, your future and that of your sisters. There are those who would kill for what is contained within those pages.

"Synnamon, are you okay?"

"Sorry." She cleared her throat. "You reminded me I need to hit the bookstore to pick up something to read."

"I was only asking because Vic had the most amazing spell for housekeeping, and I'd love to have it." Carolyn turned into the rental car parking lot. "I can only get one thing going at a time, but your mother, she could do up the entire house in minutes."

She's lying. Mama did most of the cleaning herself, by hand, and we pitched in.

"I don't remember her ever using a housekeeping spell." Syn's gaze met Carolyn's, and even though the woman's expression was friendly, Syn caught a flash of something dark behind those eyes.

"As for the book, I think the police have it. They tore the house apart that night and a great many things are missing. I must say, it isn't something I've given much thought to."

"That's too bad, I really would've liked to have that spell." Carolyn's lip stuck out like a pouting child's. "If you should find it, would you let me know?"

"Of course. Anything for Mama's best friend." Syn reached to open the door, then stopped. "That reminds me, Carolyn. Where were you the night Mama was killed?"

The other woman's face went blank, and she resembled a mannequin. There was no soul in her eyes.

In that moment Syn received an image as clear as a picture in a book. A man sitting at a table and his mouth forming the same words over and over.

Victoria is dead, Victoria is dead.

She blinked, and the vision faded. Swallowing hard, Syn dug her nails into her palms, trying to prevent herself from screaming. There was only one way to find out if Carolyn, the woman who claimed to be Mama's best friend, was more involved than it appeared.

"You're not implying I had something to do with—" Carolyn started.

"Of course not." Syn's laugh was thin. "You were her friend, I'm sure you had nothing but the best of intentions for her. I was just thinking, what with your husband at the accident scene that night, he would've contacted you first."

Carolyn gaped at Syn, her eyes were wide. "You remember that?"

Score one for me.

"I remember a lot of things from that night." Syn smiled. "Thank you so much for the ride, Carolyn, you're a *good friend.*"

Syn slammed the door and made a beeline for the door of the rental place. Not only did Carolyn want the grimoire, she was in this up to her neck.

ℤ

It took only a few minutes to determine Davidson hadn't killed himself. The body hanging from the rafters and the untidy living room had a story to tell, and it wasn't of suicide. Luckily Matt had been there only the day before, so he was familiar with the condition of the front room.

Now, hours later, Matt sat at his desk and thumbed through the crime scene photographs. The once-neat blankets on the couch were askew, as if someone had been rolling around on them. There were cigarette butts on a saucer in the kitchen, and when Matt had been there yesterday, he hadn't seen or smelled any evidence of Davidson being a smoker.

On the body, Matt noted the fresh defensive wounds,

mainly scratching and bruising on his forearms. The knuckles on his right hand were also raw and marked up. It looked as if the decedent had gotten in a few licks of his own before it was over.

The final piece of the puzzle was the whiskey bottle. He'd seen many suicides, and never could he remember one taking place with a full bottle of whiskey on the scene. Matt was pretty sure Davidson was a serious alcoholic, seeing that he'd been drinking straight from the bottle yesterday. He'd never known an alcoholic to kill himself when there was a full bottle of liquor to be had.

The timing was interesting, to say the least. Less than twelve hours before his "suicide" Davidson had agreed to testify in court about Victoria's death, only to end up dead himself.

How was that for coincidence?

This case became more convoluted every day. Every lead he received turned up yet another handful of suspects. At this point it was possible any one of several thousand people could've killed Victoria, as it seemed half the town had borne the woman ill-will. With the police department apparently going to great lengths to cover up the crime, this situation was just short of mind-blowing.

Mary walked past the door with a cup of coffee in her hand.

"Mary, can you call Pine and set up a meeting for eleven? If he puts up a fuss, tell him to clear his schedule. This is mandatory."

"Are you going to spank him, Chief? Can I watch?"

"No, but I also need you to find Sherlock and get him down here immediately. I need his services."

"Will do."

Matt gathered the photos of Davidson's house and tucked them back into their folder. With Sherlock's ability to wire a room for sound, it was time to up the ante. He would question Pine within an inch of his life and see what came up.

ℰↄ

Lieutenant George Pine was not a happy man.

From the moment he'd received the terse meeting request until he walked downstairs to Matt's office, he'd been kicking himself for not retiring sooner. The only reason he hadn't was because he wasn't sure what to do with himself without a job. How would he spend his time?

His entire life had been law enforcement, and he never known anything else. His wife had left him four years ago and his kids were grown and living their own lives. All he had left was his job.

It was the reason he got up in the mornings.

Matt's office door was open and the dragon wasn't at her desk. George knocked on the doorframe and Matt's dark head came up from the papers he'd been reading.

"Hi George, come on in." Matt wasn't smiling.

"Thanks."

"And please close the door behind you."

Only years of working the streets kept him from showing any emotion. His palms were damp as he shut the door, but he kept his expression empty, pleasant. "Looks like we're going to get some serious snow," he said, glancing out the window. "There will be quite a few accidents and injuries tonight."

"Comes with the winter," Matt said. "They're calling for eight to twelve inches, so we're in for a busy night."

"That we are."

George sat in the chair facing the chief's desk. Not only was it uncomfortable, it was also lower than Matt's by several inches. It put him at a definite disadvantage. "What can I do for you?"

"I assume you heard Doug Davidson committed suicide last night?"

"I did, and it's a damned shame. He was a fine officer and a fine man."

And a royal pain in the ass...

"He was on the scene the night Victoria Angelov was murdered."

Matt was looking at him with a directness that always unsettled George. Damn this man and his fishy Indian ways.

"Murder? Now Chief, we've been over—"

235

"George, let's cut through the bullshit. You and I both know Victoria was murdered that night and you and Davidson were on the scene. Don't you think it is past time to tell the truth—"

Shit...

"I beg to differ, Chief. I do not believe she was murdered; it was a hit-and-run accident, plain and simple—"

"That's not what Davidson told me yesterday."

Matt's gaze didn't waver, and George felt the urge to shrink in his chair as if he were five years old again. How in the hell had Matt had a conversation with Davidson? The man was a crazy as—

"George, did I lose you?"

"Of course not. I was trying to decide on a way to put this delicately. I don't like speaking ill of the dead, but I'm afraid Davidson had some pretty serious mental health issues—"

"I spoke to his doctor, and according to him Doug had been diagnosed with Post-Traumatic Stress Disorder. Doug was medicated and completely lucid at his last appointment less than one week ago. Are you trying to tell me the doctor is wrong?"

"I'm not trying to tell you anything, Chief. I'm only relaying my experiences with the man. He was a paranoid, delusional hoarder. He lived in that wreck of a house with no contact to the outside world, with the exception of a woman he paid to buy his groceries and liquor."

"He was a little peculiar—"

"A little? The man was a loon. Are you trying to tell me you believe that woman was murdered based on the ramblings of a paranoid drunk? I was on that scene; I saw everything that went on—"

"But you were tipsy, you said so yourself."

Shit.

"That I was—"

"So I should take the word of a drunken police officer over Doug Davidson's?" Matt kicked back in the chair and George wasn't sure he liked the look in the other man's eye. "Seems to me it's six of one and half-dozen of another. Neither one of you is terribly credible."

236

George remained silent, but he was both pissed and terrified. Pissed off that McNutt had fucked up by leaving the file behind. Angry as hell because that Angelov whore had come back to town, and terrified because he hadn't had enough sense to retire and leave Salem when he had the chance.

He had the sinking feeling his time was up.

"So tell me something, Pine. Why does a jury always seem to believe a prostitute isn't a credible witness to a crime?"

"Because of their lifestyle and life choices, they are deemed somehow to be uneducated and inferior." George's lips were numb.

"It never occurs to a jury that just because someone is a prostitute, it doesn't mean they have bad eyesight as well. Even the dregs of society, some of the most mentally ill, have a story to tell, and it's up to us to give them the benefit of the doubt." Matt leaned forward and braced his arms on the desk. "Including Doug Davidson."

He felt as if his heart were going to leap out of his chest, but he said nothing. He was caught, and they both knew it, though Matt would never drag a confession out of him. If he said one word, his life would be over.

Literally.

"I read through Doug's file. He was a decorated officer with exemplary attendance and numerous letters of commendation from Chief McNutt. Then, all of a sudden, he appears to have had some sort of mental breakdown about nine years ago." He picked up an ink pen and began twirling it between his fingers. "What would you know about that, Lieutenant?"

"Nothing, sir."

"So, you want me to believe you knew nothing about a man you'd supervised for roughly ten years."

George met Matt's gaze. "I'm telling you the truth, Chief."

"The truth?" Matt laughed. "I don't think any of you who were involved even know what the truth is anymore. But don't worry, Lieutenant, before I'm done everyone will know what happened to Victoria that night."

"I don't appreciate being called a liar," he ground out.

"And I don't appreciate being lied to," Matt shot back. "As of today I am putting you on suspension, Unpaid, of course. Your badge and gun will be turned over to me. You are officially a suspect in the murder of Victoria Angelov."

To George, it felt as if his entire body had been dipped into icy water. All feeling left his limbs and everything went into slow motion. The chief stared at him with a hard, unforgiving gaze.

Guilty, guilty, guilty...

With a look of disgust on his face, Matt reached for the phone. Seconds later Detectives Lark and Goldstein entered the office. Both men had removed their suit jackets, and their holsters stood out against crisp white shirts.

No, this can't be happening...

"Escort Lieutenant Pine to his office where he can gather his personal effects, gentlemen."

"Certainly, Chief."

Slowly George rose, forcing his spine to remain ramrod straight. He'd die before he'd allow Matt to see him crumble. He gave the chief a curt nod then headed for the door.

"Lieutenant, your badge and gun, please," Matt spoke.

"My gun is in my office in the cabinet," he muttered through frozen lips.

"Fine. Detective Goldstein, you will bring his gun downstairs to the armory and leave the receipt with Mary, please."

"Yes, sir."

Reluctantly, George reached into his pocket and withdrew his wallet. The gold lieutenant's badge winked up at him, and when he pulled it free of its holder, he thought his bowels would let loose.

It was everything he was and had ever wanted to be, this badge. It was the essence of George Pine, forged in gold.

Without a word, he laid the badge on Matt's desk, then turned away. On wooden legs, he left the office, the two detectives walking just behind him. Panic threatened to choke him as they walked up the steps. It felt as if everyone they passed stared at him with accusing eyes.

Guilty, guilty, guilty...

Now he knew what it felt like to be a criminal.

Guilty, guilty, guilty...

How could he have come to this?

The Brotherhood...

Just thinking of them had his stomach roiling. It wasn't worth it, none of it. Now, walking to his office, he realized all of it had been a horrible, tragic lie. His life was destroyed and for what? Money? Prestige? He'd sold his soul so cheaply and within the next few hours his word, his reputation would be destroyed.

And for what?

His heart beat loudly and the noises around him faded into a soft, muffled roar. As he walked up the steps toward his office, George's gaze landed on the stacks of brand new trashcans waiting for distribution.

That wretched woman...no one deserved to die like that.

When he reached the top step, he reached out and knocked several stacks of cans backward into the path of the detectives. Vaguely, he heard them shout and he broke into a run. His office was in the back and it seemed to take hours to make it there. His awareness had shrunk to the pounding of his heart and the air rushing from his lungs.

Kicking the door with his foot, it slammed shut, then locked it behind him. Without a pause, he snatched his keys from the desk and unlocked the gun cabinet. Withdrawing the .44 H&K semi-automatic from its holster, George noted the gun felt absurdly heavy in his hand. In all the years of his career, he'd considered himself lucky, as he'd never had to shoot anyone.

Until now.

He barely heard the pounding on his door over the roaring in his ears. Through the glass he saw the detectives' shadows and he turned away. With any luck, McNutt would rot in hell for his part in this. George sat at his desk. His blotter was orderly and his appointments were printed under each date in Alice's neat handwriting.

"I guess I won't be making my racquetball game." He swept the blotter off the desk, taking with it the lamp and a container of pens.

The pounding grew louder and the shouts increased.

J. C. *Wilder*

Staring at a photograph of his once-happy family, George could only hope some day they'd forgive him. He'd wanted to provide them with the life they'd deserved; the one he'd never had growing up.

At least in that he'd succeeded.

Picking up the frame, he slammed it against the edge of his desk. The frame and glass shattered and he removed the photo to reveal another one behind it. It was a candid shot of Victoria and her four girls. His gaze moved over their happy, smiling faces.

"Dear God, what have I done?"

Picking up the gun, he flicked off the safety. Inserting the business end into his mouth, he took a deep breath, his gaze fixed on Victoria's face.

Forgive me—

He pulled the trigger.

Chapter Twenty-Four

She had to find the book.

After picking up her rental car, Syn completed her errands, though it felt as if the entire world had slowed to a crawl. The snow had begun falling in earnest while she'd been in the grocery store, and by the time she'd finished all her shopping, more than two inches had piled up.

With her rented SUV loaded down with supplies, she was trying to get out of town, but it seemed everyone else had the same idea. Traffic was bumper-to-bumper and moving at a crawl, and it didn't look like it would be getting better anytime soon. She could only hope Maddie hadn't eaten the dining room table before she got back.

Stopping at a light, Syn slapped her hand on the wheel. From the time Syn could walk, Mama had drilled it into her head to protect the spell book at all costs. It contained the ancient knowledge, both dark and light, of the Angelov family. As a child she'd seen the massive book thousands of times. When Mama was at home, it was kept in the sunroom in the middle of the preparation table. Try as she might, she couldn't remember if she'd seen the book the day Mama had died.

Many times Aunt Bethany had come down to spend time with them, and she and Mama would practice some of the more arcane spells. At night Syn would lie in bed listening to their laughter reverberating through the house when the results were not quite as they should've been.

The light turned green and she heaved a sigh of relief. Most drivers headed to their destinations in town, while she was one of the few headed out. Holding her breath, she eased around the corner just as the light turned red again. The snow was thick and it was growing dark. She glanced at the clock.

It was only five thirty.

With luck, she would be back at the house around six. Maddie had to be frantic by now, and it was rare Syn left the dog alone for this long.

The image of Carolyn's face formed in her mind.

Syn wasn't quite sure what to make of her mother's old friend. For the life of Syn, she didn't remember Carolyn. Then again, the longer she was in Salem the more she realized large chunks of her childhood were simply gone from her mind. The only person who might possibly be able to shed some light on the situation was Aunt Bethany. She and Mama had been very close, and Bethie spent a lot of time down here. Would she remember Carolyn?

Picking up her cell phone, Syn hit the speed dial number for her aunt. By the time it was picked up, Syn had to slow the SUV to less than five miles an hour.

"Blessed be," a pleasant male voice answered.

"Uncle Joe, it's Synnamon."

"Darling girl, how are you? We've been worried." His pleased tone was enough to make her smile.

"I'm good, but I think it's freezing and I'm in danger of becoming an ice cube."

"It's called winter, Syn." His tone was dry. "You used to love it when you were a child."

She laughed. "I'm aware of that. I think I spent too much time down South. My blood may never thicken up again."

"So how is that pit of a town? Have they been nice to you?"

"Salem is Salem. I'm not sure it changed much at all. Maybe some of the houses got bigger and the cars more pricy, that's about it."

"How is the house?"

"It's in decent shape. I have a working fireplace and running water."

"Ugh, it still sounds like camping to me."

"Pussy." She laughed again. To say she adored her Uncle

Joe would be an understatement.

"I am when it's twenty degrees outside and all I have to keep warm is a fireplace. If that makes me a pussy then so be it." He laughed. "How are the people treating you?"

"Well, for the most part I'd say they're stiff, but not totally unpleasant."

"Who knows, maybe that wicked town can be saved after all."

"I don't know if I'd go that far." Syn slowed the car when she reached the base of the hill. "I called to see if Aunt Bethany was around, I have a question for her."

"Sorry Syn, she's not. She and Mother went to Nova Scotia for your Great-Aunt Alma's birthday and I'm flying up in the morning. She's turned ninety-three, can you believe it?"

"And she still works her own garden, keeps her own house and stirs up city council when it suits her."

"Where there's a witch, there's a way."

They both laughed. It was Alma's favorite saying.

"Her long life bodes well for you I'd say," Joe chuckled. "Angelovs are a hardy bunch. So what did you need to ask Beth, my darling? I might be able to help."

"I don't know, Joe, this went on before you and Bethie married."

"Give me a try, it can't hurt."

"Have you ever heard Bethany mention a woman named Carolyn Summers? She claims to have been a friend of Mama's."

"No, but I do remember Victoria talking about her once."

"What?" Syn was so startled she almost drove off the side of the road. Slowing the car, she pulled onto the shoulder and turned on her hazard lights. "When did you meet Mama?"

"I say Syn, you have the worst memory I've ever seen in a woman your age. You don't remember Bethany and me coming down for a visit that last summer?"

A feeling of unreality swept over her.

What else had she forgotten?

"No, Joe, I don't remember that." Her words were faint.

Joe made a consoling sound. "You were so traumatized by your mother's death; I guess I shouldn't be too surprised. Not to mention what those bastards did to you afterwards—"

"Let's not go there," Syn interrupted.

"As you wish." Joe's voice was quiet. "I don't remember a whole lot about the conversation. One night during dinner, Vic received a phone call and she seemed upset when she hung up. She wouldn't say anything in front of you kids though.

"I hustled you guys to bed and when I was done I came downstairs and Vic and Beth were talking about the call. I assumed they were friends and my wife knew the woman as well. Vic said she'd called specifically to ask about the Angelov grimoire. It would seem Carolyn offered your mama quite a bit of money for it."

Syn felt as if someone had just kicked her in the stomach. It was the book again.

"You're kidding me," she whispered.

"No, afraid I'm not."

"Did Mama ever mention why she thought Carolyn wanted it?"

"No. She and Bethany were laughing about it. Imagine, your mother selling the Angelov spell book. She'd have given her life for that book—"

"I think she did."

Blindly, Syn stared out the windshield. The conditions had deteriorated to a near white-out and nothing was moving outside the car. The grimoire—the very same book Mama had pounded into her head to never forget and to protect at all costs—someone had killed for it.

"Uncle Joe, does Aunt Bethany have the book?"

Silence.

"Joe?"

"Syn, we don't have it. We always assumed you'd hid it or kept it with you."

"That night, they searched the house. The police tore it apart, and I think they were looking for the book." Fear crept down her spine. "We weren't allowed to take anything from the house, not even our clothing."

"Do you think it was in the house?"

"I don't know, I can't remember if I saw it that day—"

"And you've looked for it?"

"No, I didn't make the connection until today." She was just short of wailing. "It was kept in the sunroom, but I don't remember when last I saw it—"

"Synnamon, you have to find that spell book. Did Vic tell you it should not be removed from the grounds?"

"No," she whispered.

"If it has been taken from the property then you're in grave danger, Syn."

"Joe, I don't understand—"

"It isn't for you to understand, darling girl. Some things have to be taken on faith, and this is one of those things." Joe's voice was gentle. "The book, in part, is what controls Itsy."

Itsy...

"I—"

"Chloe and Vic were the only two who could handle Itsy without the book—"

"Will she, *it*, hurt me?"

"I don't know, Syn. I don't know what Itsy is or from where it came. Itsy is the one thing no one in your family will talk about."

She swallowed hard.

"Victoria loved her girls so deeply; her beliefs ran almost as deep and she put your safety into the grimoire." Joe sighed. "That book is the key to all that is good and dark. Whatever happens, it cannot be allowed to fall into the wrong hands—"

Static drowned out Joe's words.

"Joe? Joe? Are you there?"

"...find that book..." his voice sounded tiny and impossibly far away. "...life depends on it..."

"Joe, I can't hear you!"

"...Beth...cell...not working..."

"Joe?"

A beep sounded in her ear and something cold slithered

down her spine. Fear was thick on her tongue as she looked at her phone.

The call was lost.

Joe said Carolyn had wanted the book, and she'd offered to pay for it. But what exactly did she want it for? Itsy? Was the woman desperate enough to kill for whatever was contained inside?

The snow had cut visibility to only a few feet in front of the car, and it was coming down faster. At this rate she would be cut off from town within an hour or so.

That's what they want...

Her heart was pounding and her hands shook when she punched in Matt's cell number. It never rang, only clicked, then a tinny voice directed her to leave a message.

"Matt, it's Syn—"

Loud crackling exploded in her ear, and she winced. According to the screen on her phone she was still connected, but he probably wouldn't be able to hear her through the static. She disconnected the call and tried again.

It rang once, then the voice directed her to leave a message.

"Matt, I think I know why Mama was killed—"

More static sounded, and this time the call was cut off.

"Damn it all to hell," she muttered as she redialed. "Please Goddess, I only need ten seconds."

The voicemail message sounded terribly far away, and in that moment Syn felt fear, real fear, for the first time. Sitting in her car in a snowstorm, she had the distinct feeling something or someone was watching her.

The message beep sounded and she screamed, "Matthew, I need you!"

Once again, the line dropped, and she scowled at her phone. The storm must be interrupting the reception. Looking in her rear-view mirror, all she could see was more snow. Should she go back and try to find Matt?

You must find that book...

But he was in town and maybe he'd have a suggestion—

Even as she had the thought, she pushed it away. Maddie

was alone at the house, and if the snow was bad enough Syn might not be able to get back home. Something very bad was coming and Syn wasn't about to leave her best friend to take care of herself.

No, she'd get her dog, search for the book, then come back into town and track down Matt.

Tossing her phone into the passenger seat, she carefully pulled back onto the road. While her rental was an SUV, it handled differently from her Jeep and the roads were getting slick. She gripped the steering wheel so tight her knuckles turned white.

"I can do this," she spoke into the silence of the car. "It's not like I haven't taken care of myself for the past twenty years."

Itsy...

Syn bit her lower lip as she guided the SUV around the first curve on Winding Oak. Just because Carolyn had once made an offer to buy the book, that didn't mean she'd killed for it.

She frowned. Why had Carolyn lied about her magical abilities the day they'd met? She'd hinted she wasn't a blood witch, but today she'd unknowingly admitted she was by asking for a housecleaning spell. Only a witch-born would have the abilities such as Mama's or hers...

One of the county maintenance trucks came flying around the corner, missing her car by inches. Syn sucked in a noisy breath, expelling it only after the truck had passed.

Damn, it would be easy to kill someone out here, especially in bad weather.

According to Matt, Mama had been hit near where Syn had pulled over to make her phone call. That exclusive area of housing was called Highland Hills, the swanky neighborhood for the rich and boring. The section of Winding Oak that ran past the subdivision was flat and open with evenly spaced streetlights.

Holding her breath, she negotiated the second curve. When the road straightened, she exhaled noisily.

Even in the dark of night, it would've been hard as hell to hit someone around Highland Hills unless it had been intentional. The area was too well-lit, and it was heavily traveled. There were easily a hundred houses in that area and every driver would've had to pull out onto Winding Oak to get into Salem.

How could there have been no witnesses to the accident?

She negotiated the final curve with her heart in her mouth. After going into the ravine in her Jeep, just the thought of sliding off the road was enough to give her the shakes.

Honestly, she was tired of chewing on her mother's death and all the questions that remained. More than anything she wanted only to curl up with her dog, some cocoa and watch the snow fall outside her window.

But first she needed to search the house for the book.

Even though it was less than a quarter of a mile, it seemed to take an eternity to reach the drive. Turning into the snowy lane, several times she thought for sure she was going to get stuck. Luck was with her and by the time she pulled up near the steps, she was totally exhausted.

Getting out of the car, she noticed there was at least a half a foot of snow on the ground. It was full dark and the wind was picking up, blowing the snow around and obscuring her vision. Grabbing as many bags of groceries she could handle, she hurried up the icy steps. When she opened the door, Maddie was ecstatic to see Syn, her stubby tail wiggling as fast as her butt could move.

"Baby, Mama missed her girl." Syn dropped her bags and fell to her knees to give her excited animal a hug. "Just wait 'til you see what Mama has for you."

Together they headed into the kitchen and she made quick work of feeding Maddie. Once the dog was happily munching on kibble and a bit of canned food, she stirred the embers in the stove and began feeding it small pieces of wood.

How many times had she watched her mama do the exact same thing? Syn smiled. She was amazed that Victoria had managed to turn out picture perfect cakes and pies from a stove that was over two hundred years old.

Once the fire was going, she stood up and was forced to grab the table for support. Dizziness threatened to take her legs out from under her, and she groped for a chair. In the glass front of the cabinets, she saw Victoria as clear as day. Mama looked alarmed, and she was saying something but Syn couldn't make it out. Extreme exhaustion pulled at her limbs and she uttered only one word before losing consciousness.

"Mama."

∞

"What did you mean, you didn't find out anything?" the male voice snarled.

"You heard me, Synnamon Angelov is a very bright woman—"

"Did she figure out what you wanted?"

"I don't know." Carolyn scowled at the speakerphone.

"We need that book, woman," the man's voice ground out, his impatience obvious.

"It has to be in that room upstairs—"

"That we can't get into."

"Yeah well, that isn't my problem. You men had twenty years—"

"Carolyn, you forget yourself." The voice dropped. "Not having the book is everyone's problem, yours included."

She took a deep, calming breath. It would do her no good to piss him off, she'd be found dead on the road like poor Victoria.

"The only other option I have is to go out there and tear that house apart by hand," she said.

"We've already done that," the man said.

"Then what do you suggest we do?"

"We kidnap her and convince her to tell us where it is," the man chuckled. "It isn't as if we haven't done it before."

Ice water ran through her veins, and the taste of fear was hot, coppery—not unlike that of human blood.

"Victoria Angelov was my friend—"

"You were jealous of her," the man sneered.

"—and I don't want you or any of The Brotherhood touching her daughter. That girl has been through enough."

"Loyalty," he chuckled. "How it warms my heart to hear you

speak of that whore in such a fashion. So rarely is loyalty given the respect it deserves. Too bad you didn't feel that way twenty years ago."

Carolyn ignored the jab. "I will take care of this, and I'll have the book by morning or die trying."

There was a slight pause.

"I will hold you to that, Carolyn."

She was terrified when she disconnected the call. She'd signed her own death warrant if she couldn't find the spell book. They'd spent twenty years searching Victoria's property, and they were no closer to finding it than the night she'd died.

Carolyn didn't like to think about the accident. There wasn't a day that went by in which she didn't think about Victoria and her lovely girls. Never would she let herself forget that it was her fault Vic was dead and her daughters scattered to the winds.

"Damn her for showing me that book," she snarled.

Rising from her chair, she headed for the kitchen and her magic supplies. She needed to find a way to locate the book, yet keep Synnamon safe from The Brotherhood.

Turning on the kitchen light, for a split second she could've sworn she'd caught a glimpse of Victoria out of the corner of her eye.

Carolyn spun around. Her heart was beating hard, but the kitchen was empty. Her eyes were playing tricks on her. Picking up her mortal and pestle, she held the cold marble in her hands. The sleeping potion was simple and one she'd used many times before, but never had she tried to send it to someone on the other side of town.

"Forgive me, Victoria, for what I'm about to do," she whispered.

If there was one thing she could change, she wouldn't have sent Victoria away that night. If Vic had stayed at the house just a while longer, none of this would've happened. Her friend would be alive, her daughters thriving, and Carolyn wouldn't be haunted by the images of her friend's mutilated body every time she closed her eyes.

Chapter Twenty-Five

Never in his wildest dreams would Matt have guessed George Pine would take his own life.

He closed the dead man's personnel file. They'd worked together for six years, and while they'd had thousands of conversations, Matt didn't know the first thing about George's personal life. The man had a certain reserve when it came to personal matters and Matt now wondered if his silence had hidden something much deeper and darker than he'd imagined.

A soft knock on the door broke into his thoughts.

Alice Knowles, the command staff secretary, stood in the door. Her normally orderly blonde hair was ruffled and her eyes were red and puffy from tears.

"May I speak, sir?" Even her voice was shaky.

"Of course, Alice. Please come in."

"Thank you, sir."

Matt rose as the woman entered and he waved her toward the chair. After closing the door he moved a box of tissues within her reach.

"What can I do for you, Alice?"

"I wanted to talk to you about Lieutenant Pine, sir."

"You realize you don't have to do this—"

"I need to say this now." Tears shimmered in her pale blue eyes. "I want you to know George was not a bad man," she sniffed.

"Alice, not for a moment do I believe he was," Matt said. "I think he was troubled, and I unknowingly played into his problem with the personnel issue I was dealing with."

"I know he was being put on suspension, sir." She gave him a weak smile. "There are no secrets here."

Well, you've got that right.

"Go on, Alice."

"You had to have known the man as I did, to understand why this happened." She stopped, and the pain was evident on her face. "George was a career police officer, much decorated and admired by his peers. It was all he'd ever wanted to be since he was a child."

"Did he tell you this?"

"Many times. His marriage fell apart, and when his youngest child went to college, his wife left him. He was distraught. Time after time he told me his work and standing in the community were all he had left."

Tears began to roll down her pale cheeks.

"He was a proud man, very proud. I'm sure when he received the suspension notice it just took the wind right out of him. I think he couldn't handle losing face and the resulting public humiliation was more than he could bear. He truly lived for this job." She reached for the box of tissues. "He wasn't a bad man—"

"Alice, how long were you in love with him?" Matt's voice was gentle.

The raw pain on her face wasn't difficult to see.

"Eight years." She looked away. "It was wrong. We both knew it. He was married and had children..."

"You had an affair?"

Mute, she nodded.

"And your son, is he George's?"

"Yes." She stared down at her hands. "I was divorced for years, and it didn't appear I would ever marry again. Then I got the job here, and within minutes of our meeting I was head over heels.

"He was so handsome and charismatic." A soft smile transformed her features from plain to beautiful. "He made me feel good about myself and he was so funny. George was easy to talk to, and he said the same thing about me. It seems like our love affair just began." Her smile faded. "And now it's over."

"We can't choose who we love, Alice. We have no say in the matter," Matt said. "We would like to think love is always welcome and it will make us complete and our lives full and happy." An image of Syn's face formed in his mind. "It doesn't always work like that. It is rarely convenient, usually argumentative and has just as many lows as highs."

"But we still crave it." Her voice was soft.

"That we do."

"You're in love, too," she said.

"Yes."

Her lower lip trembled, yet she still managed to smile. "Whoever she is, she's a very lucky woman, just as I was." She sniffed. "He loved me, you know."

"I'm sure he did, Alice."

"I only wish I'd been enough for him," she said. "I would've stood by him, no matter what came at him."

"I'm sure you would have," Matt murmured. "I hate to bring this up, but I need to know if George ever mentioned the name Victoria Angelov."

Her gaze dropped to her hands. "Not by name."

Matt's pulse quickened. "What did he say about her?"

"I'm sorry, sir." She swallowed hard. "I loved George Pine with all of my heart and I owe him my loyalty." Her gaze met his. "I cannot betray his confidence."

"Alice—"

"He was a good man, my George. You have to believe that, sir." Tears were welling up again.

"Alice, I know George was a fine officer and fine man..."

"When he was young he just got tangled up with the wrong people." Her tears were flowing. "He said there was no way out..." She dissolved into soft sobs.

Matt's heart ached for her, but this woman had answers he so desperately needed. He leaned forward and pushed the tissues closer.

"Alice, did he ever explain what he meant by that?"

"I shouldn't be here, I shouldn't have said anything," she whispered. "I need to go."

She lunged to her feet and headed for the door, and Matt followed.

"Alice, I'm incredibly sorry for your loss and I thank you for taking time to speak to me about George. I'm sure he loved you very much and if he'd seen another way out, this would've never happened."

With her back to him, Alice stood by the door. "I felt you needed to know the truth about George, and I wanted to make sure you knew. He had a great deal of respect for you, Chief." She wiped her nose with a mangled tissue. "He told me countless times that if he'd had a chief like you earlier in his career, his life would've been totally different."

With that, she threw open the door and practically ran out of the office, her muffled sobs growing faint as she raced up the steps.

While he felt a tiny bit less guilty than before, Matt felt pain for Alice. To have loved someone, have borne him a child, and then lose him to suicide—it was possibly one of the worst things he could imagine.

Having just found her, he didn't know what he'd do if he lost Syn now.

Walking to his desk, Matt pulled out the chair and dropped into it. He couldn't remember when he'd felt more drained. Alice believed Pine's suicide was due to the disgrace of being put on suspension. Matt wasn't so sure.

Most suicides were a culmination of multiple factors, not just one, and they could rarely be explained in a neat little sound-bite. Victoria's murder was as much of a factor, as was his fear of losing his standing in society. Somehow there was a link—

"Chief Whitefeather?"

Mary stood in the doorway, her normally animated face subdued. In her hands she held a stack of mail.

"Yes, Mary."

"The cleaning crew is done upstairs and they're packing up." She laid the stack of mail on the desk. "I'm sorry, I forgot the mail in all the upheaval today."

"It's okay, Mary. Anything that was mailed isn't too urgent." Matt said.

"Is there anything else you need?"

"No, thank you for staying so late. Now go home to your man."

"What about you, Chief? Will you be leaving soon?"

"I will." He sat up a little bit straighter. "I just want to get the paperwork finished up before I leave."

"It'll wait until tomorrow," Mary said. "You go home now, Matthew. It will do you no good to stay here any longer."

Matt smiled. It was rare Mary felt motherly enough to call him by the first name.

"Thanks, Mary, I just might do that."

"Well, you take care driving," Mary spoke over her shoulder. "It's been snowing like crazy and the roads are pretty bad. The boys have been running from one accident to another."

"I'll bet."

Matt felt guilty he hadn't paid the slightest bit of attention to the streets. He reached for the mail. Then again, his preoccupation with the suicide was understandable.

Flipping through the envelopes, he stacked them in order of importance. Most of them could wait. There was one from the Fraternal Order of Police that he could deal with tomorrow, and that left only a package.

He scanned for a return address, and it was blank. The post office was stamped with yesterday's date in Montrose, just a few miles down the road. Picking it up, it wasn't heavy, simply a standard padded envelope. It probably weighed only a few pounds.

Curiosity got the best of him and he tore open the back. Reaching inside, he pulled out a battered envelope. On the front was a sticky note and written in block letters:

I BELIEVE YOU'RE LOOKING FOR THIS.

Anticipation curled in his stomach and he dumped the contents of the envelope onto his desk. Yellowed report pages mixed with glossy photos spilled out. On top was a photo of a black car that had front-end damage consistent with striking a human being.

The missing pages of the Angelov file.

&

"Synnamon, open your eyes."

"Don't want to," she murmured.

Her body hurt. From her toes to her nose, she felt as if she'd been run over by an elephant. Slowly, she opened her eyes, and the kitchen ceiling took shape overhead.

"Why am I on the floor?" she whispered, and Maddie's funny face appeared inches from her nose. "Baby, what happened? Did I fall down?"

"That bitch Carolyn cast a spell upon you."

Mama's voice rang out, and it wasn't hard to tell she was angry. Catching Maddie around the neck, Syn used the stocky dog to pull herself upright. Weary, she propped her back against the leg of the kitchen table for support.

Victoria stood at the stove, stirring something in a small pot. She looked like an angel in a long white dress and around her waist she wore a red gingham apron. Her hair was braided into dozens of cornrows, and at the ends dangled clear crystals that chimed when she moved.

Bewildered, Syn rubbed her eyes. Her mother had always been a bohemian dresser, and Syn had never seen her dress in anything quite so ethereal.

"Mama?" she whispered.

"Darling, you need to drink this. It is a counter-spell that will clear your mind and return you to reality." Victoria retrieved a dirty coffee mug and in her hands it went from dingy to sparkling. "I just long to strangle that damned woman. How dare she cast a spell on one of my daughters?"

"Am I asleep?"

"No, Princess." Victoria glided toward her and Syn realized she had no feet. "You're in the 'tween, the place between sleep and awake." She held out the mug. "So I'm not really here. Then again, neither are you."

Syn reached for it, disappointed when her fingers passed through her mother's.

"I'm dead to your world, Synnamon. You cannot feel me ever again."

"I know Mama, I know." Blindly, she wrapped her chilled hands around the warm mug. "What's in this?"

"A touch of this and that." She smiled and Syn could've sworn she heard chimes. "Chocolate, peppermint, rosemary, lemongrass, pine and the crushed bones of an old toad."

Syn wrinkled her nose. "Gross."

"You used to adore me telling you things like that. The grosser the better."

Victoria laughed and the sound was so sweetly familiar tears stung Syn's eyes. She took a sip of the liquid, pleased when it tasted a little like grass and a lot like chocolate.

"I've grown up since then, Mama."

"I know, darling." Victoria's smile faded. "You're a woman now, very close to the age I was when I left you."

Syn nodded. She was feeling sad. For the past twenty years she'd thought only about the damage inflicted upon herself and her siblings. Her mother's life had been interrupted, and her dreams destroyed along with her children's.

"Mama, are my sisters okay?"

"You know I can't tell you, Synnamon." Her smile was sad. "I can't give you knowledge, I can only remind you of what you already know."

Syn nodded, feeling so terribly small and lost.

"I like your man, your Matthew." Victoria's voice was soft. "He's a good man."

Syn shook her head. "He isn't mine, Mama."

"It really is sad the only time we see truth is when we're dead." Victoria shook her dark head and the crystals chimed. "He's yours if you have the courage to seize him, Synnamon Angelov. You are so strong, and that man is in love with you." She smiled and a twinkling glint entered her eyes. "I didn't even have to cast a spell to help it along."

Syn's bark of laughter was loud. "Don't even tell me you'd thought of casting a spell to catch a man for me?"

"Oh really, Syn. I would never think of doing that," Victoria said. "I only meant that my daughters have been through so much, and all of you bear your scars on the inside and outside.

"You, my first born, you lack in trust. Trust in yourself and those around you." Tears shimmered in her dark eyes. "Since the day you came into this world kicking and screaming, you never lacked in courage. Now you have to learn to trust your heart again."

"My sisters?"

"You'll see soon enough." Victoria's smile was sad and a single tear slipped from her eye. "I've never left any of you, Syn, not for a moment."

"Why can I see you here? Why couldn't I see you when I needed you?" Syn began to cry.

"This place is special, Syn. But you know that, don't you?"

"Itsy?" she sniffed.

"Itsy is part of it," Victoria said. "Angelov house is within you, and you are within this place. The time you were born it became yours. Itsy and I, we were the caretakers, waiting for the day when you could take control. How I've dreamed of this moment, and now it is here."

"I'm scared, Mama," Syn whispered.

"I'd be more concerned if you weren't. There is danger all around you, and the future hinges on what you do in the coming hours."

"That makes me feel so much better." Syn downed the liquid in her cup, wincing when the final swallow reminded her of seaweed.

"When the time comes, you will know what to do," Victoria said. "All of my girls will. You, Chloe, Summer and Autumn, with all of you I achieved my greatest ambition, a family of my own. You girls are the best thing I ever did in my life."

"I love you, Mama."

"And I you, Princess." Victoria sighed. "I must go, Syn. You are starting to wake, and you have a lot to do."

"Where is the grimoire, Mama?"

"You realize the best hiding place is in plain sight, daughter."

"That tells me nothing." Syn's shoulders slumped. "How can a book hold such sway over our lives?"

"There is a price to pay for such an extraordinary gift as ours, Synnamon." A second tear followed the first. "At your birth, the idea of ever having an ordinary life was lost. We must wear the mantle of our predecessors with pride and gracefully accept the responsibility that comes with it."

"Yes, Mama."

"Every witch has a weakness, something tethering her to her mortal life. When that tether is broken, you too will leave this world."

Victoria's image began to fade; her tears gleamed like diamonds on her pale skin.

"You're courageous and strong, and it's time to gather your courage. You, Synnamon, are the child of my winter. You are my first-born, my precious child. From the moment I heard your heartbeat I knew you were destined for greatness.

"So much lies ahead of you. Your destiny isn't to die at the hands of the dark ones as I did. Trust, my daughter, trust yourself and that man of yours. He will be there when you need him."

Two tears slipped from her chin, and for a moment, they hung in the air. Syn held out her hand, and tears dropped into her palm. Instead of the wetness she expected, they were solid. Her eyes widened when she saw the two diamonds.

"Find the grimoire, Synnamon, and break your winter."

Chapter Twenty-Six

Edina Mayhew Haines removed her reading glasses and tucked them into their tapestry holder. Carefully she laid them in their customary place next to the lamp. In the morning she'd need them with her coffee and newspaper, so she was always careful to put them where they were easy to find.

The house was quiet. More and more it was like that in the evenings. Ever since Bryan moved out, she and her husband rattled around this big old house like leaves in the breeze.

Her lips tightened.

John had gone up to bed hours ago and Donnie, her eldest son, had fallen asleep on the couch. Her gaze moved over his beloved face. How could anyone not love her firstborn? He was handsome, charismatic and openly affectionate with those he loved.

For some reason his wife had thrown him out of the house earlier today, claiming she was too stressed to deal with his issues any longer. Issues? What issues? Yes, he drank a little, but didn't most men?

He'd also had an affair, which enraged Jessica to no end. Not that Edina didn't understand. Her husband had many affairs over the years, and she was grateful for it. His extramarital activities meant she didn't have to touch that thing between his legs, let alone put it inside her.

She shuddered.

Men were vile creatures; her mama had taught her that lesson from the time she'd been a young child. Women these days weren't raised properly, in her opinion. Just what kind of woman kicked her husband out into the cold because she was annoyed? If that were an acceptable way to behave, Edina would've kicked John out of the house at least once a day for the past thirty years.

Closing the photo album that was in her lap, she ran her hand over the worn cover. Since she was a girl, she'd felt her purpose in life was to be a wife and mother. When she'd married John at the tender age of nineteen, she'd thought her dreams had come true.

How wrong she'd been.

Within six months he'd had his first affair. She'd entertained the idea of leaving him for about two minutes, then she'd realized she was pregnant with Donnie. Instead of leaving, she'd learned to look away, to ignore his baser urges and concentrate on being the perfect wife and mother.

That said, she'd told her husband that if he ever embarrassed her publicly with his whores, he'd rue the day he'd discovered his penis.

Her mama hadn't raised a fool.

Donnie twitched and a low snore sounded. She sighed. Edina had had such high hopes for her firstborn. Unfortunately for her, he'd turned out to be just like his father. There'd been no saving him, but finally, after three more children, she'd had one who was like her. Bryan Mayhew Haines was a fine Salem police officer, and Edina couldn't have been prouder of him.

Rising, she returned the album to its appointed place on the shelf. Of course, with Donnie being first, his birth had been the most difficult of the four. Oh, how she'd suffered for well over twenty-four hours trying to push that one out. She should've known she was in trouble then, as he'd given her nothing but pain and grief ever since.

Now her youngest son, Bryan, he was the apple of her eye. From the moment he'd been born, he'd made it clear he wanted to do everything on his own. Donnie was the exact opposite, always needing some assistance or coaching to succeed. He'd always needed her, while Bryan rarely ever did.

Moving toward her eldest son, she noted he smelled of liquor. She could overlook that, as she'd learned to ignore anything unpleasant in her life. Her fingertips brushed his silvering hair.

She was fiercely protective of Donnie. He was the weakest of all of them and needed his family to prop him up from time to time. Both she and her husband were at fault; they'd spoiled him mercilessly as a child and now his life was slowly spiraling out of control. All too soon things, embarrassing things, would be public fodder around the water coolers.

Edina couldn't have that.

She was at a crossroads in her life. She loved her family with a fierceness, but there were times when she wanted to walk away. Edina had grown weary of picking up after her husband and three of her sons. Only Bryan had any sense whatsoever; it came from her side of the family.

She knew leaving her family wouldn't fix anything. She was old, her life had been spent raising her family and seeing to their needs, and making drastic changes now was beyond her. What would she do without her family to take care of?

ɞ

When Syn opened her eyes, Maddie was nudging and poking her with a paw.

"I'm okay, girl," Syn murmured.

She was curled in a ball on the floor and just inches from her nose was the white coffee mug. With a shaky hand, she reached for it, not surprised to find the cup was still warm. On the stove was the pot Victoria had used to make her potion.

Magic never failed to amaze Syn.

Slowly she gathered her wits and sat upright, using her dog for support. She was cold both inside and out, though her mind was crystal clear. Getting to her knees, she winced when something dug into her palm. Opening her hand, at first she thought it was a piece of ice. It took a few seconds to realize they were the diamonds from her mother's tears. Pain thrust through her heart and her eyes closed.

Mama.

Shoving the stones into her pocket, she struggled to her feet. Wavering, she took a shaky step toward the dining room. Maddie sat in the doorway, watching every movement Syn made.

"Did you see Mama, girl?" she whispered.

The dog whined and her butt started to wiggle, which Syn took as a yes. Near the door were two battery-powered lanterns. She picked up one and turned it on.

"Come on, Maddie, we're going on a scavenger hunt."

The dog fell in step behind Syn and together they climbed the stairs to the second floor. The logical place to begin was the sunroom. Seeing the police had tossed the place, then Bethie had come in and packed up everything, Syn seriously doubted the grimoire was still there now. For her own peace of mind, she had to look anyway.

The door to the sunroom was firmly shut and when Syn tried to open the door, it wouldn't budge. She had no idea where the keys were, as she'd misplaced them shortly after her arrival. Then again, what witch needed a key when she knew the spell to open the lock?

"Lock no more."

Running her fingertips over the lock, Syn was rewarded with the grinding sound of metal, and the door opened. Musty, stale air wafted out, causing her nose to wrinkle. Lifting the lantern high, Syn stepped into her mother's domain.

Running the width of the house, the empty room was bitterly cold. The entire south wall and ceiling were glass, affording an amazing view of Salem when the weather was clear. Now the ceiling was covered in snow and the windows had frozen over. If Syn were to get trapped in an ice cube, this room was what she imagined it would feel like.

Shivering, Syn made quick work of searching the room. The cupboards, shelves and drawers were all empty and the only thing she found was a dried rosebud on the floor behind the door. Fingering the crumbling bloom, she tried to put herself in her mother's shoes. Where would she have hidden the grimoire?

Her room?

Not a great idea; it seemed a little too obvious to Syn, but she decided to check anyway. Lantern in hand and Maddie at her heels, she secured the door and headed for the bedroom. Here the faint scent of roses lingered, and Syn had to smile. Maddie pressed her nose to the floor and began sniffing around while Syn set to work searching the room.

It didn't take too long to figure out the book wasn't here. The sheer size of the book made it impossible to tuck into a corner or hide on a shelf. It would take a sizeable hiding place to secret away the book and that left only one more place to look.

The attic.

She swallowed hard. That was the last place she wanted to go. It wasn't the attic so much as the room where Itsy dwelled. Just thinking about going upstairs and possibly disturbing it was enough to scare her spitless.

Then again, secreting the book with Itsy would guarantee its safety. The police couldn't get into the room and Bethany said she hadn't even tried.

That left her.

Exiting the bedroom, her feet grew heavier with each step as she approached the steps leading to the attic. Her hand landed on the railing and her mother's voice sounded in her head.

This is your journey, alone.

Syn's gaze fell on Maddie, her constant companion, where she stood in the bedroom doorway. The dog sat, then stretched out on the floor, her head coming to rest on her paws. Within moments she was snoring.

"Damn. Not my dog, too," she muttered. "I don't want to do this alone."

Watch your language, daughter.

As she stared up the steps into the darkness above, a tendril of fear unfurled in Syn's stomach. With her heart in her throat, she forced herself to climb the steps. With every step her feet grew heavier, until finally she reached the attic.

The empty room magnified the fury of the storm, and the creaking of the roof was alarming. Every slight shift of the house put her nerves more on edge, and she missed her dog more than ever. Taking a deep breath, she tried to steady herself. There were numerous hiding places in the attic, though only a few were large enough to hold the book. The girls had used the hiding places to secret their treasures away from one another, though they'd all known where the cubbies were located.

If Victoria had deliberately hidden the book for Syn to find, she might've put something in Syn's secret spot to leave a clue as to the book's location. Syn was pretty sure the book was far too large to fit in the cubby itself.

Walking toward the French doors, she dropped to her knees in the general area where her childhood bed had once stood. Moving along the baseboard, she pushed and poked with icy fingers, trying to locate the release. Because the bed was no longer in place, it took a few moments and a lot of pressing to locate the hiding spot.

A foot-long section of baseboard swung open with a squeak. Reaching in, she immediately felt something soft and crumbly.

"Better not be a rat's nest," she muttered.

Grabbing a handful, she pulled it out and frowned. Brick dust? What was brick dust doing in there? They'd never used it, not once in their magical workings. Again she plunged her hand inside to grab another handful.

"What the hell does this mean?" She dropped the dust. "Damn it, Mama, you got me into this and the least you could do is give me a real hint! I'm sick of this dog-and-pony show—"

Without warning, the door to Itsy's chamber blew open with stunning force. The wooden door exploded into small pieces when it hit the wall. A rush of icy air whipped into the room, instantly chilling her to the bone.

Syn screamed and ducked her head when the French doors, just feet away, flew outward. The glass shattered into thousands of tiny shards. The icy gust tore the remaining dust from the cubby and swept it outside into the teeth of the storm.

Struggling to her feet, Syn staggered toward Itsy's chamber, both terrified and curious as to what was inside. Would she see Itsy? Her heart began to pound.

The only time she'd seen Itsy was when she was seven or eight years old. Now, she had only the vaguest memory of an old woman in a voluminous black cloak. When she'd spoken to Chloe about it, her sister had laughed and said Itsy could take any form it chose.

That did not make Syn feel any better.

Bracing herself, she took a deep breath and peered in

through the door of Itsy's chamber. Every surface in the room was white, with the exception of a large purple pentagram painted in the center of the floor. Around the edges of the magical sign was a thick line of brick dust.

The room was empty.

Shocked, Syn stepped into the chamber and looked around in utter disbelief. This was what the police had worked so hard to get into? Where was Itsy?

All these years Syn believed this place held the answer to everything she'd ever wondered about. Where were the answers to family secrets? Where was Itsy? And the most important question, *what* was Itsy?

"Boy, don't I look stupid?" she whispered.

An octagonal window on the far wall stood open, and she moved toward it. The moment her foot touched the edge of the brick dust, she felt a sense of resistance. Carefully, she stepped around it instead.

When she moved to shut the window, the snow parted, affording her a good view of the barn. The doors were standing open and a wavering light was moving around inside.

Someone was in the barn.

Chapter Twenty-Seven

Matt was feeling both elated and sick to his stomach by the time he'd flipped through the missing file contents. It was all here, down to the last photograph, diagram and piece of paperwork. This case had been meticulously handled, though the detective in charge had neglected one thing.

To name the suspect.

There were several photographs of the suspect vehicle. It was a black 1969 Chevrolet Chevelle SS, with red flames streaming back from the hood and front quarter panels. It had been meticulously maintained and was every high-school boy's wet dream.

The passenger side was heavily damaged and the windshield smashed. Matt could clearly see where Victoria's body had landed on the car, as blood marked her position on the glass. Even if an ambulance had been on the scene waiting for the accident to occur, chances are she wouldn't have survived. Judging from the hole in the windshield, it appeared her head had actually gone through the window. This would explain a great deal of the damage to her face and neck.

But none of this explained why she'd then been dragged behind a car.

Once again, he flipped through the photos slowly to see if he'd missed anything important. None of the images were at the correct angle to make out the license plate and it hadn't been recorded on any of the documentation. This was troubling, very troubling.

Even with the missing pieces of the file, some questions had been answered, though the most important one still lingered. Who'd been driving the car that night?

Picking out a photograph of the driver's side, he reviewed every detail of the image. As far as American Metal went, this car was a classic. An economical car in the late sixties, by the early eighties it had been a popular car at Matt's high school. There'd been at least three of them among the football players alone. At the time of the accident, this car would've been at least fifteen years old, so the chances of the owner being an adult were slim. Not to mention the flames on the front, those must've been put on much later.

His gaze moved over the polished curves. It had the feel of a high school or college kid's car, and it was obvious someone appreciated it. Every inch of the body was in good repair, and even the tires looked clean. Inside, he could see a purple and white tassel hanging from the rearview mirror.

North Salem High School colors.

Whoever owned this car had recently graduated from high school and was, in all likelihood, male.

Too bad half the town was male.

His watch beeped and he looked down. It was almost eleven at night and he hadn't heard a peep from Synnamon. With the day being so hectic, he hadn't had time to call her, either. With Pine's suicide, the snowstorm—

"Evening, Mr. Matt."

Cyrus Landry stood in the doorway with his dust wand in one hand and a bottle of cleaner in the other. His baggy bib overalls hung off his thin frame, but they were spotless.

The overhead lighting shone on his bald head and behind his thick glasses his eyes sparkled with happiness. Cyrus was a simple man who couldn't read very well but had managed to hold a job with the city for all of his adult life. While he couldn't handle complex tasks, he did an excellent job of keeping the city buildings clean and he had an amazing talent for finding missing things.

"Good evening, Cyrus. I see you got into town okay," Matt said.

"Yes, sir, Mr. Matt. Ms. Debbie from Payroll had her brother come out in his truck and bring me in." Cyrus shuffled into Matt's office, making a beeline for the file cabinets. "I do like Mr.

Darrel's truck, yes I do."

"Do you enjoy cars, Cyrus?" Matt began gathering the file. He would lock it away, then head for home to grab a few hours rest.

"Yes, sir. Yes, I do. Don't like the cars today much." His nose wrinkled. "They all look alike. Now Mr. Jonas, he had him an old Barracudy one time, inherited it from his Daddy. That was a nice lookin' car. He let me ride in it once."

"He did? That was nice of him."

"Yes, he did, he's a nice man. Ms. Mamie from the diner had that there Luh Baron converteebule years back. Every now and again she'd take me for a ride with the top down. That was a fine ride." Cyrus giggled. "I like sitting with Ms. Mamie, she always smells so good."

"You have a pretty good memory, Cyrus." Matt stared at him. Was it possible the janitor would remember the car?

"Yes, sir. I reckon I do." The janitor looked at Matt and his expression was pained. "I never was one for books, all those words." He shook his shiny head. "I love the cars."

"Think back, Cyrus. Do you remember if anyone around Salem owned a Chevy Chevelle SS?"

"Oh yes, sir. Several of them. They were mighty popular years ago; don't see many nowadays." Cyrus' head bobbed as he polished the front of the file cabinets. "They were nice cars, all shiny and new."

"That they were." Matt pulled the photo of the undamaged driver's side. "Do you happen to recognize this car?"

Cyrus stopped cleaning and shuffled over to take a look.

"Well, look at that! I know that car, it's a beaut. Mister, he'd pay me a few dollars to polish that one for hours and hours." Cyrus was smiling. "I know every inch of that car."

"Who paid you to keep the car polished, Cyrus?"

He frowned. "Well, it was Mr. John that paid me."

"John Haines?"

"Yes, sir. He paid me cash money." His smile faded. "I didn't do anything wrong did I? I really love that car."

Matt gave Cyrus a reassuring smile. "Cyrus, you didn't do anything wrong at all.

"Do you remember the last time you saw it?" Matt's heart began to beat a little harder.

"I'm not so good with dates, Mr. Matt." Cyrus said.

"Was it warm outside?"

"No, sir. It was cold, cold as the devil." His mouth twisted. "It was near harvest. Mr. Ruprect on the hill paid me to come up to his place and gather apples before the frost."

Matt shoved the photograph into the envelope, his mind already chewing on the information Cyrus had given him.

Could John Haines have been driving the car the night Victoria Angelov had been murdered? According to popular gossip, the Haines family were old money and well respected in the community. Seeing that Haines and McNutt were as tight as brothers, it would begin to explain why the department would cover up the accident.

"Mr. Matt, sir, that car weren't Mr. John's." Cyrus stood in front of the desk, his head bowed slightly, and he was twisting the handle of his cleaning wand.

"It wasn't? Who did the car belong to, Cyrus?"

"His son."

"Which one?"

Cyrus looked surprised. "Why Mr. Donnie, of course. His daddy bought it new and gave it to his son when he was near to graduating. That boy didn't love the car like I did. He was careless."

"How careless?"

"Mr. John paid me to clean it 'cause it was always dirty." Cyrus shrugged. "Mr. Donnie, he dented it time after time, and the body shop would fix it up. I never felt right until I'd go over every inch of her myself though."

Interesting...

"When did Donnie stop driving the car, Cyrus?" Matt asked.

"Don't rightly know." He turned away to begin cleaning the whiteboard. "He wrecked and never drove it again. I saw it afterwards, it was a real mess."

"You saw the car after he wrecked it?"

"Yes, sir, I did."

Matt fished through the folder, then pulled out the image of the blood-stained windshield. "Was this what it looked like?"

Cyrus turned and winced when he saw the photograph. "I never want to see that car lookin' like that again. Mr. John said his son hit a deer, but Mr. Donnie denied it. Said he wasn't even driving it that day." He leaned toward Matt. "You know, when Mr. Donnie drinks, his memory isn't good."

"Yes, Cyrus, I do know he drinks." Matt shoved the photo into the envelope then moved to retrieve his gun belt. "Did he drink way back then, too?"

"Oh yes, sir. I'd find liquor bottles and beer cans in that car." Cyrus giggled. "I even found some panties once. Do you think Mr. Donnie had a girl back there?"

"I'm sure he probably did," Matt said. "Cyrus, after you saw the car with blood all over it, did you ever see it again?"

"Yes, sir, yes I did." His bald head bobbed.

"Do you know what happened to it?"

"Yes, sir. But I'm not supposed to tell." Cyrus was beginning to look nervous. "It's a secret."

"It is?" Matt gave him a wide, friendly smile. "Now why would anyone have a secret about a car?"

Cyrus' smile was twitchy. "Mr. John would not like it if I told."

"You know that Mr. John and I are friends?" Matt asked.

"Yes, sir, I know that."

"And you and I are friends, aren't we Cyrus?"

His smile turned brilliant. "Yes, sir, you are my friend."

"And I would never let anyone hurt you or say bad things about you," Matt said.

"Yes, sir." His gaze darted to Matt's gun. "I know that."

"So it would be okay if you tell me your secret," Matt said. "I would never let Mr. John know you'd told me."

"You wouldn't?"

"On my honor." Matt touched his badge. "I wouldn't betray your trust."

"You is a good man, Mr. Matt." Cyrus' smile grew wide. "Okay then, since you wouldn't hurt me. Mr. John parked the car and said no one would drive it ever again."

"Where did he park the car?"

"In that there barn up the hill."

"Which barn, Cyrus?" Something shifted in his gut then lay still, waiting for the answer.

"That haunted house."

Haunted House? Surely not...

"Do you mean the white house on the hill?"

"Yes, sir, Mr. Matt. That's the one. Parked it out there in the barn."

"What happened after that?" Matt thought his heart would come out of his chest. "When did he move the car from there?"

Cyrus looked confused. "What do you mean? It's still out there."

ও

Grabbing her coat, hat and gloves, Syn paused only long enough to retrieve her wand from its hiding place. Luckily she was already wearing her boots, and she slipped the branch into the right one.

Opening the front door, she rocked back on her heels as the storm rushed inside. Gritting her teeth against the icy air, Syn lunged out the door and pulled it shut behind her. She was a fool to be out here. With the blowing snow and wind, it was hard to see more than a foot in front of her nose. It was very possible she might not make it out there and if she did, she may not make it back.

Another, more chilling possibility was that she could miss the barn altogether and stumble around the clearing until she froze to death.

"What an encouraging thought," she muttered.

Fixing her gaze on the barn, she staggered through the snow. There were times when the storm would slow for a few seconds, just long enough to ensure she remained on course.

After spending so many years in the Southwest, she'd forgotten how tiring it was to break a path through wet, heavy snow in the middle of a storm. Inside her, the girl who loved winter wanted to roll in the untouched perfection of the snow, while the Arizona girl was screaming in horror.

Silencing her mind, she began to chant a white-light protection spell.

It seemed an eternity before she reached the barn doors. Staggering inside, it took her a moment to realize the wind was no longer an issue and the snow wasn't pelting her in the face. The best part was, she could actually stand up straight. Struggling to regain her breath, she was dismayed to realize she couldn't see anything. If there had been a light out here earlier, it was long gone now. Syn removed her wand from her boot and held it at the ready.

"Illuminate."

The tip of the wand burst into brilliant blue flame. Holding it high, she got her first good look at the changes someone had made to the interior.

It was clean, very clean, and all but the farthest two stalls had been removed. A cement floor had been laid and along the left wall were dozens of folded metal chairs in neat rows. Overhead, the beams bore some kind of flags, though she couldn't quite tell what was on them. The light from her wand wasn't bright enough for her to make them out. On the floor were strange symbols painted in red, and the only one she recognized was a pentagram.

Just what the hell was going on here?

As quietly as possible, she made her way toward the remaining stalls. The one on the right side was empty, while the one on the left held something large, cloaked in a black tarpaulin. With a shaky hand, she grabbed the black plastic cover and tugged hard. The cover shifted, then slid away to reveal a car.

Her jaw dropped.

Every inch of the car body was polished to a high gleam, and something inside her recoiled. Her shocked gaze moved over the painted flames and the destroyed windshield. She thought she would vomit.

Syn remembered this car well. It had belonged to Donnie Haines. She'd seen it countless times around town, always with a different girl in the front seat. It was in this car he'd tried to rape her. Bile burned her throat and she was going to lose her meager dinner any second.

This had to be the car that had struck her mother. But why was it here?

"Bitch, why couldn't you just stay dead?"

Chapter Twenty-Eight

"Sir, going up the hill would be suicide." Bryan Haines was blocking the back door, silently preventing Matt from leaving the station.

"Do you think I care, Haines?" Matt asked. He pulled a shotgun from the gun cabinet, taking care to stuff extra shells in his pocket before locking the doors. "Nothing is going to stop me from heading up to Angelov House, not even you. So that leaves you with a choice. If you want to stop me, you'll have to take me down. If you want to help me, then get the hell out of the way."

With Bryan's street-cop expression firmly in place, it was hard to tell what the other man was thinking. Haines had always been a quiet one, especially about his personal life. Matt couldn't help but wonder if he had any inkling as to what had occurred within his own family.

"Let me grab some chains, and we'll head on up," Bryan said.

The other man walked past him, then into the supply room. Matt was heartily glad Bryan hadn't tried to tackle him, as he had the feeling they were pretty evenly matched.

Fishing out his cell phone, he frowned when he saw the icon for a voice mail. He'd never heard the damned thing ring. Then again, he'd been so busy a circus could've come through his office and he'd never have noticed.

Accessing his voicemail, all he heard was static. Disappointed, he went to hit the delete button when he heard Syn's voice.

"Matthew, I need you!"

The sheer panic in her voice was enough to send a tidal wave of fear through his system. He slammed the phone shut.

"Bryan, let's go!"

He shoved a baseball hat on his head and burst through the back door. The wind had slowed, but the snow was still coming down in near-blizzard like conditions. Most of the cruisers in the back lot were covered in mountains of snow. When the weather was rough, even with chains they handled badly. The officers were taking calls in whatever four-wheel-drive vehicles were owned by the city, including his SUV.

"Fuck."

A flashing yellow light caught his attention. A massive city snowplow was cleaning out the handicapped parking spots at the clinic across the street.

Perfect.

Bryan came out the back door at a run with chains in one hand and a shotgun in the other.

"Lose the chains, Bryan. We won't be needing them," Matt yelled.

Keying his mike, he began to run toward the street with Bryan only two steps behind.

"Four-ten."

"Four-ten," the radio bleated.

"Three ninety-seven and I will be commandeering a snowplow and heading up the hill, break."

"Go ahead."

"All available officers should head in that direction with great care, break."

"Go ahead."

"All officers are to report to the Highland Hills entrance, break."

"Go ahead."

"Under no circumstances is anyone to run hot. I don't want any more accidents tonight. Copy that?"

"Twenty-three thirty-four."

The plow driver saw them running toward him, and he stopped the vehicle. When he rolled down his window, Matt realized it was Mike Haines, Bryan's brother.

"Hey bro," he called. "What's up?"

"We're commandeering your vehicle," Bryan called.

Mike looked surprised, then mad. "Like hell you are. Just because you're a cop—"

Matt ignored the both of them and jumped onto the step on the side of the plow.

"Do not make me pull a gun, Mike," he commanded. "You're going to drive us out to Highland Hills, where we're going to pick up some of my officers."

Mike's brows vanished into his hair. "No shit?"

"No shit."

Matt jumped down and ran around the plow to the passenger side. By the time he got there, Bryan was already inside. Climbing in, Matt barely had the door shut before the vehicle was on the move.

"We're not going to be able to fit more than one more man in here," Mike said.

"We'll manage," Matt ground out.

Mike pulled out onto the main road and Matt got his first look at just how bad the storm was. Many of the stores were snowed in, with drifts halfway up the doors. Anyone who'd made the mistake of leaving their car on the road would have trouble finding it tomorrow, as the plows and the wind had buried them with snow.

The roads were covered in a thick layer of slush, though it appeared at least some people were getting out and about.

"How bad is it?" Matt asked Mike.

"It's coming down faster than we can move it." Mike raised the plow a bit so he could drive faster. "We can only hope it stops soon. County already called for a level-three snow alert, emergency vehicles only. Nobody with any sense would be out on a night like tonight."

"You said it, bro," Bryan muttered.

"So where the hell is the fire?" Mike asked.

"Up the hill."

Mike stared at him as if he were crazy.

"There ain't no way in hell we can get up that hill, Chief," Mike said. "It hasn't been touched yet. We never get out there until the snow stops for several hours, as it's not considered a major artery."

"That doesn't matter, as that's where we're headed," Matt said. "Do the best you can, Mike. If we can't make it, then I'll be going in on foot."

∞

Syn froze and almost dropped her wand at the sound of the familiar and totally unexpected voice. When she turned, she wasn't surprised to see Edina Haines standing there with a smug expression.

The gun, however, was a complete surprise.

"You were supposed to stay dead." The other woman spoke as if she were at an afternoon tea party. "I killed you once, and it looks as if I'll have to do it again."

"You were the one who killed Mama?" Syn blurted before she could stop herself.

"Shut up, whore." Edina's face contorted, then smoothed into a perfect mask of calm. "You knew it was me driving the car. Just seconds before I hit you our eyes met."

"I don't remember much from that night." Syn's voice was faint. This woman thought she was Victoria, alive and in the flesh.

Edina chuckled. "I'm sure you don't, what with the way your head went through the windshield and all." Her smile was pleasant. "When I left the house that night, I never meant to kill you, I only wanted to talk. By the time I saw you on the road, it was too late."

Syn swallowed hard, the impulse to gag returning with a vengeance.

"Well..." An odd little smile played around Edina's mouth. "I might've hit the gas. Just a little, anyway."

"Why?" Syn gasped, desperate to keep her stomach under control. "Why were you looking for me?"

"As if you don't know." Edina sniffed. "You'd been going around town telling horrible lies about my son, Donnie. I wanted you to stop before you ruined his future." The smile returned. "I never anticipated it would take running you over to do it."

"They weren't lies," Syn said. "Your son—"

"My son is not a rapist," Edina shouted.

"Attempted rapist—"

"You were telling people my Donnie had touched your dirty girl. That brat of yours was just like you, opening her legs for any boy that happened to pass by."

"That's a lie."

Syn's gaze fixed on the gun in Edina's hand. It wasn't pointing at her any longer, but that didn't make her feel any safer.

"My daughter was a good girl—"

"Is that why you named her sin?" Edina crowed. "Just like her mama. She looks like you, too. Her return to Salem has done nothing but dig up bad memories for our family. She must leave, tonight. Once I get rid of you, I will deal with her. This town doesn't need any more whores in its midst."

"You're going to kill her?"

"Seems like the easiest way to me." Edina shrugged.

The light of madness gleamed in the other woman's eyes. What kind of person could speak of killing someone in such a cavalier fashion? Had this woman no soul?

"Why were you driving Donnie's car that night?"

Syn began moving backward, slowly easing Edina away from Syn's only escape.

"What a stupid question," Edina said. "My car was in the shop, and it was the only solution." Her smile was pleasant. "Donnie applied to the college here, and if they'd ever gotten wind of your lies he would've been denied entrance. There was no way I was going to allow you to ruin his chances—"

"So instead you chose to destroy the lives of four innocent children."

"Better them than my children. Besides, there was nothing innocent about them girls. Witches, all of them. Evil to the

279

bone, they were. Salem was much better off when they were taken away."

Syn's mind reeled. She never would've guessed Edina Haines even knew about her mother's murder, let alone would've been the one driving the car. As far as Syn knew, Victoria had never spoken to Edina before Donnie tried to rape Syn.

And this was why her mother had died? Because she was defending her daughter?

"You're wrong, Edina." Syn spoke in a low voice. "This town wasn't better for their leaving. Salem has always had an Angelov living here, and when you killed Victoria, this town was torn apart."

The shock on Edina's face would have been comical if it weren't so pathetic. This woman was sick, very sick.

"Lies," she snarled, the perfect mask dissolved. "You're lying again."

"No, Edina, I'm not. You killed an innocent woman, and your son did try to rape Synnamon when she was fourteen. I have proof."

Okay, so that was a lie...

The other woman's face flushed, and it looked as if her hair was going to explode into flames. Edina took a step forward, and the gun hung at her side as if she'd forgotten she was holding it. Syn knew it was now or never.

Pointing her wand in the direction of Edina's feet, she called out, "Bind!"

Edina screamed and her arms came up. Syn didn't stay to see what happened. Running toward the door, she was within feet of making her escape when she heard a gunshot and fire tore through her body.

₭

The drive up the hill had been harrowing, and there had been several times Matt thought for sure they were going into the ravine. The cab was crammed with five people, and Mike was cursing every inch of the way.

When they finally made it to Syn's driveway, Matt heard someone mutter, "Thank God."

Thank God, indeed.

Mike pulled into the drive and lowered his plow to push forward. Less than ten feet in, they realized there was a car in the way.

"What the hell?" Matt muttered.

"That looks like Mom's car," Mike said. "There's no way she'd be up here in this weather. Do you suppose someone stole it?"

"That is her car, bro." Bryan's voice was low.

"It can't be. You know she hates to drive at night, let alone in a storm—"

"Trust me, bro, that is Mom's car." Bryan's voice held a tone of finality.

"You're full of shit. Someone must've stolen it and abandoned it out here—" Mike started.

"Push past it, Mike," Matt said. "Someone's life is in danger, and now your mother's could be as well."

"You're all fucking crazy," Mike muttered. He took his foot off the brake and they moved forward. The plow shuddered when it kissed the bumper of the car, but in less than a minute the car was pushed to the side, leaving them room to maneuver around it.

Matt looked at Bryan. "It was you, wasn't it?"

Bryan nodded, his gaze was fixed straight ahead. "I've had it since my first year with the department."

"And you left a few pieces behind, just enough to raise suspicion."

His nod was abrupt. His voice dropped to barely above a whisper and Matt had to lean in to hear him over the roar of the plow.

"McNutt was going to destroy it. I overheard him and Dad talking about it. I didn't know what the file contained, and I became curious so I searched it out. McNutt was transitioning his job to you and he forgot all about it. Once I saw what the file contained, there was no way I could let it be destroyed. Someone had to know the truth."

"So you hid the rest."

"For a long time I didn't know what to do with it. I could barely look at myself in the mirror at times. The knowledge has weighed me down like the proverbial albatross around my neck.

"When I saw Ms. Angelov, I knew I had to do something. It was her mother that had been murdered, and the girls paid the ultimate price. It wasn't right to keep those secrets any longer."

"You did the right thing, Bryan."

"Sure doesn't feel like it."

The plow lumbered around the bend and Angelov house came into view. A light burned in the living room but Matt wasn't concerned with the house. It was the odd, bluish light coming from the barn that snared his attention.

"Head that way." He pointed toward the barn.

"We might get stuck," Mike said.

"Then we'll get stuck," Matt shot back. "Men, be alert for anything."

The massive plow lumbered toward the barn, and the occupants were forced to find ways to brace themselves as the vehicle lurched over the terrain like a drunk. Less than a hundred feet from the door, the plow came to a stop.

"We're stuck—"

Matt didn't wait for the end of the sentence before bailing out of the cab. The snow was up to his knees and the wind blew much harder out here than in town.

"Bryan, Rick, I want you to head for—"

A single gunshot rang out and Matt thought his heart would stop.

Synnamon.

Rick Brown, who was a tall, thin officer, took the lead and broke a path through the snow with ease. Falling into step behind him were Matt and Bryan, with Officer Roy Card in the rear.

Every instinct in Matt's body had him wanting to barge in and grab his woman. Luckily for him, Rick was in front. When Matt made the move, Rick bodily restrained him from doing something stupid. Silently, the other man pointed to a crack in the open barn door.

Leaning against the barn, Matt could scarcely detect a woman's voice over the scream of the wind. Peering through the crack, he saw Edina Haines standing over Syn, who lay on the floor. A foot or so from her lay something that resembled a tree branch, and the tip threw off a brilliant pale blue glow.

Matt's gaze met Bryan's, and the other man was stoic. He gave a curt nod, then stepped away from the wall.

"Mom, are you in there?" he called.

Edina looked up, clearly startled. "Bry, is that you?"

"Yes. Mom, are you okay?" he called.

"I'm fine, son, just taking care of some unfinished business. You go on home now—"

The hand holding the gun shifted and Rick made his move. The officer ran in the door and took Edina down with a flying tackle. Officer Card followed and it was Roy who located the gun when it fell out of the woman's hand.

Edina Mayhew Haines, member of the Junior League and president of the Salem Garden Club, began to scream at the top of her lungs.

"She has to die! She must, she must!"

Within seconds Matt was beside Syn, helping her sit up. She gave him a thin smile.

"What took you so long there, cowboy?" Her teeth chattered.

He wrapped his arms around her, pulling her tight to his chest. "The snow slowed me down," he said. "Just a bit, anyway."

"L-l-likely story," she muttered.

"Are you hurt?" he asked. "Were you shot?"

"She got me in the leg. I think it's just a graze, though." She gave a choking laugh. "Thank goodness she wasn't wearing her glasses."

Silent, Matt kissed her forehead.

"Is Ms. Angelov okay?"

Bryan stood over them both, his expression carefully blank. Only a few feet away, his mother was on the floor, screaming her head off, with two police officers standing over her. The fact that his first thought was for Synnamon's safety said a lot about the man.

"I've got her," Matt said. "See to your mother, Bryan."

He turned away.

"How sad for him." There were tears in Syn's eyes. "I'm sorry he has to go through this."

"Me too, Syn. Me too."

ಬ

Hours later, the sun raced for the noon position and Syn felt empty. Her eyes were dry and her body had been numb for hours. Sitting in the window seat in Mama's room, she watched the crime scene team as they packed to leave. For the past twelve hours, dozens of officers and crime scene techs had crawled over every inch of the barn. They'd emerged with bag after bag adorned with the all too familiar EVIDENCE tags.

Edina Mayhew Haines. Who would've ever guessed the woman was a murderer?

Certainly not Syn. Even now, she reeled from the events of the past twelve hours. If she'd had to draft a list of potential suspects, Edina would've never entered her mind. Yeah, the woman was crazed. Yes, the woman had attacked her at the grocery store, but never would she have imagined Edina, one of Salem's finest social matrons, had killed her mother.

Matt walked out of the barn, and automatically Syn's gaze moved to him. He had to be as exhausted as she, though from watching him, she couldn't tell. Standing tall in his dark blue uniform, Matt covered the distance between the barn and the house with his long, easy strides.

When she needed him, he'd been there. What else did she need to know about him?

Something warm broke free in her chest and spread through her belly. Turning, she looked into the mirror over the makeup table. Her mother still lay on the bed with a pleased smile. Maddie was beside her and Victoria was cooing over the mutt as if she were the most magnificent creature ever born.

"Still watching over me, Mama?"

What do you think?

Syn turned away to look outside. The brilliant sunshine coupled with the snow forced her to squint or be blinded. Overhead, fat clouds dotted the sky, casting shadows on the frozen landscape below.

Earlier, she'd had the most dizzying sense of déjà vu. Her journey had begun with a yard full of police officers, and this chapter closed in the same way. Except this time around, the cops were the good guys.

The front door opened and Maddie took off in a flurry of dust and yelps to greet Matt downstairs. His deep voice mingled with the dog's excited whines and after a few moments, he called out.

"Syn?"

"Up here."

His footsteps sounded on the steps, and Maddie came flying into the room followed by Matt. He stopped in the doorway and his gaze met hers.

"What are you doing in here?" He looked around the room with undisguised curiosity.

"This is my mother's room. Bethie never had the heart to pack it up, so instead, she closed the door and left everything as it was."

"So this is the damage the police did?" He stepped into the room, nudging the papers and clothes on the floor with one black boot.

"They really tore things up."

"That they did. I can't help but wonder what they were looking for." Matt walked toward her, coming to sit on the padded seat beside her.

"They were looking for my mother's grimoire, or spell book."

"Is this another woo-woo thing?"

She rolled her eyes but couldn't help smiling. "Yes, so hold onto me and I won't let you go spinning off into spooky land."

"Good."

Matt reached for her, and Syn went into his arms willingly, sliding her arms inside his jacket. Even with the bulk of his vest and gun belt, it was heaven to be in his embrace. He was so solid.

"The book isn't to leave the house, or we'll be in grave danger, Matt. Mama secreted it away, and when the cops tore the house apart they never found it."

"What's in the book?"

"Hundreds of spells to do almost anything imaginable." She laid her head on his shoulder. "Mama pounded into my head how important it was that the book not be removed from this place, and for some reason it just completely left my mind."

"Did you find it?"

"I believe it's upstairs in Itsy's room."

"What is an Itsy?" His shoulders tensed.

"Now that is a question I can't answer," Syn said.

"More woo-woo?"

"Yeah."

They fell silent. Maddie had resumed her position on the bed, though Syn knew her mother was gone. She'd waited until Matt arrived to take her leave, satisfied someone was keeping an eye on her daughter.

"Syn?"

"Yeah?"

"Why didn't you tell me about Donnie?" His hands stroked her back.

"I thought I had."

"You downplayed it. Made it sound like it was a high school prank."

"Sorry. It certainly wasn't funny, not to me at least. When I was in my early teens all I wanted was to fit in, and when a football player noticed me, I was naïve. It never occurred to me he'd grab me the way he did."

"It's understandable. Everyone wants to be liked for who they are."

"I was lonely as a child. Looking back, I think all of us were in our own way. Our lives were very isolated here." She raised her head. "But not bad. It was never bad."

"I think I understand what you mean. The town didn't accept you, the kids made fun of you and—"

"All I ever wanted was to be normal. Just normal."

"Do you still feel that way?"

"Sometimes, but not really. I've come to understand myself and my family. My only regret is Mama. Her life was cut short and for what? Defending her daughter." Tears stung her eyes. "I don't know if I'll ever be able to forgive Edina."

"You don't have to. Everyone makes such a big deal about forgiveness but, in my mind, you don't have to forgive her. That said, you do have to let the anger go at some point. It will eat you alive if you don't." His chin brushed her forehead. "But that process will take time."

"Yeah, a long time."

Outside, the tow truck lumbered out of the barn with the Chevy on the flatbed. The sun gleamed on the black paint, and Syn's stomach tightened.

"I don't ever want to see that car again." Her voice was low.

"That can be arranged." His voice was a reassuring rumble in her ear. "It's over, Syn."

"No, I don't think this will ever be over, Matt. In fact, it's just begun." Syn swallowed hard. "Edina killed my mother, but there are so many more unanswered questions. The men who were ultimately responsible for Mama's death are still out there, and I won't rest until they receive the punishment they deserve."

"Neither will I."

"My sisters are still out there somewhere." Syn allowed her eyes to close. "I need to find them, Matt. This will never be over until I do."

"They'll return," Matt said. "If not, we start tracking them down."

"I hope you're right."

It felt so good to sit in his arms. To be this close to another human being was such a wonder to her. With any luck, it always would be. The sunlight warmed her skin and Syn felt safe, protected.

"Do you have to go into work?"

"No. I've arranged for a few days off. I might have to go in for an hour here and there, but I thought it was more important

I take care of my girl." He kissed her forehead. "You're a lot more important than some paperwork."

"Hmm, who knew you were such a romantic?" Syn giggled.

"Yeah, you rank right up there with clean socks and hot coffee."

"Honeymoon's over already, eh?"

"It hasn't begun yet."

Syn raised her head, leaning back until their gazes met. "So you're keeping me around then?"

"It would be easier if you'd asked me if I needed my next breath." His fingers brushed her forehead, pushing her hair behind her ear. "We don't know each other very well, but we have time. If we take things slowly—"

She shook her head. "I'm not very good with slow..."

"Good." His smile was warm. "Neither am I." He dropped a noisy, smacking kiss on her mouth. "So tell me, do you have a spell to make money?"

"No, you did not just ask me that." She started to laugh.

"Purely a question for professional purposes." His eyes gleamed with amusement.

"Honestly, I don't know. Mama was careful about leaving us alone with the book for limited periods of time. I have no idea even half of what it contains." She unwound herself from his arms. "Let's go upstairs and see if we can retrieve it." Syn took his hand and pulled him from the seat.

"I was thinking if the book contains some way to create cash, double money, something like that, it would be a good motive for murder."

Together, they walked up the steps.

"Sounds good to me, but I'm not convinced money is the answer we're looking for. That said, there is at least one person who wants the book and made an offer to Mama for it."

"Who?"

"Carolyn Summers."

Matt frowned. "The owner of that pagan store on the square?"

"That's her. It would seem her dead husband was there

when Mama was killed or shortly thereafter. She knows more than she'd admitted to me."

"Interesting."

A thin layer of snow covered the attic floor and the remains of the French door swung in the breeze. Pieces of Itsy's door crunched underfoot as they made their way to her chamber.

"What the hell happened up here?" Matt asked.

"More woo-woo stuff."

"Tell me one thing. Does this woo-woo stuff ever end?"

"No." She turned and looked at him directly in the eye. "With me, the woo-woo will never end, Matt. It's a part of me, and I suspect I'll always be surrounded by all sorts of things that will set your teeth on edge. You need to decide now if it's something you think you can come to terms—"

Matt hushed her by laying his finger across her lips.

"You don't have to keep testing me, Syn. I'm here for the long haul, woo-woo or not." He removed his finger and gave her the sweetest kiss she'd ever experienced. Her eyes began to burn with unshed tears.

"I'm sorry."

"No need to be." He wrapped his arms around her and squeezed. "We all have our baggage, Syn. Just try not to let yours push mine out of the closet."

"Okay."

She hugged him back then released him. Blinking away the tears, she led the way into Itsy's chamber. In the daylight, it was even more austere than it had appeared last night. The paint wasn't white; it was pale blue, making the room look like an ice cube. The octagon-shaped window was open again.

"There's nothing in here," Matt said. "What's with the pentagram? Is that ochre?"

"Brick dust. It is used for protection by practitioners of voodoo. On the surface it looks like nothing is here." Syn retrieved her wand from her boot. "Didn't you know the best place to hide things is in plain sight?"

Pointing her wand at the pentagram, she gathered her energy and focused on the ancient wood in her hand. With a slow exhalation, she cast her spell.

"Reveal."

Lavender smoke appeared in the center of the pentagram and Matt's breath was sharp. When the smoke started to swirl around the painted lines of the pagan symbol, Syn reached for his hand. A cloud formed and lifted toward the ceiling to reveal the grimoire lying on the floor.

"I'll be damned," he muttered.

"I knew it had to be here somewhere." Syn's voice came out a little squeaky, excitement tightening her throat. "Last night I tried to walk through the pentagram, and I felt resistance. It was only later I realized it had to be the book, it was what—"

"What the hell is that?" Matt was staring at the cloud slowly spreading out across the ceiling.

"I think it's Itsy."

"That's Itsy? A cloud?"

"Uh, no, and please don't piss her off." Syn stepped over the dust and into the pentagram to pick up the book. "She could hurt you pretty easily, and she isn't one to be trifled with."

"She?"

"I don't know if she is a she. It was always my gut feeling Itsy is female." She looked up at the lavender smoke, and the edges had turned pale gray. "As for what she is, I'm not sure, but I know she must be an Angelov."

The cloud turned pale pink.

"I think she's happy with that announcement."

Matt reached for the cloud, and it gathered to swirl around his hand like a puff of cotton candy. In the blink of an eye it made a beeline for Syn. Twirling around her, the cloud spun her in a circle.

"That tickles," she shrieked.

The smoke released her, then vanished between the floorboards.

Syn blinked. "Wow. That was amazing."

"I hear you." Matt looked at the book she held wrapped in her arms. "Is that it?"

"Yes, and it's finally back where it belongs. I guess, in the end, I didn't fail my mother after all." A tear ran down her cheek. "And speaking of Mama, she likes you, a great deal."

His brow arched. "And this is a surprise how? Women adore me."

"Come on, Casanova." She laughed, and together they exited the room. "You and I have a date with my bed and a long nap."

"Mmm." He dropped his arm around her shoulders. "Now you're talking."

Epilogue

It's almost time, daughter.

Chloe Angelov was dismayed when she heard her mother's voice move through her mind. Cautiously, she lowered the black eyeliner to look around the crowded dressing room. Ten women were crammed into the tiny space, each fighting for a piece of mirror to finish their makeup before taking the stage.

A shiver slipped down her spine. It had been twenty years since she'd heard her mother's voice, but that didn't mean she'd forgotten how it sounded. Her nerves were on edge and she took a deep breath. Deep inside, she was terrified of the thought Angelov House was calling her back.

Damn it, why did she have to run out of dope this morning?

Sometimes she thought it was the drugs that kept her sane. At least when she was high, the voices of the dead were reduced to meaningless whispers that were so much easier to ignore than when she was sober.

Her jaw tightened and her gaze met her reflection. Why had she chosen black hair on today of all days? The face staring back at her looked too much like her mother. She licked her lips.

Never as long as she lived would she forget the night Mama had been killed. The shock, sitting on the couch for what seemed like hours, cold air, and dozens of empty eyes watching her.

Images from that day crowded her mind. The house, the red and blue lights against the white paint. Men in uniforms tearing the house apart. Her sister, Synnamon, trying to convince Chief McNutt to listen to her. The screams of her younger sisters.

That man.

That horrible man had touched her, forced himself on her. Bending her body, breaking her soul when he forced himself inside.

The blood.

The pain.

Chloe pushed the troublesome memories away. She was older now, an adult, and it didn't matter what had happened to her in the past. She'd done whatever she'd had to do to keep her mind and body together and never, ever did she want to return to the house or face her sisters again.

"Hey, babe, you look hot tonight."

Marissa, one of the dancers, gave her a wolf whistle. The woman's massive breasts threatened to spill out of her skimpy pirate costume. At her waist was a leather bullwhip.

"Pirates again?" Chloe hurriedly finished her eyeliner, then reached for the gloss.

"The men like the whip; it gives them an erection."

"Which means more money, ladies." Cheryl, a beautiful woman dressed in nearly nothing, gave a raucous laugh.

"What's up, doll? You look just a little pale." Marissa touched Chloe's shoulder.

"Jonesing. Ran out early this morning." Her hand shook as she tried to put on her lipstick.

"Sorry, babe." Marissa reached down and pulled a flask from her garter. "This might help. It's vodka."

"Thanks." Chloe opened the flask. "Is Bobby stopping in tonight?"

"Oh yeah." Marissa leaned forward to fluff her curls. "We're going to party. I'm sure he can hook you up. Chooch got some good stuff from Argentina. Blacker than my pussy hair, girl!"

Cheryl cackled, and Chloe forced herself to smile. Taking the flask, she downed half the contents, enjoying the burn of cheap liquor.

"I guess you needed that." Marissa squeezed Chloe's

shoulder. "Come on girl, let's get moving. Our public awaits."

"Ah." Chloe rose and gave her hair a flip. "There's no business like show business," she muttered to herself. She took a final swig of the liquor, praying it would kick in quickly and keep the voices away until she could get her dope and smoke herself into oblivion.

About the Author

J.C. Wilder left the world of big business to carry on conversations with the people who live in her mind—fictional characters, that is. In her past she has worked as a software tester and traveled with an alternative rock band, and she currently volunteers for her local police department as a photographer. She lives in Central Ohio with 6,000 books and an impressive collection of dust bunnies.

To learn more about J.C. Wilder, please visit www.jcwilder.com. Send an email to J.C. Wilder at wilder@jcwilder.com or join her Yahoo! group to join in the fun with other readers as well as J.C. Wilder! http://groups.yahoo.com/group/thewilderside/

Printed in the United States
148878LV00002B/2/P

9 781599 989860